PRAISE FOR THE GREEN DRESS

"A haunting story fraught with danger and intrigue, *The Green Dress* will leave you with a bittersweet remembrance of the characters long after you read the last page. Some you'll love and cheer for—others you'll love to hate. Author Liz Tolsma blends historical fact and fiction seamlessly in this tale of murder and romance."

—Michelle Griep, Christy Award-winning author of *Once Upon a Dickens Christmas*

"I'm always up for a true crime read, and Liz Tolsma's latest foray into the seedier days of life insurance policies, poisonings, and early forensics had me turning the pages as fast as possible. It's difficult to believe such villainous stories grace our history books, and Tolsma does a wonderful job in bringing them to fictional form."

—Jaime Jo Wright, author of *Echoes among the Stones* and Christy Award-winning, *The House on Foster Hill*

"Suspense rooted in the impossible and wrapped in love. Liz Tolsma tells a fascinating but harrowing tale rooted both in justice and compassion. Chilling without being gruesome, *The Green Dress* will keep you up long past your bedtime, and you might lose a few fingernails along the way. Recommended for anyone looking for an excuse to stay up into the wee hours and shiver at the slightest shifting shadow."

—Chautona H̶ bestselling
Agg̶ ̶ard series

the GREEN DRESS

Liz Tolsma

BARBOUR BOOKS

An Imprint of Barbour Publishing, Inc.

©2020 by Liz Tolsma

Print ISBN 978-1-64352-475-7

eBook Editions:
Adobe Digital Edition (.epub) 978-1-64352-477-1
Kindle and MobiPocket Edition (.prc) 978-1-64352-476-4

All scripture quotations are taken from the King James Version of the Bible.

This book is a work of fiction. Names, characters, places, and incidents are either products of the author's imagination or used fictitiously. Any similarity to actual people, organizations, and/or events is purely coincidental.

Published by Barbour Books, an imprint of Barbour Publishing, Inc., 1810 Barbour Drive, Uhrichsville, Ohio 44683, www.barbourbooks.com

Our mission is to inspire the world with the life-changing message of the Bible.

Member of the
Evangelical Christian
Publishers Association

Printed in the United States of America.

To my quarter friend, Janet. Thank you for always being there, for loving me, and for supporting me through thick and thin. I couldn't do life without you. I love you. You are worth far more than one hundred pennies.

Cast of Characters

Sarah Jane Robinson – Widowed Irish immigrant living in Somerville, Massachusetts

Moses Robinson – Sarah Jane's late husband. He passed away on July 23, 1883, at the age of 45

Elizabeth A. "Lizzie" Robinson – The oldest of the Robinson children, born on January 29, 1862

William "Willie" Robinson – The oldest Robinson son, born c. 1864

Charles "Charley" Robinson – The second Robinson son, born June 15, 1868

Emma May Robinson – Another of Sarah Jane and Moses's children, born c. 1874, died September 6, 1884

Grace W. "Gracie" Robinson – The youngest of the Robinson children, born June 27, 1879

Annie Freeman – Sarah Jane's younger sister. She passed away on February 28, 1885

Prince Freeman – Annie Freeman's husband. He passed away on June 27, 1885

Thomas Freeman – Prince and Annie's son, born November 13, 1878

Dr. Charles C. Beers – A friend of the Robinson family

Thomas Smith – A friend of the Robinson family

Harriet Peters – A friend of Lizzie Robinson

Dr. Michael Wheaton – A Somerville, Massachusetts, physician

Dr. Emory White – A Somerville, Massachusetts, physician

Dr. Edward Wood – A professor at Harvard University

Chapter One

February 1886
Somerville, Massachusetts

The note in Harriet Peters's hand trembled as she read it, the words scrawled across the page in obvious haste making sense in her brain but not in her heart.

Come quickly. I'm ill and need you.

Lizzie

What would make Lizzie Robinson send such a letter? Of course, Charley would be the one to deliver it. Good, sweet Charley. His sister Lizzie had been ill before, but she had never sent word through him for Harriet to come.

No, oh no.

A shiver coursed through Harriet, and an odd fluttering sensation settled in the pit of her stomach. Her head told her not to panic, but her heart said something was very wrong. This couldn't be happening. Not to Harriet's best friend. The person she held dearest in this life. Her only family after she fled from her home. To lose Lizzie would be akin to losing half of her heart.

Harriet bit her upper lip. *Heal her, Lord. Please, don't let it be what the others had.*

She peered at Charley as he stood with his hands clasped, his grip so tight his knuckles were white. "Is it like the other illnesses?"

With a single nod, Charley shattered her world.

Because his father, aunt, uncle, and sister had died of the same mysterious illness.

Mrs. McGovern's hat would have to wait. Harriet shoved aside the flowers and threw the needle and scissors in her work basket. Once she turned the sign to CLOSED on her millinery shop, she grabbed her dark green cloak and flung it around her shoulders.

With a quick glance at the ribbons, thread, and notions scattered about her small workshop, she left the mess behind.

Lizzie needed her more.

Harriet dashed into the inky night. A bitter north wind tore through her cloak and bit at her ears. She bent her head to fend off the sleet that stung her cheeks. Though she did her best to hurry, the walks and streets were icy, slowing her too much.

Charley clung to her by the elbow, holding her from slipping on the glazed street. The howling gale kept them from all conversation.

What if they were too late? No. Harriet pushed the thought from her mind and concentrated on picking her way to her friend's house. She had to make it in time to speak to Lizzie, to tell her she loved her, to thank her for all she had done for her.

By the time they reached Holland Street, her toes had frozen to the point that she had no feeling remaining in them.

She climbed the steps that led to the front porch of the gray Greek-revival-style house, the ornate portico sheltering her from the icy pellets. Darkness settled like a blanket around Harriet as she stood on the crooked stoop. The blackness was almost a physical presence, weighing down her shoulders. She couldn't draw a deep breath, the air around her thick and heavy.

With shaking hands, she drew her cloak tighter. As she waited for Charley to open the creaky door, sleet pinged off the dirty upstairs windows.

Willie Robinson, his brother, stood just inside at the bottom of the stairs that led to the second-floor apartment the family occupied. As usual, he didn't smile but grasped her by the upper arm and all but dragged her up the steps. "I'm so glad you came. We really need you."

"Is it bad?"

"Awfully terrible."

When they reached the top of the steps, Harriet unbuttoned her cloak, but Charley and Willie were already racing toward Lizzie's room. She threw her garment on the new blue davenport that the family had purchased after moving to this larger place almost four months ago. Black crepe was draped over the mirror above the fireplace, marking this as a home still in mourning. Mourning for the loss of Lizzie's uncle six months ago.

She hustled to follow the young men to the back of the house. "What are her symptoms?"

Charley whirled and swallowed several times, his prominent Adam's apple bobbing. "Like I said, same as the others. Exactly the same."

Knees buckling, Harriet leaned against the wall for support, her mouth dry. "Just like your uncle?"

Charley nodded. "And Papa and Emmie and Auntie and Uncle. Severe stomach pains, vomiting, the whole bit. She's in agony, Harriet, sheer agony." He sucked in a breath, his face devoid of all color. "No one seems able to do anything about it. Dr. Beers is with her now, but as usual, none of his remedies have worked. I sent Mama to rest, though she resisted it something fierce."

"I'm sure it was hard to tear her from her daughter's side." Harriet followed Charley into the room. Willie already sat at the foot of the bed.

Though she put on her best smile, the odor of vomit and decay was gagging. Harriet restrained herself from reaching into her reticule and pulling out a perfumed handkerchief. Instead, she went to Lizzie's sickbed, falling to her knees at her friend's side. "Oh sweetheart, I'm so sorry about this."

Lizzie lay pale against the pillow, curled into a ball. "Harriet." She croaked the word.

"Yes, dear, I'm here. Just relax. Everything will be fine." Yet Harriet's own stomach clenched. Sweat beaded her friend's fair forehead. Harriet wiped away a damp tendril of Lizzie's brown hair. "Don't you worry about a thing."

"I'm so sick."

"I know. Charley brought me your note."

"Good old Charley."

"Yes, he is." Charley was like one of the brothers she had left at home when she ran away from what would have been a disastrous marriage.

Dr. Beers, a short, balding elderly man with a paunch, stood on the far side of the bed. "It's good of you to come, my dear, and on such a night." He withdrew a gold watch from his vest pocket and flipped open the cover.

Did he have somewhere better to be? He'd been retired for a while, or so she understood.

She'd met him on numerous occasions at the Robinson home. Lizzie had told her that he'd proposed to her mother several times, but the widowed Mrs. Robinson always turned him down. He was persistent, though. "How is she?"

He gave the smallest shake of his head.

Harriet bit her lip to keep from crying out. Why, why was this happening to someone as sweet, kind, and caring as Lizzie? One of the few true friends Harriet had in all the world. When Harriet had come to the Boston area four years ago, she'd met Mrs. Robinson outside of the Methodist church, hunger gnawing at her insides and her pockets empty. Lizzie and her mother had taken Harriet in and had been a true family to her.

Charley touched her shoulder, the warmth of his hand working to relax her shoulders. "Why don't I get you a cup of tea, Lizzie? That might help settle your stomach."

The once-vibrant young woman made a vain attempt to raise her head from the pillow. "No. I can't, can't even think about it." A moan escaped her chapped lips.

"Well, then, we should let you rest. Harriet, Willie, Dr. Beers, shall we?"

Harriet stared at Charley and raised a questioning eyebrow, but he exited the room. She trailed him, the floorboards groaning as Dr. Beers followed close behind her.

Willie remained in the room. At least Lizzie wasn't alone. Faithful, solid Willie.

Charley leaned against the papered wall and finger-combed his straight hair. "There has to be something we can do. We can't let her go. We've lost so much of our family. Now Lizzie. I won't stand by and watch her die." With his fist, he banged the wall.

Harriet covered her mouth, her reticule swinging from her wrist. Die? No, no, it couldn't be. Losing Lizzie would be the worst kind of tragedy. "I agree with Charley. Some doctor must have some medication that can help her, that can cure her. She's suffering so." Several tears slid down her cheeks. "Isn't there anything we can do?"

Dr. Beers shook his head. "I'm afraid not. We couldn't help the others. There's little hope for her. It's just a matter of time."

Harriet's legs shook, and she crumpled to the ground. She fought the sobs that threatened to tear from her throat. "I won't accept it. We'll get every doctor in Somerville and Cambridge and even Boston to examine her until we find one who can save her."

"That won't help."

At the firm, feminine voice, Harriet glanced up through tear-laden eyes. Mrs. Robinson's black crepe dress with its high neckline rustled as she swished down the hall, tall and regal, with a long, sloped nose. "There isn't the money to pay for a doctor."

"No funds?" Charley pushed away from the wall. "What about the insurance payout we got when Uncle died?"

Charley and Mr. Freeman, his uncle, had been very close. Losing him last summer was a great blow.

"There was no payout from my brother-in-law's death."

Charley stood in front of his mother, peering down at her. "But you went to Wisconsin and purchased new furniture and got a bigger apartment."

"Now the creditors are coming after me. How was I to know Lizzie would get so ill?" Mrs. Robinson's voice warbled and cracked. Her eyes widened, and she stiffened. She pulled at her hair, then glanced all around, as if following a buzzing bee in an erratic flight path. "What is it that you say?"

Who was she talking to?

Charley stepped in front of Mrs. Robinson. "Mama?"

She stared straight through him. "Moses? Is that you, Moses?"

He rubbed his forehead. "Not another one of your crazy visions."

Lizzie had told Harriet about them. Mrs. Robinson had at least one before each of her loved ones died. Harriet didn't put much stock in them, but Mrs. Robinson did.

She was always right. Cold shot through Harriet. If only her cloak weren't in the parlor, she might make an escape.

"Tell me what you want to tell me, no matter how much it hurts. What? You're here for Lizzie? Please, Moses, I beg you not to take her. What will I do without her?" She closed her eyes and scrunched her forehead. "Yes, yes, I understand. You need her more than I." With that, Mrs. Robinson sagged. Charley caught her a moment before she hit the floor.

Harriet's breath hitched in her throat. Not this time. Mrs. Robinson couldn't be right this time. God wouldn't take Lizzie from her. Though the others might stand around and do nothing, Harriet wouldn't.

She wiped away her tears and struggled to her feet. "Not far from my shop, a new doctor has just hung his shingle. Fresh eyes. A young man, perhaps knowledgeable about new medications that weren't available before. I'll fetch him. Maybe he'll know what to do. Don't worry about the bill. I'll pay it. I'll do whatever I have to in order to save Lizzie's life."

Dr. Beers frowned. "I don't see what good bringing in a new doctor is going to do. We've tried that before. No one has had any success treating any of the cases. Not a single one of them knows definitively what is causing this, and not a single one of them has been able to cure any of the patients. You are wasting your time and money, Miss Peters."

"Then I will gladly do it for my very best friend. I need her. We all need her. Who will look after Tommy and Gracie when everyone else is at work if Lizzie isn't around? No, I'm getting the doctor.

I'll leave now and hope to be back in the next hour. Tell Lizzie I love her."

Before any of them could brook a single objection, Harriet raced to the main living area, grabbed her cloak from the settee, and still clinging to her reticule, hurried into the frigid night.

All the way to the doctor's place, she prayed that Lizzie would live.

And all the way, she feared for Lizzie's fate.

The carriage bumped along the slippery, uneven road, jostling Michael Wheaton. He clutched his black doctor's bag harder with his sweaty hands and stared at the raven-haired woman across from him, her intricately braided hair slipping from its pins. She returned his stare, her dark blue eyes intense and just a bit watery.

"Can you describe for me again the symptoms your friend, Miss Robinson, is experiencing?"

"Vomiting, great stomach discomfort, profuse sweating." There was a catch in her words.

"And you say this is something that runs in the family?"

"It seems to." Miss Peters drew in a deep breath. "Just last June, her uncle passed away of a similar ailment. Poisoning from the factory he worked in, that's what the doctors guessed. Several others have died too. No explanation has been given in those cases, to the best of my knowledge." She fussed with the reticule on her lap, twisting the ribbon that closed it around her finger.

"Hmm. Unusual symptoms. No fever or chills? No one else in the home ill at the same time?"

She shook her head then leaned forward as the sleet and wind buffeted the carriage, the interior dim but dry. Even in the low light, he didn't miss the firm set to her lips. She clenched him by the wrist, her black-gloved grasp strong. "Please, Dr. Wheaton, there has to be something you can do for Lizzie. Anything. She's…" Miss Peters released her grip and sat back. "She's the only friend I have in the world. There must be some medicine you can give her, some remedy the others have not tried. Each time someone has fallen ill, Mrs. Robinson has brought in a different doctor, each one less effective than the other. Perhaps, being so new to the profession, you are familiar with some new discovery."

He wrinkled his brow. How was it that this woman knew he had only just become a qualified doctor?

"Word gets around, Dr. Wheaton." She answered as if she read his mind. "I own the milliner's shop a few doors down from your office. A number of my clients have mentioned to me how kind and compassionate you were to them in their illnesses and how pleased they were with you, even though you were new."

He warmed through and through despite the aching cold blowing through the thin carriage shell. "Thank you. That's very nice of you to say." There were many who wouldn't share such polite words about him. Those who would be downright mean and nasty. Or worse. He clenched then relaxed his fists.

"So you see why I immediately thought of you when Lizzie took ill. All of this is so sudden. I visited her only last evening, and she was quite well. We played checkers with the children, and nothing was amiss at the time. She gave no indication of feeling the least bit poorly."

Michael chewed on the inside of his cheek. Several family members passed away from similar ailments. The last one from poisoning, supposedly from the factory where he worked.

None of it made sense. He wiped his damp palms on his pants. How was he ever going to figure this out and save the young woman when others had failed? "I'll know more after I examine Miss Robinson."

"Thank you." Miss Peters blew out a breath. "And thank you for the conveyance. It was rather a cold walk on the way to your office." The pale light of the gas streetlamps penetrated the storm enough for him to catch the brief smile that crossed her pink lips.

They pulled up to a large duplex home, a porch reaching almost to the street, two doors along it, elaborate carvings decorating its triangular roof. He stepped out, the wind howling like a pack of wolves. He pushed his bowler hat down further on his head lest it blow away.

After he paid the driver, he assisted Miss Peters from the carriage, her hand tiny but her step sure. She led the way across the porch, her deep purple skirts sweeping the light dusting of snow and sleet that covered it.

Once upstairs and inside the almost-dark apartment, only one lamp lit in the parlor, she took his hat and coat and led him to the sickroom. "I've brought the doctor."

A short, older gentleman with a rounded belly glared at Michael. "I told you no other physician was needed. I can attend to Miss Robinson myself just fine. I may be retired, but I'm not dead."

Michael stepped backward. Miss Peters had not informed him that another doctor had been brought in on the case. "I'm sorry. I didn't know—"

"And as I told Miss Peters, your services won't do any good." This from the tall woman in a high-necked black gown sitting beside the patient. "My husband is expecting her in heaven. He told me so. She won't recover."

Goose bumps broke out on Michael's flesh.

What had he gotten himself into?

Chapter Two

The weak, early-morning, late-winter sunshine attempted to poke through the window as Michael leaned back after examining Miss Robinson. Praise the Lord, the young woman had lived through the night.

He focused his attention on Miss Peters and Mrs. Robinson, both sitting in tall kitchen chairs on the other side of the bed. "I'm going to prescribe some bismuth phosphate, each dose to be dissolved in three parts water and taken at regular intervals to ease her stomach discomfort. Be sure she drinks plenty of tea since she is losing so many fluids." Beyond that, he didn't know what to tell the young woman or her family.

Though still alive, Miss Robinson was much weaker than she had been last evening when he first saw her. If she continued in this state much longer, he didn't hold out any hope for her recovery. The next few hours would prove critical.

The young woman's mother rubbed her red eyes. "I've been giving her plenty to drink, doctor. Nothing wants to stay in her stomach."

"Whatever you can get into her will be helpful. Just keep up the good work."

"Thank you. I was so hoping Moses would be wrong this time. But he's never wrong."

"Moses?"

"My dear, dear late husband. He comes to me in dreams, always right before death visits this home." She pulled a black-lace trimmed handkerchief from her apron pocket and dabbed her eyes.

At her words, shivers ran up his arms, and he shook his head.

He'd heard of spiritualists before but had never met one in person. She might have very vivid dreams, but her husband didn't warn her of death. Michael couldn't believe in such things that weren't in the Bible.

"Thank you, Dr. Wheaton." The shadow of a dimple appeared in Miss Peters's right cheek. "I'll show you out."

On his way to the door, he stopped in the comfortable parlor, the heavy maroon brocade curtain drawn, and he placed the medicine bottle next to another vial on the carved oak fireplace mantel. He picked up the amber bottle and rolled it around in his hands. No label on it. That was strange. "What's in this?"

Miss Peters shrugged. "I don't know. I believe Dr. Beers left it there last evening or perhaps the evening before that when he was here. Probably something he gave Lizzie for her stomach upset."

"Well, I would discontinue the use of whatever this is and start with bismuth phosphate. What Dr. Beers prescribed isn't working."

With a soft, fleeting touch to his arm, Miss Peters kept him from leaving. "Please, I beg you, be honest with me. What is Lizzie's prognosis?" She gazed at him with intense, dark blue eyes that pleaded with him to save her friend's life, a shimmer of a tear sparkling in the low lamplight.

He scrubbed his unshaven cheek, his whiskers rough beneath his fingers. "I really can't say." He didn't have it in him to break her heart. Delivering bad news was the worst part about being a doctor. His mentor, Dr. White, said he would toughen the more he did this, but how could one grow so calloused to human suffering?

"Can't say or won't say?"

She was too perceptive for her own good. "You want me to be honest?"

"More than anything." Her voice was breathy, her shoulders stiff.

"What baffles me is that this is a recurring illness in this home, always resulting in death. I would characterize it as a family ailment, but you said your friend's uncle through marriage recently died from similar symptoms."

"That's correct."

"And you characterized that as poisoning."

"From his workplace. Yes, that's what the doctor said."

"Was that Dr. Beers?"

"No. Mrs. Robinson brought in another physician at that time as well, though Dr. Beers concurred."

"Where is Miss Robinson employed?"

"She isn't. She stays at home and keeps the house and watches after the smaller children."

If the uncle died from chemical poisoning and this young lady was suffering very similar symptoms, what could the correlation be? Probably nothing more than a coincidence.

"Truth be told, this case has me exceedingly puzzled. I can treat the symptoms, but I have no idea of the underlying cause. That makes a cure all the more difficult."

"What you're telling me is there isn't any hope for Lizzie?" Miss Peters crushed her spotless white apron in her hands.

"I have no idea how many days the good Lord has in store for your friend. My feeling is that it may not be many."

Miss Peters closed her eyes for a long moment before opening them and gazing at him. "Thank you for your honesty. Difficult as it is to hear, it is good to be prepared."

"Tell me, does Mrs. Robinson often speak of hearing from the dead?"

"She merely has strong dreams, that's all. She's a good, God-fearing, church-going woman. One who saved my life."

Perhaps that's all it was. Nothing more than strange dreams during the night. He himself often dreamed of things that were happening in his life. After all, he didn't know the woman. He should give her the benefit of the doubt. Then again, he knew all too well what insanity looked like.

"I will check in again later today. If there is any change either way in Miss Robinson's condition, please send for me at once."

"Thank you very much, Dr. Wheaton. We appreciate it."

After a short walk down the block, Michael hired a carriage and rode to his office. If he didn't have many patients to see today, he would spend the rest of the morning poring over his medical books to determine the mysterious cause of Miss Robinson's illness. Still, he couldn't quite shake the notion that something was not quite right in that house.

As Michael pulled up to the building, an older gentleman with a tall top hat and his coat collar turned up against the February wind was knocking on the office door. Michael hurried to pay the driver, then approached his caller. "Dr. White, how good to see you."

"Ah, Michael, I was afraid I had missed you."

"And so you almost did. But I'm glad I caught you. Come inside and warm up. I have a case I'd like to ask you about."

In short order, Michael had his mentor sitting on the davenport with a cup of coffee to warm him through. "First I should ask what brings you out on such a cold day."

"Cooped up in my house for too long. I'm not about to sit inside all day waiting for life to come to me. I may be retired, but I'm not going to spend my time rocking and knitting."

Michael chuckled at the image that conjured. "Well, I'm glad you're here."

"You mentioned needing to speak to me about a patient."

Michael filled him in on Lizzie Robinson's case. "I don't know what to think. I can't come up with any reasonable cause for this same disease to strike so many in the household, including one who wasn't related to them by blood. Not to mention that it's always fatal."

Dr. White stroked his drooping mustache. "Interesting that you mentioned the man's case of poisoning from the factory. I wonder if he could have been carrying something on his person in some way when he came home that sickened his family members."

"That might make sense in some of the cases, but not in Moses

Robinson's death. Mr. Freeman wasn't living with them then, and not in Miss Robinson's case either, as Mr. Freeman has been gone for about six months."

"That is quite unusual. Let me do some research, and I'll let you know what I find."

"You have a hunch, don't you?"

"Not really. You do some hunting in those books of yours too, and let's see what we can come up with."

When Dr. White left, Michael pored over the texts, just about ripping his hair out when he couldn't find anything that fit the symptoms.

He kept at it until the light in his office dimmed and his eyes burned. Then he slammed the book shut.

All day, and he had no reasonable explanation for the illness.

Was he about to fail another patient?

The house on Holland Street sat still and quiet, the black and gold mantel clock ticking away the precious moments Lizzie had left on this earth. Harriet leaned over her friend's sickbed and replaced the cool cloth on her sweaty brow. "Oh, my sweet, you should have been able to marry Fred and should have had many, many happy years with him. You should have been able to be a mother to your own houseful of children." This loss stabbed Harriet in the heart. "Why don't you let me send for him?"

"No. Mama wasn't happy when I told her about my beau. I don't want to upset her."

"It's time you think about yourself and about your beloved and not worry about your mother."

"She cried and cried so when I told her we wanted to live in Cambridgeport. The thought of losing me broke her heart. I sent Fred a note telling him not to come. Besides, I don't want him to see me such a mess."

"If he loves you less because of it, then he isn't the man for you. I'm going to notify him. He can come during the day while I'm here to chaperone. Now that's settled." Harriet sat back in her chair.

Mrs. Robinson, Willie, and Charley had all gone to work. Though Lizzie lay near death's doorway, they needed the income to survive. Harriet had her shop to think about, but the only pressing order she had was Mrs. McGovern's hat.

That would have to wait. The shop would still be there tomorrow. Lizzie may not be. Her friend needed her. Not to mention that someone had to watch after Tommy and Gracie. Harriet had given them each a slate and a piece of chalk and set them at the kitchen table to draw. A few moments of peace and quiet Harriet might spend with her friend.

She sat in a chair beside the bed and dashed off the note to Fred. Perhaps when Lizzie slept, there would be an opportunity to get the note to the box to be delivered to Fred.

Lizzie thrashed and moaned, and Harriet rubbed her warm hand. "Try to rest." Another round of sleet and snow pinged at the bedroom window, the storm demanding to be let in but unable to clench its icy grip around the patient.

Lizzie moaned. "The pain. The pain. It burns so. Like the hottest fire."

Harriet took a few deep breaths. To watch her friend in such agony tore at her heart. "I wish there were something I could do." Sitting there, helpless against the onslaught of the disease, was the worst. Nothing she did, nothing anyone did, made Lizzie better. "Shall I get you more tea?"

Lizzie shook her head. "It makes my stomach churn more."

"Some water then. Dr. Wheaton said you need to drink plenty. Just a few sips. For me. Please? I promise, this isn't mixed with anything so foul as the medicine he left."

"For you, anything."

Harriet lifted Lizzie from the pillow and held the glass while her friend swallowed a tiny bit of the liquid.

"That's the way. Keep that up, and you'll be feeling better in no time."

"Mama says I won't." A dark-brown lock of Lizzie's hair curled on her damp cheek.

"Hush now. We all dream crazy things from time to time. It doesn't mean that everything we see in the night is going to come to fruition in the light of day."

Lizzie clenched her stomach. "Oh, I can't bear it. I'm going to be ill."

As she was sick, Harriet held her, stroking her head, holding her silken strands out of the way. "Sweetheart, don't worry, it's going to be fine. You're going to be fine."

Once the nausea subsided, Harriet cleaned up Lizzie, changed her nightgown, and freshened the room. "How are you feeling now?"

"A bit better, I think. The pain isn't so bad. Perhaps I'll try a little more water."

This time, she sipped much more. Some of the weight that had pressed on Harriet's shoulders lifted. "That's so good. What did I tell you? Keep doing what Dr. Wheaton said, and you'll be better in no time." She wouldn't share with Lizzie what prognosis the man had pronounced. "I can't lose you, my dear, dear friend. My only friend."

"You are so good to me. To us."

"After you and your mother took me under your wing when I first came to town, I could do no less for you. You became my family after I fled mine. I owe each of you a great debt."

"No debt in friendship."

Harriet couldn't halt the stream of salty tears that cascaded down her cheeks and dripped from her chin. "You took me in and had pity on me when no one else would. Your sweet mother even gave me a little money to start my shop. Without you, I'd be living on the street, doing who knows what."

"Hush. Don't talk like that. You've been good to us, nursing my uncle in his illness, helping with the children. You are a true friend."

"And what about the very handsome Fred Fisher?"

A wan smile crossed Lizzie's face, and she shifted positions in the bed. "Mama, though not happy at all about it, agreed to meet him. To at least see how wonderful he is and how much he means to me. Nothing made me happier than that. Oh Harriet, we have the most terrific place to live all picked out. Now that I'm so ill, I don't know when the meeting will happen."

"I have the note to him all written. I just have to drop it in the box. My guess is that you didn't make your illness sound that serious."

"Please, don't post it yet. When I get feeling a little better, then he can come."

By the slight blush in Lizzie's cheeks, Harriet could almost believe that Lizzie would recover. That she would rise from this bed, go about her usual chores, and perhaps one day marry the dashing Fred Fisher and have a family of her own. "How is your pain?"

"Much less. I'm as weak as a cup of Mama's tea but feeling ever so much better. And all thanks to you and your nursing."

Harriet gave a one-note laugh. "I don't think that is true. Nursing is not my calling, I'm quite sure. I'm glad you're improving, though. I couldn't stand to lose you."

"You would be fine. Everyone would be."

"What about the little ones? They adore you."

"I would miss them horribly, but they would soon forget about me."

"No one who has ever known you and loved you could ever forget about you." Harriet shook her head. "This is morbid. I don't want to think about it."

"But it's going to happen to all of us one day, whether we think about it or not. This might even be my time. I don't know."

"I can tell you that it isn't." Harriet scraped her chair back and stood, clapping her hands together. "That's enough of that kind of talk. I hereby declare that Elizabeth Robinson will recover from this illness and will be my very best friend and companion from now until forever."

Lizzie chuckled. "You are a goose, but that is why I love you so."

"And I love you too." Harriet kissed Lizzie's smooth forehead. "Now, I'm going to slice some bread for you to eat. You need to get your strength back."

But you couldn't wave a wand like the magician at the circus did and make everything right again. All Harriet could do was pray that Lizzie had survived the worst and would live.

Chapter Three

Harriet's horse's hooves pounded underneath her, matching the throbbing in her head. She dug her heels into the mount's side, urging him to run faster. She had no idea where she was going, only that she had to hurry, had to reach her destination as fast as possible.

The urgency wrapped around her throat, and she had a difficult time drawing in a deep breath.

The hooves pounded, pounded, pounded.

With a gasp, Harriet awoke and sat up straight in bed, her heart racing as fast as the stallion in her dream.

Still, the pounding continued. Not only part of her dream, but part of reality.

"Miss Peters, wake up. Miss Peters!"

Was that Dr. Wheaton's voice? As she dashed down the stairs to the door, she threw a wrapper around her shoulders.

She flung open the door to discover the doctor did indeed stand on her front step. "What on earth are you doing here this time of night? You'll wake my neighbors."

"Hurry and dress. There isn't time to lose. Charley just came for me. Miss Robinson has taken a turn for the worse."

That strangling sensation from her dream returned. Her breath came in short spurts. "No. No! She was fine when I left her. Talking. Laughing. Eating. No, this can't be happening."

"The horse cars aren't running this time of night. I've been to the livery and saddled my mare. That will have to do. Please, from what Charley told me, there isn't much time."

"I'll be down in two minutes." Though her limbs shook, Harriet raced up the stairs, pulled on a skirt and a shirt, and covered it all with a heavy sweater. No time for a corset. She shrugged on her green cloak as she stepped through the doorway.

Dr. Wheaton boosted her into the saddle, and they set off through Somerville's darkened streets. In the distance, a dog barked. A cat scurried across the icy path, but the doctor held to the horse's reins and urged her forward.

Harriet held tight to him, his body firm beneath her grasp. She huddled behind him to cut the bite of the wind that whistled in her ears. The temperature had risen a couple of degrees, and a frigid rain slashed at them. How could he see?

With no wagon or pedestrian traffic to dodge, they arrived at the Robinson home in record time. Charley waited for them on the porch, running to greet them as Dr. Wheaton pulled to a stop. Charley gave Harriet a hand then took the reins from the doctor. "Go and see her."

Lifting her sodden skirts, Harriet raced to the apartment behind the doctor. She didn't bother to shed her soaked cloak but burst into Lizzie's room just after Dr. Wheaton. A small lamp on the bedside table provided little light in the enveloping blackness that consumed the bedchamber.

As before, Lizzie moaned and thrashed, the sheets twisted around her legs. Sweat glistened on her face, and the room stank of vomit.

Mr. Smith, the Sunday school superintendent from their church, stood over Lizzie, laying hands on her and praying.

Harriet gazed at Mrs. Robinson. "What happened? She was fine just a couple of hours ago, and now she's worse than ever. I thought, I thought she was going to live."

Mrs. Robinson shook her head and brushed a tear from her drawn, lined face. "I don't know. The illness returned so suddenly and violently. I knew this would happen. I just knew it would. Didn't I tell you? You never listen to me. You really should."

Harriet knelt on the floor at Lizzie's bedside. "My darling, my poor, poor darling. What can I do for you?"

"The pain. The burning. I want it over."

"Just hold on. It will go away as it did before. I promise." Harriet rubbed Lizzie's shoulder to calm her, but her friend didn't respond to her ministrations. Mr. Smith mumbled more prayers for Lizzie and her soul.

"Listen." Lizzie's voice was so soft, Harriet had to strain to hear her.

"I'm right here. I'm not going anywhere."

"Do me a favor."

"Anything. You know I would do anything for you. Just say the words, and it will be accomplished."

"Promise me, Harriet. Take care of Tommy and Gracie. I know you have your shop." She paused to catch her breath. "Don't give that up. But help them."

"Don't worry about them. They are sleeping now."

"When I'm gone."

"You aren't going anywhere." *Dear God, she can't go anywhere. I beg You to please not take her from me. Without her, I have no one. I'll be lost and alone in the world. You wouldn't do that to me. Please, don't do that to me.*

"I am. God is calling me home."

No, He couldn't be. Lizzie had her whole life in front of her. What about Fred? He would be devastated at Lizzie's loss. This was too much, entirely too much.

Rain slashed at the windowpanes, the dampness settling in Harriet's bones.

A gentle touch to her shoulder brought her focus back to the sickroom.

"Let me examine her." A dripping wet Dr. Wheaton, his long brown oilskin coat reaching beyond his knees, set his black bag on the bed and opened it, withdrawing a stethoscope.

Harriet rose from her knees and gave him room to do his work. Mr. Smith stepped backward, his eyes closed, his lips moving as he incanted prayers. After listening to Lizzie's heart and lungs and pressing on her belly, Dr. Wheaton stood back. "Has she been able to keep any food or water down?" He directed his question to Mrs. Robinson.

"Not since I've been home from work."

"She ate some bread while I was with her this afternoon, and that went well." Lizzie's condition had changed so drastically in such a short time. That shouldn't be so. Such a vibrant woman couldn't deteriorate this fast.

"I don't know why Charley sent for you." Mrs. Robinson's words, directed at Dr. Wheaton, were sharp, but the woman had to be in an awful state. "Dr. Beers has come and gone and pronounced this to be the end."

Dr. Wheaton nodded. "I have to concur. It won't be long now."

Harriet returned to Lizzie's side. "You could be wrong, couldn't you?"

Mr. Smith opened his eyes and stared right at Harriet. "Though we pray for her recovery, her life is in God's hands. If it's His will to call her home, that is what shall happen."

Lizzie gave Harriet's hand a little gentle pressure. "He's right. The Lord's call is louder, stronger now than the call of this world. If you could but see it, Harriet. Oh, it's beautiful. Lord Jesus, I come."

Lizzie went limp.

The pinks, peaches, and oranges of dawn had just lit the sky when Michael returned to the office that doubled as his residence. He mussed his hair. Who cared how disheveled he was?

He had lost a patient.

Not his first one.

Not his last, no doubt.

Something about this one, though, stung more than any other.

There had to have been more he could have done. A clue that he had missed in his examination or diagnosis of Miss Robinson. But what was it? If only he could figure it out.

Strange how she had been better the past afternoon and was gone by the morning. Very strange.

Who knew? Maybe the kids in school were right. He was not cut out to be anything other than the town crazy. After all, precedent was on his side. Perhaps that was all he could aspire to be.

Even all these years later, heat raced up his neck and into his cheeks at the thought. Becoming a doctor had been the worst idea of his life. Yes, helping people was the best part of the job.

But watching someone die, someone so young and full of life and with so much potential ahead of her, was gut-wrenching. And the way Miss Peters mourned over the loss of her friend. He would never shake the sound of her wails from his head.

A light tap came at the door a moment before it cracked open. "Are you seeing patients yet?"

Anyone other than Dr. White, and Michael would have turned them away. "Come in, come in. What brings you by so early?"

The gray-haired man gave Michael a quick appraisal. "You look like something the cat dragged in."

"Good morning to you too."

"I understand that you had something of a rough night."

"Word travels fast. I thought Somerville was big enough that it was immune to small-town gossip."

"I happen to know the undertaker." Dr. White shrugged. "Hazard of the business. He stopped by and let me know you might need a friend this morning."

"I don't even have coffee brewed yet."

Dr. White waved him away. "Don't need any. After so many years of doctoring at all hours of the night, my body has adjusted to being up any time. You'll get used to it. Probably already are, after working with me like you did."

"Was it hard?"

"Hmm?" Dr. White raised his bushy gray eyebrows. "Was what hard?"

"Losing those first few patients once you were on your own."

"Watching anyone die is difficult. That's not the way life was supposed to be. Sin changed all that."

Michael pushed his chair back and made a circuit of the claustrophobic room jammed with medical books and littered with papers. Once around the space, he turned and headed in the other direction. "I don't know if I'm cut out for this."

"What do you mean?"

"It isn't right that a healthy twenty-four-year-old woman should suddenly get so violently ill that she dies in a couple of days. Her death was one of the most horrific I've ever heard about or witnessed. She suffered so much, and there was nothing I could do but stand by and watch. Nothing I could give her to ease her agony. I had to have missed something. I have this feeling there was more going on that I didn't pick up on."

Dr. White stood in front of Michael to stop his pacing and grasped him by the shoulders. "You can't beat yourself up every time a patient dies. In this profession, that happens all too often. As doctors, we work as hard as we can and use every tool at our disposal to save our patients, but in the end, it's up to God whether the people under our care live or die."

"I understand that. I do. This case is different, though. There's this undefinable quality about it. This feeling deep in my gut that everything isn't as it first appears in the Robinson house. It's curious that so many of them have passed away and all of them under similar circumstances."

"What is it that bothers you about the case?"

"I can't put my finger on it. Maybe that's the problem. I have no diagnosis. It's not diphtheria or scarlet fever or anything readily recognizable."

Dr. White rubbed the top of his head. "You're right. Nothing comes immediately to my mind, and the research I did yesterday didn't get me any closer to an answer. I'll keep working on it. But don't doubt yourself. You're a good doctor."

Michael puffed out a breath. "Am I? A good doctor, I mean?

Because right now, I don't feel like it. I feel like I failed that family. They came to me for help, and I wasn't able to aid them. Their daughter, their sister, their friend, died despite my assistance. Or maybe because of it." He closed his eyes, and the image of Miss Peters leaning over Miss Robinson's body had engraved itself onto the backs of his eyelids.

"That's no way to think. You did nothing wrong in the case. You treated it exactly as I would have. No matter how much you may want to, you can't save everyone."

But the taunts of the kids Michael had grown up with rang in his ears. He couldn't shut them out. Perhaps they had been right all along. Maybe he was like his mother after all.

Dr. White gave him a small shake. "I know what you're thinking. That's enough of that. No more. I've watched you grow. You're good. You know your science. You understand the workings of the human body as well as anyone today does. Not to mention that you're compassionate with your patients and their families. Maybe too compassionate."

"What you're saying is that I have to become more hardened?"

The older man released Michael and took his seat once more, one leg crossed over the other. "Not hardened. Just learn how to carry on after each case. You did the best you could, and now it is over. Don't allow yourself to dwell on it. That could be your ruin."

But how did one go about not feeling anything? Especially when, in his wake, he left a home already struck by tragedy in even deeper mourning.

The weight of that grief he understood all too well.

Chapter Four

A gust of wind lifted the black veil that covered Harriet's face and froze the tears that streamed down her face. In front of her, the undertaker lowered Lizzie's coffin into the grave dug from the frozen ground. Mrs. Robinson had dressed Lizzie in a pale blue gown she had made. Lizzie said she was saving it for her trousseau.

Mrs. Robinson squeezed Harriet's hand. Harriet hugged Tommy and Gracie closer to her, in part to keep them warm, in part to ward away their grief. Both of them clung to her black skirts, thick woolen mittens covering their hands.

Reverend Crawford intoned the service. "We don't always understand God's ways, but we acknowledge He is sovereign and holy in all His ways, and we trust that His child, Elizabeth, is now resting safe in His arms."

No, Pastor Crawford was wrong. This death made no sense to Harriet. None at all. Lizzie, bright, vibrant, fun-loving, caring, should not be lying cold in that grave. Her only friend, ripped from her forever. Why did God have to do this to her? This wasn't fair.

No one much would have missed Harriet. Her family in Connecticut had wanted to be rid of her years ago. That's why father arranged the marriage to their despicable, wife-beating neighbor. Lizzie, on the other hand, was needed.

Harriet glanced at Tommy and Gracie, both huddled against her. These children depended on Lizzie to take care of them. What would happen to them now?

Reverend Crawford's words broke through Harriet's musings. "Ashes to ashes, dust to dust."

The mourners, including Harriet, stepped forward, and each

tossed a clump of icy dirt into the gaping hole in the earth, Lizzie's final resting place. Every *thunk* on top of the pine box pierced Harriet's heart until it bled without ceasing.

Mrs. Robinson pushed Gracie forward. The six-year-old threw in her handful of earth then ran back to Harriet and hid herself in the folds of Harriet's dress. Harriet drew a black-edged handkerchief from her pocket and wiped the little girl's eyes. Then she folded it over and dabbed at her own tears.

Once the service had concluded, members of the Methodist church where Mrs. Robinson worshipped gathered around her, murmuring their condolences. Harriet stood to the side between the children.

A light snow now fell, driving away those gathered to pay their last respects. At last, no one was left but the family, Harriet, and Dr. Beers.

Mrs. Robinson approached her. "Thank you so much for being here, dear. You don't know what this means to me and to the children." She nodded to Tommy and Gracie.

"It's what Lizzie would have wanted. She showed me kindness, you all did, when I ran away from home. Without Lizzie and your family, I don't know where I would be. Either dead or in the workhouse."

Mrs. Robinson squeezed Harriet's hand. "We don't know where we would be without you. Thank you for your tender care of Lizzie at the end. You were a great comfort to her in those final minutes."

Charley and Willie joined them. Willie wrapped her in a cool embrace and squeezed her. "I have lost one sister but gained. . ." He pulled back and gazed into her eyes.

She touched Willie's whiskered cheek. "You've gained another sister. I can't take Lizzie's place, but I will be there for you and Charley and the little ones. You can count on me."

While Charley stared at the ground and kicked at a lump of snow, Willie smiled at her. "That's good. The holes in our hearts won't seem so large."

What did he mean by that?

She shook it off. Gracie clasped Harriet's hand. She gazed at the child, whose blue eyes were wide. Harriet's almost constant tears threatened to fall again. "I wouldn't have been anywhere else."

"I was wondering. . ." Mrs. Robinson twisted the handkerchief that she held, a large *L* embroidered in the middle of it. Lizzie's.

"Yes?"

"I was wondering if you might consider. . . No, I couldn't ask it of you." Mrs. Robinson shook her head and sniffled.

Harriet leaned forward. "Please, ask me anything. If it's in my power to make it happen, I will."

"I have to keep working at the R.H. White department store to support the family. The boys too have their jobs. Their incomes help. Every little bit does. Though the money from Lizzie's life insurance policy will provide for us for a while, it won't last forever."

Not with the way Mrs. Robinson spent it. Harriet pushed away the unkind thought. The poor woman had lost yet another daughter. Three had died in infancy. Emma had died a few years ago under circumstances similar to Lizzie's. No one could blame her if she was reeling.

"I know you have your shop to think about, but I could use help watching Tommy and Gracie while I'm at work. I guess I'm asking you to move back in and live with us like you did before. You haven't been gone that long, just a few months. What a great burden would be lifted from me if you would be their caretaker, just like Lizzie was."

Harriet sucked in her breath. That was a big commitment. She did have her millinery. She'd worked with all her might for a long four years, apprenticed to a hard-nosed woman who taught her the business, but she had finally done it a few months ago.

Opened her shop. Her piece of the world. Something that belonged to her and to her alone.

Little by little, she was building her clientele. Perhaps she could continue to work at her store while the children were at school and do the rest of her millinery from the Robinsons' home. She had promised Lizzie she would care for the little ones. The vow she'd made to her best friend, her one true friend she'd had, rang in her head.

No matter what the cost, this was a promise she would have to keep. "If I am able to continue my work, if the business doesn't suffer because of it, I will do it. For Lizzie and for you and for the children. You're right. With you, Charley, and Willie working, there is no one to take care of them. The children are in school now, so I can work then. In the summer, they can come to the shop with me. It will take some juggling and finagling, but because I love Lizzie, for her, I'll lend you a hand."

She wouldn't give up her dream of being a milliner. There had to be a way she could make a go of her shop and care for the children as well. With God's help, she would find that way.

Mrs. Robinson kissed Harriet on both cheeks, her lips cold. "Thank you, my dear. It is such a relief to my soul to know that I can share one small part of my burden with someone."

"It's my pleasure." Harriet's throat threatened to close. She bit the inside of her cheek to keep the ever-threatening tears from falling.

Dr. Beers touched Mrs. Robinson's shoulder. "We should head to the house to greet the guests."

Mrs. Robinson nodded. "You're right. We'll see you there in a few moments?"

"Yes. I'll be there to give you a hand."

Mrs. Robinson and her doctor friend strolled toward the waiting carriage.

"Thank you, Harriet." Willie also kissed her cheek while Charley stood to the side. "This is such a relief to Mama." The two brothers followed their mother.

The children remained beside Harriet. She knelt to their level. Gracie hugged Harriet's neck so hard, she couldn't draw a deep breath. She had to loosen the girl's grip.

"Papa, Emma, and now Lizzie are dead. And Auntie and Uncle." Gracie stared at Harriet with the big, pale blue eyes so common in her family. So sad that her uncle passed away on her sixth birthday. "I miss them. Are they in heaven like Reverend Crawford said?"

"Of course they are. They are happy and aren't sick anymore. While we are sad and miss them, we can be happy that they are happy."

Gracie nodded, but her lower lip trembled. Harriet pulled her close and allowed the child to sob. Tommy snuggled into her and shed his own tears. Lizzie had handed her a great responsibility. These children were grieving so much loss, and now it was up to Harriet to step into her shoes and take her place.

No one, though, could ever replace Lizzie.

Mourners packed the Robinsons' parlor. Michael grasped his coffee cup and kept watch as Miss Peters circulated through the crowd. Chairs and other furniture in the parlor hugged the papered walls, leaving a large space for the guests. Miss Peters carried a coffeepot and refilled the callers' mugs.

The elderly woman beside Michael, a black hat perched on her snowy hair, patted his hand. "Bless that Peters girl, for all she's doing for this family. Lizzie loved her without limit. She's a good girl for standing by them through this great tragedy, even though her own heart must be breaking."

"I've noticed that about her. She nursed Miss Robinson so tenderly."

Miss Peters meandered in their direction, the smiles she gave the guests tight, her face pale. A small light brightened her eyes as she reached Michael. "Can I warm your coffee?"

"Are you feeling well?"

"I'm fine." Even as she spoke the words, though, she teetered.

He grabbed her by her elbow. "Give me the pot."

She did as he bid. He set it on a table and led her from the room, down the stairs, and to the porch. "I saw you were overcome."

The brisk air teased a wisp of black hair from its pins. "Thank you. I couldn't take it anymore."

"Have you slept much?"

She shook her head.

"You need to rest before you fall ill yourself."

"Oh, I can't get sick. Tommy and Gracie are depending on me now."

"Don't worry. I don't believe the illness that claimed your friend is contagious. No one else in the house has symptoms." Not that he could guarantee she would remain healthy, but in that moment, she appeared so vulnerable. Like she needed someone to take care of her.

She nodded and hugged herself. What had he been thinking, dragging her outside? She might not catch whatever had taken Miss Robinson from this earth, but she might catch her death of cold because of him. Some kind of doctor he was.

He slipped off his jacket and wrapped it around her shaking shoulders. She leaned into him, fitting perfectly into the crook of his arm, and sobbed. For a moment, he stiffened. A woman had never wept in his arms before. What did he do? When she snuggled closer, he wrapped her in a one-arm embrace.

"What am I going to do without her?"

He had no words to offer, nothing to say to console her. Instead, he stood there and allowed her to grieve.

The door behind them clicked open, and Miss Peters jumped from his embrace, wiping the remnants of her tears from her eyes.

"I was wondering where you had gone." Mrs. Robinson, tall, regal, with hooded eyes, stood in the doorway. The wind tugged on her black skirts, tangling them around her legs.

Miss Peters shook more than ever. "I'm sorry, Mrs. Robinson. I just needed some air."

What must the woman think of him? Had he sullied Miss Peters's reputation? Though their actions were innocent, some may not take them that way. He stepped forward, between the two women. "This is entirely my fault. I saw that Miss Peters wasn't well, so I suggested we come out for some air. I'm afraid her grief overtook her, and I comforted her."

Miss Peters moved from behind him. "I'm feeling much better now. Thank you, Dr. Wheaton." She tugged off his jacket and handed it to him. "I appreciate your kindness." With that, she disappeared into the house.

Mrs. Robinson, however, stood her ground, her hands on her slender hips, a frown on her care-worn features. "I believe your services are no longer needed. I have a responsibility to Miss Peters, you understand, and can't allow you to take advantage of her."

"Of course. I meant no harm. I came to pay my respects and to check that no one else in the family had fallen ill."

"How very. . .caring of you, Doctor. We are all well."

"I only wish I could have done more for your daughter. Again, you have my sympathies."

"There was nothing anyone could have done. I hope you also understand that I don't have money to pay you. I have a large household to provide for, and even with Miss Peters coming to live with us and paying her own way, that burden only grows."

"Oh, I didn't know that Miss Peters would be boarding with you." Why would she leave her home above her shop?

"She is a generous person, Dr. Wheaton, willing to sacrifice for others. That is why Lizzie asked her to take care of the younger children, so we can work and provide for the family. That, sir, is what Christian charity looks like." A swish of her skirts and a slam of the door, and she was gone.

Michael startled. Mrs. Robinson left no room for misinterpreting where he stood, at least with her.

He made his way to the street and stared at the upstairs apartment, mourners passing in front of the parlor window. He shuddered. Something about this house struck him as strange. Sinister.

A warmth spread through him as Miss Peters came to mind. The way she had leaned into him for comfort. Of course, he was the nearest person at the time, so it was nothing more than that. But it had been his honor to be the one to try to ease her suffering.

If she was going to be living here from now on, what would become of her shop? He didn't know her well and to this point had only passed the storefront with casual interest. Would the building become vacant?

Oh, well. He probably wouldn't have a chance to meet the family ever again. Hopefully this would be the last of the mysterious deaths. No one else was exhibiting concerning symptoms.

Just as he stepped from the porch, he peered up one more time.

Inside, someone covered the window with a black curtain.

Chapter Five

Michael scrubbed at his stubble-covered cheek as he stumbled down the boardwalk to his office. A drip, drip, drip from the eaves ticked out a steady rhythm. A thaw had set in while he was gone overnight to deliver Mrs. Yount's new baby.

His toes hadn't gone numb on the long walk from the young couple's house to his office, and his nose wasn't frosty. The pink and orange sun peeking over the two- and three-story buildings of Somerville promised to raise the temperature further.

He climbed the two steps to his front door and inserted the key into the lock. A movement out of the corner of his right eye caught his attention. A dark figure moved down the street toward him. From the swish of the hips, it must be a female. She trotted at a brisk pace, even for so early in the morning. Perhaps someone come to seek his services.

As she approached, the sun slanted across her fair face, the blackness of her dress highlighting the paleness of her skin. And then those intense blue eyes pierced him.

Harriet. He shook his head. No, he had to refer to her as Miss Peters. Without a second thought, he left the key in the lock and retraced his steps to meet her as she came to her shop. "Miss Peters, what a pleasure. You and your friend's family haven't been far from my thoughts or prayers these days since the funeral."

Whether the sun dimmed or her eyes did, he couldn't tell. "Thank you for your well wishes. It has been a very difficult time for the family." Her voice caught.

"And for you."

She nodded. "There's an empty spot in my heart I doubt will

ever be filled. I had no other friend than her."

"What brings you by so early this morning?" Up close, the dark circles under her eyes were more prominent. "Not able to sleep?"

She shook her head. "My only comfort is that Lizzie is no longer suffering. But Charley, Willie, and Mrs. Robinson have returned to work. I'm busy with Tommy and Gracie. And that Tommy. . ." For a moment, a bright smile turned up the corners of her lips before disappearing.

"He's a handful?"

"That's an understatement. I don't know how Lizzie managed to keep him under control. She had this way about her that commanded respect and obedience from him. I don't possess it."

"Give it time. It's only been a few days, and the poor child has been through quite a loss. His entire family is gone, and now his well-loved cousin. That's enough to upset anyone, much less a young child."

This time, a genuine light lit her eyes. "You're very wise for a younger man. Yes, I agree, I must learn to be patient. In the meantime, I'm here to pick up some of my belongings. I'm moving back into the Robinson home to help with Tommy and Gracie."

"Back into the home?"

"I lived with them for about three years before renting this space just a few months ago. Mrs. Robinson was very good to me then, and I owe it to her now."

"That is gracious of you. I do hope you won't be giving up your shop."

"Of course not. When Gracie and Tommy are in school, the shop will run as usual. Whatever work I don't finish during the day, I can complete at the house after the children have gone to bed. On weekends and school holidays, they can come with me to the store. I've worked too hard to start the millinery to see it fail now. Without it, I have nothing."

"I'm glad we'll continue to see you in the neighborhood."

"I've struggled these past six months or so to build a clientele, too hard to just give it up. Things will work out. I'm sorry. I shouldn't have dumped my problems on you."

Mrs. Robinson was right on one point. Harriet was selfless and giving. "No trouble at all. I'm happy to be a listening ear." He glanced at the deep brown valise she held in her slender left hand. "What can I help you with?"

"Nothing right now, thank you. I'll take items to the Robinsons' a little bit at a time. Tommy and Gracie can help me. Some of it will have to stay here for clients." She sighed.

"I insist. Pack up all you need, and I will call for a carriage."

"That's very kind, sir, and I'm most appreciative, but I don't have the funds."

"I will take care of hiring the transportation."

"I couldn't allow you to do such a thing. Please, I don't want to be beholden to you. If the bags grow too heavy, I can always take the horse car."

"Consider it an act of friendship."

Miss Peters sucked in her breath then bit her lip, as if considering his offer.

"You know how much time and trouble it will save you. More time for you to spend with the children in their grief and to comfort Mrs. Robinson. You'll also have more hours to create your fabulous hats."

For the first time since he'd met her, she laughed. "And you know that my hats are fabulous? You have a good grasp on women's fashion? Perhaps you're in the wrong profession."

"I would expect no less of you, that's all."

"They say that flattery gets you nowhere, but in this case, I believe flattery might just have gotten you a job helping me move."

"Then it's a deal. I'll bring over some crates and trunks I have and then call for the carriage. In no time, you'll be well and truly settled in the Robinson household. I hope they appreciate what you're doing."

"I have many sisters, Dr. Wheaton. Five to be exact, though all of them are much younger than I am. Lizzie Robinson was closer to me than any of my blood sisters." Like the sky before a storm, her countenance darkened, and water pooled in the corners of her eyes, threatening to stream down like the rain.

Great. Now he'd gone and done it. Made the poor woman weep. He touched her arm, her dark green wool cape soft beneath his fingertips. "I'm sorry."

"No, it's not your fault. They cannot help what a heartless man my father is." She gestured as if cleaning a slate. "I miss Lizzie tremendously." With the back of her hand, she wiped the tears from her eyes. Within a moment, she had composed herself.

"What do you say we get started?"

"That sounds like a grand plan." She unlocked her door and slipped inside, then turned to him. "Just one thing. When we get to the Robinsons' home, perhaps it would be better if you didn't let them know you were with me."

As the carriage approached the Robinsons' house, Harriet slid forward on the leather seat, so far that she almost bumped knees with Dr. Wheaton, who sat across from her. Though more than happy to do what Lizzie had asked her to do, shivers still raced up and down her spine every time she approached the large, ornate gray house on Holland Street where her friend had lived and died.

They hadn't even resided there that long. But this house in particular, though nicer than any other home the Robinsons had occupied, sent Harriet's stomach flipping around her middle. She held tight to the edge of the seat to keep from sprinting all the way back to her small, neat rooms over the millinery. She would miss the freedom she had gained at last.

The driver pulled the horse to a halt, and Harriet glanced at the upstairs window overlooking the street. Just as she did so, the black curtain fell into place. And it wasn't a child's face she had glimpsed at the pane. There was no doubt about who it was. A woman with an angular jaw and hard lines.

She turned to Dr. Wheaton. "Thank you so much for your help. I do appreciate it more than I can say. To have to lug this many belongings here or take them on the horse car would have been quite the chore. You have made my task that much easier."

"I'll carry the trunk upstairs. You can't lift it."

"No, I beg you not to." The words shot from her mouth.

"Why not?"

"Mrs. Robinson is still quite upset about Lizzie's death, as you can imagine. She is searching for someone to vent her hurt and her anger upon. It seems she's chosen you. Despite all you did for her daughter, and I know you did all you could, she won't forgive you for her death. She complains about you without ceasing." Her pulse thrummed in her ears.

"I can take care of myself when it comes to Mrs. Robinson. Don't worry about me. I've been trained to handle such situations."

Harriet curled her bottom lip under her teeth, then caught herself and stopped short of biting it. "It's no problem. Because it's Saturday, Charley should be home from his job early. Between him and Willie, we'll be able to handle the cases. We can leave them on the porch until they arrive."

"I insist. Let me help you in this way."

Why did he want to do this? Most of the time, Mrs. Robinson was a kind woman. She had a deep love and protective spirit when it came to her family, so when she got the idea someone had wronged a relative, she went on the warpath. When that happened, you wanted to be sure to give her a wide berth. "You will only be making trouble for the family if you do."

This brought him up short. "I wouldn't want to cause problems. Very well. I'll remain downstairs."

"Thank you." She slid from the carriage, glancing over her shoulder as she scurried up the walk to the door, just to be sure he wasn't following. True to his word, he stayed with the carriage. She expelled a breath she hadn't realized she'd been holding.

As she headed up the stairs, Charley and Willie trotted down.

"Good. I'm glad you both are home already."

Willie screwed up his face, much like he would have had he eaten a sour lemon.

Charley peered over her shoulder at Dr. Wheaton standing beside the carriage. "Mighty fancy conveyance you have there, Harriet."

If she had been ten years old, she would have stuck out her tongue at him. Charley was a tease. "I'm a fine lady, you know. Only the best for me. Actually, I was coming to find the two of you. I have more with me than I anticipated. Could you help me bring my belongings inside?"

Willie was already out the door. Charley brushed by her. "Just like a big sister. Already ordering us around. How I've missed you."

Harriet turned and followed him outside. The teasing was a welcome break from the heaviness that filled the house.

She stepped from the porch to find Dr. Wheaton standing on the carriage's step, assisting the driver in untying her trunk from the top. Charley and Willie each took a valise and headed inside.

"What is he doing here?"

At Mrs. Robinson's words, Harriet just about jumped a mile. Clutching her chest, she turned to Lizzie's mother, who stood on the porch. "He hired the carriage and helped me bring my belongings and hat-making materials. This will save so much time. Less running around for me. I'll be better able to take care of the children."

Mrs. Robinson pushed by Harriet and marched in front of Dr. Wheaton. She pointed at him, almost boring her finger into his chest. "You. I blame you in part for Lizzie's death."

He widened his hazel eyes. "Me?"

"Yes, you."

"Dr. Beers was unable to do anything to save your daughter's life either."

Harried had warned him. This wasn't going to make the situation better.

"Dr. Beers brought elixirs and tried everything within his

power. He worked hard to save my daughter's life. You threw up your hands and declared there was nothing to be done. At least he put in some effort. You didn't."

"If you recall, I did give Lizzie some medication, and she did improve for a time. You yourself declared that, no matter what we did, she wouldn't survive. So, according to you, nothing I did or didn't do would have made a difference."

Harriet winced. He should have heeded her warning.

Mrs. Robinson stepped even closer, her beaked nose almost even with Dr. Wheaton's. "Because I knew you were incompetent from the moment I laid eyes on you. Great heavens, isn't there a single doctor in this city, other than Dr. Beers, who knows what he's doing?"

"Please, Mrs. Robinson, it's not good for you to become so distraught." Somehow, Dr. Wheaton managed to keep his composure. For that, Harriet had to give him credit.

"Come, Mrs. Robinson." Harriet took Lizzie's mother by the arm and spun her in the direction of the house. "Let's go inside. I'll make you a cup of tea, and you'll feel better once you drink it. Dr. Wheaton will be on his way." She shot him an apologetic glance over her shoulder before steering Mrs. Robinson up the steps to the family's apartment. Good thing the older gentleman who lived downstairs was hard of hearing.

As they reached the porch, Mrs. Robinson turned again. "Please, leave my family in peace. Don't come around anymore. Let us mourn in private."

Chapter Six

Blue smoke from Dr. Beers's cigar filled the parlor as Harriet sat near the sputtering oil lamp to mend a ripped pair of Tommy's too-small pants. He'd been running away from another boy on the school playground today and had fallen. Just like that, a tear in one of his best pairs of trousers. Not that he had many.

Harriet coughed and waved away the smoke. The doctor and Mrs. Robinson huddled beside each other on the settee, their heads bent together, a length of gorgeous green fabric in Mrs. Robinson's lap. From time to time, Harriet glanced at them. Sometimes they frowned, deep furrows in their foreheads. Other times, they chuckled, almost giggled, like young girls sharing a secret.

A weight pressed on Harriet's chest. She glanced up to find Dr. Beers glaring at her. After she rubbed her neck, she returned her attention to her mending.

"I won!" Tommy's shout broke the parlor's relative stillness. "I beat you at checkers!"

Charley slapped his knee. "You most certainly did. You are getting to be quite the player. How about another game? I have to beat you at least once tonight."

Dr. Beers puffed out a stream of stomach-churning smoke. "I think it's about time for Tommy to go to bed. It is a school night, after all. You too, Gracie."

Harriet raised one eyebrow. Who was Dr. Beers to tell the little ones when it was time for sleep? He was old enough to be their grandfather. She shook her head. Just as well. This way, she could head to bed too, and be out of his presence. "Come on, children. Dr. Beers is right. Time for sweet dreams. I'll bid you all a good night."

She gathered her mending basket while Gracie kissed her mother on the cheek.

"Wait a minute." Willie caught up with her as she made her way down the hall.

"Yes?"

"Take a turn about the block with me once the little ones are asleep. I mean, I know it's cold, but it will be a short walk."

What was this? She tried to smile but failed. To her, Willie was like a brother, not a possible suitor. The thought of it was too bizarre.

Then again, she had been so busy, she'd had little time for herself. Getting out of the house and away from her duties for a bit was a welcome thought. Perhaps it wasn't such a bad idea. Brothers and sisters often did such activities together. It meant nothing. Right? "That sounds wonderful. Let me get the children settled and grab my cloak, and we can be off."

Mrs. Robinson, who was moving her needle in and out of the material, raised an eyebrow. Thankfully, she said nothing.

For some reason, it took longer than usual for Harriet to get Gracie and Tommy to bed. They each wanted just one more story and yet another glass of milk. Finally, she put her foot down and insisted it was time to sleep.

The walk with Willie was sounding better and better all the time.

At last, she closed the door on Tommy and made her way to the smoky parlor. Willie waited by the head of the stairs, tapping his foot.

"My apologies. The children didn't want to settle down tonight. I hope I haven't kept you too long. I know you have to get up for work in the morning."

In typical Willie fashion, he mumbled something or another but then smiled and led the way down the stairs. Once outside, he offered his elbow. Refusing him might cause too much of a fuss, so she linked her arm with his, and they were off.

She glanced at the sky, scattered clouds skittering across the yellow-orange full moon. "It is a lovely night, isn't it? Spring will be in full bloom in short order."

"I like summer better."

"Oh. Well. Yes, summer can be very pleasant. The warmer weather is a welcome relief from the harsh winter."

"Exactly."

They walked almost a block before Harriet tried a different turn of conversation. "How is your job going?"

"I don't like the railroad." A strand of hair fell over his eyes, and he pushed it back. His lips remained in a tight line.

"That's too bad."

"I'll find something else."

Harriet sighed. After another block, she tugged on his arm to pull him to a stop. "I think it's time for us to head back. I still have a few things to finish before retiring."

"Fine." He spun in a circle so fast, it left Harriet rather dizzy. They hustled all the way back to the gray house on Holland Street. When they arrived there, he paused on the front porch. Before Harriet knew what was happening, he pulled her close, very close, and planted a hard kiss on her mouth.

She pushed away, ready to bolt inside, panting to catch her breath. "Willie, I—"

"Harriet, I've loved you for a long time."

No, no, no. This wasn't what she wanted. She squeezed her eyes shut then popped them open. "Listen, Willie, you're a good, hard-working man. But you aren't the right man for me. You are dear to me, but I consider you another brother."

Bright red flooded Willie's cheeks. "Were you stringing me along?"

"What? Of course not. I never treated you in any other way than a sister would treat a brother." Hadn't she? Perhaps she had unwittingly done something that caused Willie to believe she was interested in him.

"That's not how I saw it."

"Then I'm truly sorry for the message my actions were sending. Please, don't let this affect our relationship. We have to live in the same house. Can we pretend this didn't happen and go on with our lives the way they were?"

Willie grunted. "This may be one decision you regret."

He entered the house, slamming the door behind himself, leaving Harriet on the porch trembling.

After several minutes of deep breathing to steady her nerves, she entered the house.

Mrs. Robinson rose, a waterfall of green material cascading from her lap. "What on earth have you done to my son?"

"Nothing, I assure you."

With the way the red rose in Mrs. Robinson's weathered cheeks, Harriet's words had done nothing to placate her. Then again, Mrs. Robinson didn't need to be privy to everything Harriet said or did. "Good night, Mrs. Robinson, Dr. Beers."

Both of them grunted their replies.

Harriet almost raced down the hallway to her room, donned her flannel nightgown, and slid under the quilts beside Gracie.

Creak, creak. The house's old floorboards groaned and squeaked as the house settled in for the night. Harriet lay in bed, Lizzie's old bed, staring straight up at the ceiling. Beside her, Gracie slept, a light whiffling snore coming from her from time to time.

The heavy black curtains at the window blocked out moonlight. Harriet padded from the bed, the floor beneath her bare feet as cold as ice, and lifted the drapes. The bright moon reflected off the still-bare trees, illuminating the night so it glowed with a dawn-like brightness.

Harriet pressed against the window, the glass chilling her from the outside in. If she went across the room for her wrap, she might awaken Gracie, so she stayed put.

Across the top of the back fence, an orange cat scampered on silent feet. He stopped, stared at the ground on the other side of the fence, then pounced. One less mouse or rat in the world. And a good thing. Harriet had found a box of rat poison in one of the kitchen cabinets the other day. Though theirs was a nice apartment in a decent part of town, the Robinsons still had a rodent problem.

Her breath steamed the window, turning to frost almost immediately. With her fingernail, she scraped a peep hole. Two dark figures appeared, their moon-soaked shadows long and stark in the slanting moonbeams. One was rather shorter than the other and rounder, while the other was taller and thinner.

Mrs. Robinson and Dr. Beers. They must have stepped outside for some air. Or else he was finally leaving for the night. Harriet must stop her unkind thoughts. If he had no wife or children, he must get lonely.

They spoke to each other, though their voices were low enough Harriet couldn't make out their words through the closed windowpane. Dr. Beers gestured, his shadow's arms flailing.

Mrs. Robinson shook her head and drew herself straight.

With each word they spoke, their voices grew in pitch. At last, Harriet managed to make out what they were saying to each other. And she didn't have to raise the window to hear.

"I'm not sure. I'm not sure about anything anymore." Mrs. Robinson paced in a circle.

"You can't falter now. There's too much at stake."

"Don't you think I know that? Do you take me for that much of an idiot?"

"No. Not at all."

"Because I'm warning you not to underestimate me. Too many have done that."

"I never would. You know I love you. You know I want to marry you."

"I've told you at least a thousand times now, that is never going to happen. I don't need or want another husband. One was more than enough for me. I'm done with spouses and children. No more of either."

Harriet spun from the window and headed to bed. No matter which way she turned, she couldn't get comfortable. Gracie flipped over, so Harriet attempted to stay still and not disturb the girl.

Get out of the house.

Harriet shot up. Who had said that? Who was in the room? The words hadn't come from either Mrs. Robinson or Dr. Beers. If not them, then who?

She must have been having a dream. Forcing her breaths to steady and her shoulders to relax, she drifted into the land between waking and sleeping.

Get out of the house.

Michael paced behind his desk, wiping his hands on his pants as he made each pass. A stack of thick leather-bound medical books teetered on the edge of the desk. "Tell me what you know about Dr. Beers." As Michael peered at Dr. White, he loosened his collar to release the heat building around his neck.

Dr. White crossed his legs and relaxed against the back of the leather armchair. "He's an elderly gentleman, as you well know, who doesn't see patients anymore. Much like me. Though he has lived in this area for quite a while, he did go to New York state for a time. There was talk he ended up in prison there."

Michael frowned. "Prison?"

"Something about robbery. I'm not quite sure. You know how rumors can be. I would wonder at their validity."

"Was he even qualified to practice?"

Dr. White heaved a sigh. "People have called him a quack. Does he have the best reputation around town? No. Then again, others speak highly of him. In any case, he's not active anymore."

"Other than treating the members of the Robinson household."

"Other than that."

Michael leaned over the paper-strewn desk to stare at his mentor. "Something is rotten in Denmark, I tell you. Not quite right.

Every time I go over there, I get this feeling. I don't know. I can't describe it."

"By the sound of it, the feeling is that they don't want you there. You have to remember they are a house in mourning. Over the past year or two, they have suffered many losses. Their grief is raw. People often say and do things they don't mean when burdened with so much sorrow."

Michael knew all too well what grief did to people. He'd watched the sorrow erode his mother to an even greater degree. Because of his situation, he couldn't sit in judgment on a family dealing with a great deal of loss.

Dr. White curled down the corners of his mouth, his gray mustache following along. "Losing a child is the greatest grief of all, something you never quite recover from. My wife and I lost our beautiful five-year-old daughter to scarlet fever years ago. I think about that little girl, time freezing her as a child, every day."

"I'm sorry about your daughter."

"Medicine is advancing all the time. Someday, I pray, people will live longer, and mothers and children will no longer die in childbirth, and young people will no longer pass away from disease. But that's not the case now."

"So you have experience with people who have lost this much?"

"In a word, yes. I treated a family where all of the children and the mother came down with scarlet fever and died one after the other. Six in all in a matter of weeks. So it's not unheard of."

Michael deflated. Perhaps he was allowing his imagination to run away from him. This funny flutter in his stomach, though, told him something else. He couldn't shake it.

"Don't go making waves where there is no ocean."

Michael couldn't help the chuckle that escaped from deep within his chest. "You should have been a writer. You have a way with words."

"You're a good doctor, Michael. I know it was hard for you to lose your patient. Truth be told, it never really gets any easier. But you learn how to callous your heart."

"What if there was something I missed? Something I could have done?"

"Dr. Beers wasn't able to save her, was he?"

Michael shook his head.

"And he tried?"

"Miss Peters told me he did give Miss Robinson some medication."

"Do you know what it was?"

"No. I prescribed bismuth phosphate."

"That's what I would have done. It didn't help, did it? Whatever illness overtook Miss Robinson, there was nothing to be done about it."

"So I have to sit by and accept it?"

"Pretty much, yes. You aren't God. You can't save everyone." Dr. White pulled himself to his feet. "I need to be going. If I'm not home on the dot of noon, my wife gets testy about having to keep my dinner warm. Now that I'm retired, she likes to eat promptly on the hour." He flashed a wide grin.

"Thanks for listening to me."

"Anytime, my boy, anytime." Dr. White left Michael alone with his thoughts.

He needed to clear his head. After leaving a note in the window indicating what time he would return, he stepped out and strolled down the street. Two- and three-story brick buildings were organized around squares, the Baptist church spire rising above it all. Up on Cobble Hill stood the former home of the McLean Asylum for the Insane.

He was all too familiar with the place.

Tearing his attention away from that house of horrors, he tipped his bowler hat to the woman coming from the general store and to the stooped-over older lady strolling down the street, tapping her cane as she went. When he crossed the street to avoid the tinny piano music streaming from the saloon, he stepped around the horse droppings and scurried in front of a wagon full of sacks of something or another.

He strolled along, ignoring the clanging call of the horse car, until he found himself in front of the police station, built of brick like so many of the other buildings in the city. He stared up at the facade. A uniformed officer stepped out the door and down the stairs.

His mouth went dry. Maybe this was where he had been headed the entire time without even knowing it. Yes, this was the right thing to do. He had no other choice.

Drawing in a deep breath, he climbed the steps and entered the warm interior. Men hustled here and there while others huddled together, no doubt discussing the latest leads in their cases.

He made his way to the counter where an officer in a long blue coat sat, a tall, billed hat on his head.

"Can I help you?"

All Michael could do was nod.

"Sir?"

"I need to speak to an officer. A detective, probably." As his heart thudded in his ears, it drowned out all the background noise.

"And what is this in regard to?"

"A possible crime."

The man gazed up from his paperwork without raising his head. "A possible crime?"

"Yes. Please, just allow me to speak with someone."

"Certainly. I believe Chief Parkhurst is in now. Wait while I see if he's free to speak to you." The officer slipped from behind the desk.

Michael crossed and uncrossed his arms and tapped his foot until the officer returned. "He said he would be willing to see you. Follow me."

They made their way down the long corridor to the back of the room where a middle-aged gentleman with thinning hair and a long, wild beard sat at a table. The pile of file folders on the desk resembled the Leaning Tower of Pisa, about to topple over at the slightest breeze.

The detective motioned toward the straight-back wooden chair opposite him. "Have a seat. I don't believe I have your name."

"Dr. Michael Wheaton." He had a difficult time forcing the words through his tight vocal cords.

"And what brings you in today, Dr. Wheaton?"

"I treated a patient a couple of weeks or so ago who suffered from incredible stomach pains, vomiting, and the like. She died in agony."

"I'm sorry to hear that." The chief's words rang with sincerity.

"She wasn't the first member of this family to pass in such a manner. In fact, a good number have. I believe something nefarious is happening in that home."

"What has led you to this conclusion?"

Michael swallowed hard. "Just a feeling I have."

"No proof?"

He shook his head. "I wish I had some."

Chief Parkhurst leaned back in his chair and chuckled. "In my humble opinion, doctor, along with many years of experience, where there is no smoke, there is no fire."

"But there is. I'm more convinced of it every day."

"The world is a cruel place, Dr. Wheaton. You're a young man yet. You don't know what lurks out there. Still, you can't go peeking around every corner and finding crimes wherever you look. If every doctor who lost a few patients from the same family came in here, I would never get any other work done."

"I understand, sir, but—"

"My hands are tied. Until you bring me absolute proof that a crime has taken place, I cannot help you." The smile fled from the chief's face. "If that's all, I must bid you a good day."

Michael stumbled from the chair and fled the station, humiliation once again nipping at his heels.

Chapter Seven

Heavy clouds hung over Somerville, a light mist falling from time to time, and a chilly spring wind blew from the east. The dampness settled deep into Harriet's bones. After stretching her sore muscles, she dressed herself and made her way to the kitchen.

"Good morning, Harriet." Mrs. Robinson turned away from the stove, a spatula clasped in her hand. "Pancakes for breakfast this morning?"

"They're really good," Charley mumbled around the forkful of flapjacks in his mouth. He winked at Harriet.

Willie stared at her, his eyes narrow. Under his scrutinizing gaze, Harriet squirmed.

"That sounds wonderful. Thank you, Mrs. Robinson. I have to get Tommy and Gracie up for school, but we'll be in shortly."

"I'll have warm pancakes and syrup waiting for you girls."

"What about Tommy?"

Mrs. Robinson cackled. "Him too."

Lizzie's mother did little for the children, little in the house, in fact. To give her credit, she did work hard all day at R.H. White department store as a seamstress. She had to be exhausted most of the time. Especially with how late Dr. Beers stayed each evening.

For all that, the one thing the woman did was prepare breakfast. Each and every morning, she poured the coffee and the milk and fixed the family pancakes or eggs or hash. It helped Harriet get the children ready for school and herself ready for her workday. So far, their system was operating well. Harriet had lost a little business, but not too much. She still made enough to pay Mrs. Robinson for what she ate and to keep her dream alive.

She roused Tommy first. He was the hardest. In order to get him moving, she had to shake his shoulder.

"But I don't wanna get up. I don't wanna go to school."

"Whether you want to or not isn't the issue. You must. Your papa would want you to grow into a fine, strong, smart young man. For him and for your mama, you must get out of bed and attend classes."

He sat up, his brown hair sticking up in clumps at various angles. He leaned forward and grasped Harriet in a full hug, clinging to her by the neck. "I miss them so much. I'm the only one left. Then Lizzie went away too. Will you go away, Miss Harriet?"

She brushed the boy's wild hair in a vain attempt to get it to lay properly. "I promise you, Tommy, I won't go anywhere." Was it a promise she could keep? Life was unpredictable. Just last week, a young woman in town was run over by a carriage. Life could be over at any moment.

Lizzie's was.

Harriet's could be.

She shut her eyes as if she could shut out the thought. Her hands went clammy. If she died, what would happen to her? Sure, she believed in God, but was that enough? Had she done enough good things? She had certainly done many, many bad things. All the time, in fact.

Where did that leave her in God's account book?

"I'm glad you're taking care of me."

Tommy's voice popped her back to the task at home. "I wouldn't be anywhere else." She tweaked his nose. "You are very special to me, Master Freeman. Don't you forget that. Now let's get cracking and off to school. It won't do for you to be late."

Tommy crawled from bed, his skinny arms and legs sticking out from underneath his night dress. When he pulled it off, Harriet stifled a gasp. His ribs showed through his thin, pale skin. He hadn't been eating much, but she didn't realize until just now how it was affecting him. "You have to eat more."

"One day, when you were at the shop, Auntie told me she doesn't have much money, so I shouldn't ask for extras. And I shouldn't take a big helping."

"What?"

"That's what she said."

Harriet shook her head. The rest of the family wasn't going hungry. Mrs. Robinson had never scolded Gracie or Harriet or anyone in the family. Goodness, she had enough to feed Dr. Beers almost every evening. What a ridiculous thing to tell a child.

She handed Tommy a clean shirt. "Don't you worry. You eat all you want. You're a growing young man. In order to be strong and tall, you have to have good meals." Even if she had to take the money from her own account or food from her own mouth, Harriet would see to it that Tommy had what he needed to sustain and nourish him.

While he dressed, Harriet roused Gracie. She was much easier to get going in the morning. Soon, the three of them made their way to the kitchen. At the sweet smell of cinnamon and syrup, Harriet's mouth watered. Mrs. Robinson was a good cook.

She entered the room ahead of the children. Willie and Charley had finished their pancakes and were readying for their jobs. Willie cast Harriet a dark glance. She focused on the table. But only two places were set. "Aren't you forgetting something?"

Mrs. Robinson stared at Harriet, her brows scrunched together. "I don't believe I have."

"There are three of us who haven't had our breakfasts yet."

She gave a one-note laugh. "Oh my. I do believe I've forgotten Tommy again. Such a little thing. So easily overlooked. I'll get his plate."

"He told me you said he shouldn't ask for seconds and should only take small portions. Is that true?"

Mrs. Robinson crinkled her forehead. "Of course not. Why would I tell him such a thing?"

"I'm sure it's nothing more than a misunderstanding." Hopefully, that's all it was. Though it was strange that Mrs. Robinson continued to seem to forget about Tommy's existence. "Don't worry about the plate." Mrs. Robinson would likely forget Tommy's cup of milk too. "I'll take care of it. You need to be off yourself soon." Harriet pulled the plate from the cabinet and the silverware from the drawer and placed them on the table.

"I do have to get going, but before I leave, I hope I might speak to you about something."

This sounded serious. "Yes?"

Mrs. Robinson gave each of them a flapjack then pulled out a chair and settled herself at the table. "Oh dear, this isn't an easy subject to broach. So many find it uncomfortable, even though it is absolutely necessary."

Harriet's stomach churned, and the breakfast that had smelled so heavenly a moment ago now sent waves of nausea through her. "What is it?" Perhaps she expected more money for room and board. Maybe she thought Harriet wasn't doing a good enough job with the children.

"You know I belong to the Order of Pilgrim Fathers. In addition to being a social group, they offer life insurance policies to their members. I do believe everyone should have their lives insured. You never know what will happen. Why, take a look at my poor brother-in-law when my sister passed away. He was always a lazy good-for-nothing."

Harriet couldn't contain her sharp intake of air. The man's child was seated at the table beside her. How could Mrs. Robinson say such a thing in front of the boy?

"Of course, I couldn't leave him and Tommy in such dire straits, so I had them come and live here. The money from Annie's policy helped us out of a pinch."

"I see." Where was all this leading?

"Do you have a life insurance policy, Harriet?"

"No. I've never thought about it." And she didn't want to start.

"You know, just burying someone is a huge expense. That's why so many end up in paupers' graves. I wouldn't want that for you. If something should happen to you, especially while you are under my care, I would want to be able to give you a proper funeral, like I did for Lizzie. It would also help with other expenses I might incur, especially doctor's bills."

To think of her own death? Harriet pressed on her stomach to still its flip-flopping. What would it feel like to die? Would it hurt? Lizzie had suffered plenty. What would it be like to stand at the pearly gates? Would Jesus let her in?

What was heaven like? If only Lizzie could come back and give her the answers to these questions.

"I see I've made you uneasy. I realize it isn't a pleasant subject." Mrs. Robinson patted Harriet's hand.

No, it wasn't pleasant at all. Yes, she believed in God, but did she love Him enough for Him to allow her into heaven? Then to lie under the ground, in the cold and rain and heat, with the vermin and the worms, until the trumpet sounded. . .

Harriet shuddered.

"Yes, thinking about our deaths causes so much distress. But isn't that all the more reason to get the life insurance?"

Harriet gave two slow nods.

"Wonderful." Mrs. Robinson clapped her hands. "I'll have the man from the organization here tonight with the paperwork."

Why so soon? What was the rush?

A headache pounded behind Michael's right eye. Outside his window, the birds chirped, ready for spring to make its full showing. The trees were about to burst into bloom.

Here he had to sit inside and finish this infernal paperwork. He picked up his pen and dipped it into the ink. When he applied it to the paper, he smudged his words. Blast it. He threw the pen to the table, jumped up, and stretched. Perhaps he would get more done if he went for a walk.

Then again, he didn't want to find himself in front of the police station once more. Why had he even gone there in the first place? He had no proof other than a bad feeling. The police couldn't investigate on that basis. Chief Parkhurst had laughed him out of the station.

A knock on the door halted all thoughts of escaping his tiny office. With a sigh, he strode to the door and answered it. There stood Miss Peters on his step, her dark hair peeking from underneath a deep green bonnet, her cheeks flushed. "I'm so sorry to disturb you." She licked her lips.

This was the kind of disturbance he didn't mind. Not one bit. "Come in. I've missed seeing you at your shop lately."

"I've been there. I think it's you, Dr. Wheaton, who has been busy and away."

"That is true. You understand the demands of running a business. How has the new arrangement been going?"

"Not too bad, when all is said and done. When the children are at school, I've been able to keep up. On Saturdays, it's harder, because then I have two young children running around underfoot. I don't know what I'll do this summer."

"You have a few months to figure that out. I'm glad you've been able to keep your business going."

He motioned her for to enter.

"Oh, I'm sorry. Here I've gone and poured out all my troubles to you before I even stepped foot inside."

"That's not a problem."

"Thank you for listening. I've given my heart and soul to this shop. Mrs. Robinson rescued me from starving to death, and I have no intention of going back to that position. Anyway, that's not the reason I'm here."

"I'm glad to be a friend to you, Miss Peters."

A softness filled her face, only increasing her beauty. "Please, if we are to be friends, call me Harriet."

"And you may call me Michael. Can I offer you a cup of tea?"

"That would be very nice. Thank you."

While he put on the kettle and measured the tea leaves, he forced himself to take deep breaths. Why was he having this reaction to Miss Peters? No, now she was Harriet. Perhaps it was that she was providing a welcome distraction to his demanding work.

He carried the teacup into the little waiting room where Harriet sat in one of the flowered armchairs. The china rattled as he brought it in and set it in front of her.

"Thank you."

He positioned himself in the chair beside her but in a way that he would still be able to peer at her. "You must have had a purpose in coming here."

She blew across the top of the cup, sipped her tea, then set it on the saucer. "You are astute, Dr. Wheaton."

"Michael."

"Yes, Michael. Though it is very nice to see you again and chat with you, I do have a purpose for my visit."

"What is that?"

"As you know, I've been living with the Robinsons for a few months now, helping take care of the children. Though I hate to say anything bad about anyone, much less someone with as many troubles as Mrs. Robinson, it seems to me that she is quite neglectful of Tommy Freeman."

"That's her nephew, correct?"

"Yes. He's been living with her since the death of his mother two years ago. His father passed away last summer."

"I do remember you speaking about them."

"Tommy is terribly thin. I'm so concerned for his health. I do make sure that she is feeding him, and I pay him as much attention as I possibly can, but I'm still fearful for his overall health. Yesterday, he took off his nightclothes while I was in the room, and I noticed his ribs sticking out. I've had to take in his pants twice since Lizzie's death."

Michael wriggled in his chair. Another troubling situation in that house. Then again, he had learned his lesson about jumping to conclusions. "Do you believe he's still mourning for Lizzie?"

She patted her high lace collar. "I don't believe so. I know he misses her. We all do." She squeezed her hands together. "It's more than that. I've been spending Saturday afternoons and Sundays at my shop. Of course, I don't work on the Sabbath, but I work until midnight on Saturday, trying to fulfill as many orders as possible. After church on Sunday, I go there to rest. Tommy is so relieved to see me when I return. He's also ravenous."

"So his appetite is good, but you see that he's losing weight?"

Harriet nodded. "He told me Mrs. Robinson said she doesn't have much money to feed him. That's ridiculous. He's her nephew, the son of a much beloved sister. Mrs. Robinson wouldn't let him starve. I'm worried there is an underlying medical condition."

"That most certainly is worrying. I can't make a diagnosis without examining him, though. Has Dr. Beers seen him?"

"Dr. Beers brushes off my concerns. He says that Tommy's losing his baby fat, but I don't believe that to be the case. I would like your opinion on the matter."

"Does he have any other symptoms? Coughing? Vomiting? Diarrhea?"

"Nothing I've noticed."

Michael fiddled with the pen on his desk, rolling it around, tapping it on the desk pad. Should he tell Harriet what he had done? And what he'd been told?

He studied her. She too had lost weight, her blue eyes larger and more piercing than ever in her thin face. If his assumption was correct, she needed protection. They all did. "I have to tell you something I did."

She clutched her black reticule until her knuckles turned white. "What?"

"I was out for a walk a couple of weeks ago, pondering all that has happened to the Robinson family. As providence would have it, I found myself in front of the police station. I went inside and spoke to Chief Parkhurst."

Her mouth dropped into an O. "What about?"

"I told him about the deaths that had occurred in the family and the manner of those deaths."

"I'm not sure I like what you're implying, Dr. Wheaton." Her tone was strident, and she had returned to addressing him in a formal manner.

"Don't you find it all very strange?"

A shadow passed across her face, an emotion he couldn't define. Like a flash of lightning, it was gone. "What I find is that it is tragic."

"I'm not accusing anyone of anything. I'll just give you this warning. Please, be careful. Keep your guard up and your eyes open."

She scraped her chair back and rose. "The Robinsons are good, upstanding, church-going people."

"I'm not saying anything bad about any of them." He worked to temper his words with a calm demeanor. "I don't want to see anyone else come to harm. That's all. Please, do bring Tommy by to see me when you can. I would like to have a look at him."

"Thank you. My concern for him grows by the day."

Michael's hands went clammy.

Harriet swept out of the room and exited the building with a firm shutting of the door. The thought that he might have upset her unsettled him. That was the last thing he wanted. With a sigh, he rubbed his aching temples. *Dear God, how is this all going to end?*

Chapter Eight

As it turned out, Mr. Albert Bugbee from the Order of Pilgrim Fathers hadn't been able to come to the Robinsons' a few nights ago. He'd had a personal matter come up, and they had to reschedule for tonight. For some reason, every time anyone mentioned the life insurance policy, Harriet's throat closed so much she had a difficult time drawing a breath.

She stood in the small, warm kitchen commanding her lungs to drag in a gulp of air, her hands in the dishwater and a stack of plates awaiting washing.

"Don't just stare into space and daydream." Mrs. Robinson's words in Harriet's ear startled her so that the plate slid from her hands to the bottom of the sink. "We have to get those dishes cleaned up before Mr. Bugbee gets here."

"I'm sorry. I'll try to hurry. But I'm not sure I can sign these papers."

"Why ever not? Lizzie had a policy, and so does Willie, and I'm working on Charley getting one. I explained how this operates to you already and why it's important."

"I know. And you're right. If anything would happen to me, I wouldn't want you to be burdened." Though the thought of her own death sent her heart to the races.

"That's the spirit." Mrs. Robinson's voice softened, and a smile graced her thin lips. "I tell you what. I'll even help you dry. That way, we'll be sure to be done by the time our visitor arrives."

"Thank you."

"You miss my Lizzie, don't you?"

"Very much. She was my best friend. My only friend, really.

My clients are nice enough to me, but Lizzie was the first person I could tell all my troubles to. I valued her. When I had to run away from home to avoid marrying that awful man Papa promised me to, I lost what few relationships I had. You and Lizzie filled the void I had from leaving my family." Harriet blinked back tears. "With her gone, that hole in my heart is larger than ever."

Mrs. Robinson touched Harriet's shoulder. "I understand, my dear, I truly do. Annie, my sister, was also my best friend. She was my everything, especially after I lost my dear husband. When she left me, well, my world was a darker and sadder place. That hasn't changed."

Harriet turned and hugged Mrs. Robinson. At first, Lizzie's mother stiffened, but then she relaxed in Harriet's grasp, and they clung to each other. For a short minute, Harriet had a mother again.

The arrival of Mr. Bugbee and Dr. Beers interrupted their moment. Mrs. Robinson hustled out of the kitchen then turned to Harriet. "Pour them a cup of coffee, and I'll show them in here. We'll need a table to sign the papers."

Harriet did as Mrs. Robinson bid. In a few moments, she brought in a light-haired man who carried a battered briefcase. He set it on the table and moved to shake Harriet's hand. "Albert Bugbee. I'm pleased to make your acquaintance, Miss Peters."

"And it's nice to meet you, Mr. Bugbee. Won't you please have a seat?"

Dr. Beers also entered and took his customary place at the table at Mrs. Robinson's right elbow.

"Thank you." Mr. Bugbee sat in the seat where Harriet had set the coffee cup, opened his briefcase, and drew out a rather intimidating sheaf of papers.

"All of that?"

"Yes. We keep extensive paperwork. It's good to make sure everything is in order. If there are problems after someone's passing, it can complicate the matter to no end. Because our purpose is to provide peace of mind for the one who leaves us and security for those remaining behind, we don't want there to be any difficulties in distributing the money."

Dr. Beers sipped his coffee. "You want to be sure there are no problems after you're gone, don't you?"

"Of—of course."

Mr. Bugbee nodded. "Very good, then. Shall we get started?"

Harriet clasped her shaking hands together. While Mrs. Robinson sat at the end of the table without saying a word, stitching some dark green fabric, Harriet and Mr. Bugbee worked through the stack of papers, Dr. Beers interjecting from time to time. The man from the Order of Pilgrim Fathers was beyond patient with her, explaining each paper as they went along, and Harriet signing on each line as he indicated.

He grabbed the next sheet from the pile. "Now, let's move on to the beneficiary section. This is the person who will collect the insurance money upon your death. This is the person you want to provide for when you are no longer here. Is that clear to you?"

"Yes, I understand."

"On this line, we have Mrs. Robinson listed as your beneficiary. She'll be the one to receive the payout. If you'll sign down here, we can move on."

Harriet set her pen on the table and wiped the dark ink from her fingers. "Why did you assume Mrs. Robinson would be my beneficiary?"

"That's what she told me."

"I thought that was what you wanted, my dear." Mrs. Robinson set the green fabric aside and pushed the paper closer to Harriet, her thimble still on her finger. "After all, I'm the one who will have to bury you and pay for any medical expenses you might incur in the course of an illness. We discussed this the other night. If something happens to you and I don't have this money, I would have trouble paying my bills."

Dr. Beers nodded, his jowls jiggling with the motion. "Of course you want to do right by Mrs. Robinson."

"But shouldn't it be my parents?" Not that her father truly deserved anything from her, but her mother and siblings did. "Maybe even Tommy or Gracie?"

Mr. Bugbee straightened his stack of papers. "The beneficiary can be anyone you choose. If you like, we can change it to them." Mr. Bugbee took up his pen to strike Mrs. Robinson's name.

"No." Mrs. Robinson jumped to her feet, knocking over her sewing basket, spools of thread spilling over the floor. She bent to pick them up. "Who took you in and fed you when you were nothing more than skin and bones? Who got you a job so you would have the means to support yourself? Haven't I been more of a mother and father to you than your parents ever were?"

Mrs. Robinson spoke the truth. Without her Christian charity, Harriet might not even be alive today. As it was, she had given her a family when her own family didn't want her anymore.

"Yes, dear." Dr. Beers's voice was confectionery sweet. "Think of all this dear woman has sacrificed for you. This is the least you can do to repay her for her kindness. You wouldn't want your death to put a strain on her finances."

Of course, Mrs. Robinson had been kind to her and treated her as her own daughter. Didn't Harriet owe it to her to make her the policy's beneficiary? "What do you think, Mr. Bugbee?"

"That decision is entirely up to you, Miss Peters. I cannot tell you one way or the other. It's all a matter of personal preference. If you'd like to take a few days to think about this, I can come back later to finish the paperwork."

Mrs. Robinson pinned Mr. Bugbee with her glare. "That won't be necessary. Miss Peters knows everything I've done for her and what is right."

Harriet took up the pen again and chewed on the end of it for a moment.

"Stop it, child. Quit stalling and just sign the paper."

With a glance at the older woman, Harriet added her signature to the document naming Mrs. Robinson as beneficiary.

"Good morning, Harriet." Michael stood on the Robinsons' porch, twirling his bowler hat in his hands.

A damp spring morning wind gusted in Harriet's face. She pulled her old green shawl tighter around her shoulders.

She stared at the man in front of her, a dark curl falling over his left eye. When he flashed her a grin, she grabbed the doorpost. Goodness, he was handsome when he smiled.

After a restless night of very little sleep, his visit was not what she needed this morning.

Not because she didn't want to see him. Just the opposite. After her evening and the visit with Mr. Bugbee from the Order of Pilgrim Fathers, she hadn't slept well. Her hair was a mess, and she wore an old work dress.

For the little good it did, she smoothed her dirty apron. "What can I do for you this morning?"

"I deduced it might be difficult for you to get Tommy to my office for an examination, so I thought I'd come to you. I figured since it was Saturday morning and I didn't see you at your shop, the children would be here and that Mrs. Robinson would be at work."

"The problem with that is that Charley is home today with a bit of a bug."

"He doesn't need to even know I came. Bring Tommy to me in the parlor. I'll perform the exam in the kitchen, and no one will be the wiser. I've been worried about the lad since you came to see me."

She could offer no objection to that. Tommy's condition was a cause for concern. If anything, he'd lost more weight in the few days since she'd been to see Michael. "It's very kind of you to remember him and think of his welfare. I'm sure you have many other patients who require your assistance."

"You amaze me with how much you care for children, ones that aren't even yours, sacrificing time from your business to be their caretaker. Your dedication to them is commendable."

"I'm not doing it for the thanks. When I was growing up, there were so many other children in the home, my parents never had time for me." The pain of it still ached. "Tommy and Gracie need an adult in their life who will pay attention to them and care for them the way they deserve. I can run my business and be there for the children." At least, she prayed she could. Her client list had ceased to grow and was starting to shrink.

"I'm glad they have you."

"Come in, then, and see Tommy. Please, don't send a bill to Mrs. Robinson. I'll pay you."

Because Mrs. Robinson blamed Michael for Lizzie's death, Harriet had to keep this a secret from her. She'd have to be sure to let Tommy and Gracie know not to say a word about the doctor's presence in the house.

She led the way up the stairs. Since Charley had a cold, the two little children were playing in the parlor, blocks strewn over the floor. "Tommy, Gracie, you remember this man, Dr. Wheaton, don't you?"

Tommy stood, knocking over his tower in the process. "Yes. You're the doctor who came when Lizzie was so sick. You were here when she died."

"That's right. I'm sorry I couldn't help your cousin."

"Doctors aren't much use."

Heat rose in Harriet's neck and burned her cheeks. "Tommy, that is not a polite way to speak to Dr. Wheaton."

"It's the truth. They haven't been able to help anybody."

Michael lowered himself to the midnight-blue settee and gazed straight in Tommy's eyes. "Sometimes that's true. Doctors can't help everybody. When God says it is a person's time to go to heaven, there isn't much we can do. Hey, why don't you show me this tower you're building?"

They spent the next five or ten minutes chatting and playing together. Even the normally shy Gracie crept over and watched what they were doing, her sky-blue eyes wide and observant.

Finally, Michael got to the point of his visit. "How have you been feeling, Tommy? Are you getting enough to eat?"

The boy kicked at the blocks, sending them skittering across the floor. "I'm fine." His voice was flat and unconvincing.

"That's good to hear. Then you wouldn't mind if I take a look at you, listen to your heart and such?"

Tommy shrugged. "Sure. That's fine, if it's okay with Miss Harriet."

She nodded, and the two scuttled to the kitchen. They hadn't been in there very long before the boys' bedroom door creaked open. Charley appeared at the end of the hall. He'd pulled on a shirt and a pair of pants. She hurried to him. "What are you doing out of bed?"

"I woke from my nap feeling better. The worst of the cold is over. I'm even a little hungry, enough that I'm going to get a slice of bread and see how that goes."

"I'll get it for you. You really shouldn't be up. Let me help you back to bed."

"I said I'm feeling better. I'm tired of lying around like an invalid. I'd like to sit up for a while."

"That's not a good idea. You should really take it easy until Monday morning. You want to be sure to be completely better so you can go back to work. You don't want to miss another day." She said a silent prayer he would listen to her.

"If I didn't know better, I'd say you were trying to keep me out of the kitchen."

"Nonsense." Except that it wasn't.

"Then let me get my bread. I'll sit in the chair and let you put the kettle on for some tea. How's that?"

"What's even better is if you go back to your room and allow me to bring your meal to you on a tray before you go fainting on me. If you do that, how will I ever get you back to bed? Go on with you now." She shooed him like a stray cat.

Charley sighed. "There's no arguing with a woman."

"You're right about that." With a giggle, she pushed him down the hall. He nearly made it to his room.

Then the kitchen door flew open, and Tommy scampered out. "Charley, you have to see who came to visit today. Dr. Wheaton even let me listen to my heart beating with his steth. . . What was that thing called again?" Tommy peered over his shoulder.

Michael appeared in the doorway. At least he had the decency to stare at the floor and shuffle his feet. "I'm sorry. He got out before I could stop him."

Charley turned to Harriet. "Why is he here? I thought Mama told him to stay away and allow us to grieve."

"She did. It's been months, though, and I was a little concerned about the amount of weight Tommy has lost. Haven't you noticed? Besides, I didn't invite him here. He showed up today of his own volition." She narrowed her eyes in Michael's direction.

"Well, it's almost noon, and Mama will be home soon. Please, everything has been so hard on her since Lizzie's death, don't make it worse by having her discover this man here." The quietness of Charley's voice almost broke her heart.

Harriet wiped her damp hands on her apron and marched to Michael, who stood in the middle of the parlor. "Charley's right. Thank you for stopping by, but you'd better get going before—"

"Before I get home."

At the sight of Mrs. Robinson in the doorway, Harriet's knees buckled, and she slumped to the settee.

Chapter Nine

The weight of Mrs. Robinson's stare bore down on Michael's chest, the air around him heavy, his legs weighted.

But right now, the sight of Harriet, fainted on the couch, was his focus. He knelt beside her. "Harriet. Harriet, can you hear me?"

She remained unresponsive.

He nodded to Tommy. "Get me the black bag from the kitchen."

The boy ran to obey Michael's command, and when he returned, Michael withdrew the smelling salts from his bag and waved them under Harriet's nose. In a moment, her eyelids fluttered, her long, dark lashes like butterfly wings brushing her cheeks. Then she came fully awake. "Michael? What happened?"

Mrs. Robinson leaned over Michael's shoulder. "I'll tell you what happened. You allowed this man into my house though I asked him to stay away. Can't I be allowed to live my life in peace?"

Harriet scrambled to sit up, her mouth open. Michael arranged one of the embroidered throw pillows behind her for support. "I only went to him because I was concerned for Tommy and his weight loss. There's almost nothing left of him. Dr. Wheaton is a good doctor."

At her compliment, warmth spread through him. Though it may not be true, it was good to hear it from her lips. "Just a quick examination of the boy. No charge at all."

A muscle jumped in Mrs. Robinson's jaw, but she kept her voice steady and even. "Thank you, Doctor. Now, however, I must insist that you leave."

"I'm sorry to have bothered you, ma'am. I'm only here for the welfare of your family." And to get to the bottom of the mysterious deaths that plagued the house. That, of course, he couldn't tell Mrs. Robinson.

"Don't blame him." Harriet stood, still teetering, her face white. He reached out to steady her. "I'm the one who went behind your back and asked him about Tommy. He came because I inquired of him if there might be something done to improve Tommy's health and weight."

"Tommy is just fine." Mrs. Robinson's words were tight. "I told you, he's not eating because he is mourning Lizzie. This has been so hard on the boy. You are reading too much into the situation. I'm taking care of him. Yes he's lost some weight, enough that I have to sew him a new shirt, but he's a child with a broken spirit. Nothing more."

Michael sighed. There was no doubt that the boy was underfed and malnourished. He would need to speak to Harriet about this, but not in front of Mrs. Robinson.

Harriet swayed on her feet, and Michael tightened his grip on her arm. "You need to sit down and rest." She too was peaked and pale. Probably overworked, between caring for the children and trying to keep her millinery business afloat.

"I'm fine." She shook him off. "In fact, I'll walk you out." She steered him toward the door and past a dress form draped with dark green material. Then they headed down the stairs, halting on the porch. She caught sight of their gray-haired downstairs neighbor peeking out the window. "What did your examination reveal?"

"Tommy isn't eating enough."

"I'm not a doctor, and I could have made that diagnosis."

"Not because he has no appetite. Who takes care of his meals?"

"Mrs. Robinson. She goes so far as to insist on packing his lunch for school. I try to buy extra treats for him when I can on my way home each afternoon."

"She isn't feeding him enough."

Harriet rubbed her temple. "Yes, sometimes she gets distracted and forgets about him. But that's only natural after the grief she has endured. I've been keeping an eye on him. I'll do a better job from now on."

"Can't you see the kind of person she is?" How could Harriet defend that woman and her actions?

"I know she's not kind to you, but if you ask people, you will hear how generous and good-natured she is. She always has been to me. You heard her. In her spare time away from the shop where she sews all day, she's making Tommy a shirt. She loves the boy. I don't know why she dislikes you. Probably it has something to do with you being here when her beloved daughter died. This is my fault. I was wrong to go to you and drag you into this situation." With a swish of her skirts, she spun toward the house.

"You again?"

Up the walk came Dr. Beers. Just what Michael didn't want to deal with right now. "I'm on my way out."

"Mrs. Robinson was clear with you about leaving this family to mourn in peace."

"I asked him here." Harriet grasped the doorknob. "But he was just about to leave, and this time, he's given me his assurances he won't return. Isn't that right, Dr. Wheaton?"

Michael stared at his shoes. He might as well be ten again and on the school playground with the other boys who teased him, laughed at him, told him they didn't want to play with him.

His existence had been miserable. Because of who he was, the boys didn't befriend him. Or rather, because of who his mother was.

Even though his pace was slow as he ambled from the home, his breathing was rapid. All these years later, it still stung. Perhaps it was from fear that someone would discover his secret. As long as he could keep it from being discovered, life would be good. If his colleagues or his patients found out what he labored so hard to keep hidden, it could spell the end of his career.

Back then, he didn't stand up for himself, either at school or at home. He didn't share with his Grandpop what was going on, even though he must have seen Michael's bruises from where the other boys kicked him.

He never asked about it, and Michael didn't enlighten him.

Nor did he go to the teacher, who also chose to turn a blind eye. More than once, when a ring of boys surrounded him, Michael glanced up to find the teacher staring at him through the window, her mouth drawn into a frown.

The woman never left the schoolhouse to address the situation. Not a single time.

Now, just as then, he slunk away without defending himself.

He didn't take the horse car home, but chose instead to walk, his feet heavy, his steps plodding. When he was young and bullied, the stakes weren't as high as they were now. This time, his livelihood was at risk. Lives hung in the balance.

Harriet had told Dr. Beers that Michael wouldn't return. He hadn't made that promise. When he was picked on in school, he allowed the boys to take his lunch and the lunches of some of the girls.

This time, no matter what Harriet thought of him, he had to take action. He wouldn't be the boy who didn't speak up. The boy who allowed his lunch to be stolen. The boy who was bruised.

Michael refused to be bullied anymore.

Tommy wouldn't suffer because of Michael's fear. Tommy didn't have a voice. Michael would be his.

"Wait." Dr. Beers's single word stopped Harriet in her tracks, her foot on the bottom step of the staircase leading to the Robinsons' apartment.

She faced the man, his green eyes dark and stormy, his lips pressed into a tight line. Her skin itched, as if a thousand ants crawled over her, their tiny pinchers nipping at her. Most of the time she did everything she could to stay out of this man's way. He looked her in the eyes, but she stared him down. "What can I do for you?"

He took a single step closer to her, and she held her breath.

"Why don't you trust me? Do you think I don't know what I'm doing? I'm a trained physician and have been for more than fifty years. I have the experience, much more than some just-qualified doctor. He doesn't know a stethoscope from a scalpel. Half the time, he's guessing. Flailing in the dark. If you were concerned about Tommy's health, you should have come to me."

She swallowed hard. "Begging your pardon, but you are here almost every evening. You observe Tommy for yourself, up close. As a medical doctor, you should be able to see the boy is losing weight. He should be a growing child, and he's not."

"Sarah Jane does the best she can under the circumstances. She has many mouths to feed. We all have to make sacrifices. Sometimes, not everyone gets quite enough to fill their stomachs."

"Four of us in the household have jobs. That's plenty to support ourselves and two small children. Gracie isn't neglected the way Tommy is. Not to mention the life insurance money Mrs. Robinson should have gotten from Lizzie's death."

"Well, she hasn't received any money."

"Even still, there surely is enough to fill Tommy's belly. No one else in the house is going hungry." She clenched her fists and ground her teeth. She had made a promise to Lizzie to look after the children, and that was what she would do.

No matter what it took.

"Are you accusing Sarah Jane of something?" Dr. Beers hissed.

"Of course not. I know she loves the children very much. I've witnessed her distress over Lizzie's death. She doesn't have an easy life and never has, from the time she was born in Ireland. Then she immigrated with her younger sister to the States when she was but a child herself. My pity for her runs deep."

Dr. Beers wriggled his mustache. "She doesn't require your pity. What she requires is for you to help her and be a friend to her. More than anything, she needs you to trust her so she can trust you. Going behind her back the way you did breaks that trust."

Harriet leaned against the doorjamb. The back of her throat

burned. Of course the doctor was correct. It had been wrong of her to deceive Mrs. Robinson. Harriet owed her a great deal.

Other than a brother in Wisconsin, the woman had very little family. Just her nephew and her children. They must be important to her. She was devoted to Tommy, had taken him in along with his father when his mother died, even though Harriet was living with them at the same time. "I apologize for my behavior, Dr. Beers. My action was uncalled for. I didn't take Mrs. Robinson's feelings into account, and for that, I am truly contrite."

"You should be apologizing to her, not to me." Dr. Beers pointed to the stairs, giving a silent order for her to go.

She obeyed him at once, almost running up the steps. The children had returned to playing with their blocks. "Where has your mother gone?" she asked Gracie.

Gracie turned out her lower lip and motioned toward the kitchen. "I think Mama was crying."

Oh goodness, what had Harriet done?

She followed Mrs. Robinson's heart-wrenching cries into the kitchen where she sat at the table, a cup of no-longer-steaming coffee in front of her, white material in her lap, a needle in her hand.

Harriet pulled her handkerchief from her apron pocket and handed it to Mrs. Robinson, who blew her nose and wiped her eyes before gazing at Harriet. "I'm sorry for my display. That was not very mature of me."

Harriet sat across from Lizzie's mother and squeezed her hands. "No, I'm the one who needs to beg your forgiveness. I should never have confided in Dr. Wheaton about Tommy's health. You're absolutely right. He is still missing Lizzie. We all are." A tear seeped from her own eye and trickled down her face. Her heart ached. So many times, she caught herself wishing she could confide in Lizzie. To share her joys and sorrows with her best friend.

Now when she wanted to do that, she had to go to the cemetery. Lizzie never answered.

"I'm so lost without my daughter. She was everything to me."

"I know." More tears fell, racing each other to drip off Harriet's chin. "I miss her more than anything in the world. I'd give my right arm for one more day with her. Just to hear her voice and see her smile."

Mrs. Robinson nodded. "How wonderful that would be. You know I love my children and my nephew. He's all I have left of my sister. I hurt for him. He's so much like me, young and alone in the world. No parents. No one to care for him. None of us has been right since Lizzie left."

"That is true. Can you forgive me?"

"Oh child, there is nothing to forgive."

Harriet rose and moved to the opposite side of the table, knelt beside Mrs. Robinson's chair, and hugged her.

For the longest time, they remained in that position, crushing the material between them, each of them sobbing for their losses. Life had robbed them both of so much and so many loved ones. They shared that common bond, one that would tie them together forever.

Behind them, someone cleared his throat. Harriet wiped her eyes. Willie stood in the doorway.

"Oh Willie, I didn't see you there." Harriet released her hold on Mrs. Robinson, rose to her feet, and smoothed her skirt.

"Is everything okay?" He glanced between Harriet and his mother.

Mrs. Robinson covered her face with the handkerchief, so Harriet answered. "Just a misunderstanding between your mother and myself. I've apologized for causing her distress. We've made our amends."

"Don't upset Mama. Ever."

"Of course not. I shouldn't have, and I won't anymore. I'm not here to cause trouble but to take a burden from her shoulders and to help care for all of you. In fact, let me make dinner tonight while you have a nap, Mrs. Robinson."

With a noisy blow of her nose, she shook her head. "No. Thank you for the kind offer, but I can manage. It's the one thing in my life that brings me pleasure. I work hard to put food on the table. I enjoy cooking it."

"Very well, then. I'll see what the children are up to."

Willie followed Harriet from the kitchen. He spoke in a low growl. "You've come into this house and turned life upside down."

Oh, dear. He was still angry with her. "You know how much I love this family. I'm risking my business, my livelihood, my life-long dream to be here." She worked to control her voice. "I would never intentionally hurt any of you. Your mother has been kind to me. I owe her a great debt. We all make mistakes. After an apology, it's time to move on."

Willie straightened himself and tightened his shoulders. "There was no need to upset her. You knew what would happen inviting that man here."

"Like I said, it's over and done with. Your mother has forgiven me. We've reached an understanding, and all will be well from this point on." She sidestepped in an attempt to disappear down the hall.

He grabbed her by the upper arm, squeezing so hard there would be a bruise there tomorrow. "Let's make one thing clear. No one hurts my family. No one."

Chapter Ten

July 1886

Though morning had just broken the horizon, the Robinson household was already awake and buzzing. Mrs. Robinson had stirred the fire, the heat of the kitchen enveloping Harriet, threatening to suffocate her. The sweet spice of cinnamon wafting from the pot of oatmeal beckoned her to eat, but the warmth and humidity pressed on her, and a bead of sweat trickled down her back. In the distance, a roll of thunder broke the quiet of the morning. After deciding to forgo her usual cup of tea for a glass of water, Harriet went to rouse the children.

She pulled aside the curtain in the boys' room. Charley and Willie were already at work. "Good morning, Tommy. Time to rise and shine."

"No."

Harriet suppressed a laugh. The boy never changed. "I'm afraid that isn't an acceptable answer. You must get up and get dressed. Auntie has your breakfast ready and waiting, and she'll be sore if it gets cold."

"I don't feel good."

Harriet's heart seized. Five months had gone by since Lizzie's death, but any illness still sent Harriet into a tailspin. She sat on the bed beside the pencil-thin boy. With the back of her hand, she felt for a fever. He remained cool. That was a good sign. "What's the trouble?"

"My stomach hurts so much."

Indeed, he lay in a fetal position, clutching his midsection.

Just like Lizzie.

No. Dear God, no. This couldn't be happening again. "You stay right here. I'm going to tell Auntie." Harriet scampered from the room and, holding her skirts, dashed into the kitchen.

Mrs. Robinson glanced up from a pot she was stirring on the stove. Sweat glistened on her high forehead and above her lip. "Ah, there you are. Where is Gracie? Don't you have her up yet? Breakfast is ready."

"Never mind breakfast. It's Tommy. He's sick. Says he's having awful stomach pains."

"That boy will do anything to get out of chores. He knows I was planning on having him help you beat the rugs today. He didn't want to work, so he's made up this ridiculous farce to get out of the job, leaving more for you and Gracie to do."

Lightning flashed, brightening the dark, close room. "No, I believe he is genuinely ill. His color is not good at all." The building shook with the thunder, the tremors racing up Harriet's legs.

"Tell him to get up and come for breakfast at once."

"But—"

"I'm not going to argue this point with you." The muscles in Mrs. Robinson's neck tightened. "Get Tommy at once."

Harriet returned to Tommy's room to find that he had vomited and was crying. The hot room stank. Even though raindrops pinged against the roof, she threw open a window.

She smoothed his brown hair from his forehead. "Hush, now. There's nothing to cry about. I know you aren't feeling well. Let's get you cleaned up, and then I'll bring you a cup of tea. That will settle your stomach in no time."

She held her breath as she changed the sheets, washed Tommy, and got him into clean nightclothes. Before she left the room, she kissed his forehead. "Please, don't worry. You'll be fine in no time. Just wait and see."

Once she exited, though, Harriet had to lean against the rose-papered wall in the hall to catch her breath. His symptoms mirrored Lizzie's to a T. This was how her final illness started. Despite Harriet's best efforts, the poor boy was so thin already, he didn't have much strength to fight whatever plagued him.

"No, dear God, you cannot take this sweet boy from me. I would be devastated to lose him. He's so young. He has his whole life in front of him. He's so sweet and bright. Please, Lord, spare this child's life. If You have any goodness and compassion, don't take him home. We need him here."

Gracie emerged from the room she shared with Harriet. "What's the matter?"

Harriet pushed herself upright and wiped the moisture from her cheeks. "Tommy is sick."

The color drained from the little girl's face. "Is he sick like Lizzie and Emma and the others?"

Harriet knelt beside Gracie. She had already lost her father and two of her sisters, among other family members. If Harriet thought this was hard and scary, what about this poor young girl? "I don't know. We need to pray that God makes Tommy better. I was just going to get him some tea."

"Can I go talk to him?"

"I think it's best if you stay out of his room. We don't want you to catch whatever sickness it is that he has."

Gracie gave a solemn nod, her blue eyes wide. No one could blame her for being frightened. Even Harriet's pulse thrummed in her wrists.

"You mother has breakfast ready. You'd best come and eat something."

Hand in sweaty hand, they went to the kitchen where Mrs. Robinson stood at the stove. "Well, where is he?"

"He is not faking this illness. He has lost the contents of his stomach and is in a great deal of pain."

Mrs. Robinson sighed. "Just what I need to deal with. A sick kid. As if I didn't have enough problems. Very well, then. I'll make him a cup of tea. I do have to hurry to work. There is no way I can miss at the store. I'll try to stop along the way and alert Dr. Beers of Tommy's illness. He can come and see what can be—"

Mrs. Robinson went as stiff as a board. She took several shallow breaths before she collapsed onto the floor, her eyes rolling to the back of her head. She foamed at the mouth.

What was going on? Was she having a fit? Harriet's heart raced. She spun in circles in a desperate attempt to figure out what she was supposed to do.

Then Mrs. Robinson spoke, her voice low, dark, and deep. "This is Moses Robinson."

Harriet gasped. Mrs. Robinson's late husband.

"I have come from the great beyond to deliver a message." Mrs. Robinson, speaking as her husband, sat up straight, her blue eyes, usually stormy, now bright.

Harriet trembled from head to toe. Gracie clung to her by the hand.

"This illness of Master Thomas Freeman, my wife's nephew, is serious indeed. In fact, this illness will cause his death. He will not recover but will soon join his parents in glory.

"Don't be afraid. God has ordained this." A loud clap of thunder, one that shook the house and rattled the windows, punctuated the words. "It is His will that He calls Master Freeman home to himself."

With a scream, Mrs. Robinson fell backwards to the hard floor and went limp.

Michael stood in front of Harriet's millinery shop and stared through the window to the inside. Lace and ribbons were strewn about her worktable, an explosion of yellows and pinks and greens and blues, of lace and tulle, and other materials Michael had no idea what they were.

On a Saturday afternoon, when Harriet was usually busy at work in her shop, it stood silent. Dark.

A heavy cloud passed over the sun and deepened the shadows over Michael. Though it was the middle of July, he pulled his jacket tighter around himself.

Should he go to the Robinsons and see what was the matter? No, that was a ludicrous thought. He'd been told in no uncertain terms to stay away. Yet something nagged at him. Tugged at him and refused to let go. An urging to disobey Mrs. Robinson's very firm order and stop by the house.

No, he wouldn't. He shook his head as if to seal the deal. Only because of Harriet. Only because he didn't want to bring trouble on her. She hadn't asked for it. She didn't need it.

Yet she occupied his thoughts day and night. What was she doing? Was she well? Did she think of him?

He had seen her at her shop from time to time, had waved to her through the window, had even stopped in for a brief conversation or two.

Those small snatches weren't enough.

He had to stop these crazy feelings that invaded his heart. She was a beautiful, kind, and compassionate person, and under different circumstances, they might have been friends. If she hadn't gone to live in the house on Holland Street, they might have gotten to know each other better.

Best he keep his mind on his work.

To that end, he turned to go back to his office. Before he managed to take three steps, a young man with a long, scruffy beard approached him. Michael recognized those dark brown eyes and the eye-watering stench of an unwashed body.

"I've been looking for you." The man spit a stream of tobacco juice on Michael's just-polished black boots.

The voice was familiar to Michael too.

"You don't remember me, do you?"

"I feel I should, but I'm afraid I don't."

"Does the name Paul Gilliland ring any bells?"

Michael covered his mouth.

"Ah, by your reaction, I can see that it does. You killed my Lily. And our baby." Paul poked Michael in the chest, driving him backward. "You told me they would be fine. That Lily was strong.

That the baby was in some distress, but you thought he would survive too."

A crowd gathered on the walk around them, spilling onto the street. Michael now understood what a caged animal felt like. "Could we talk about this in private?"

"That's where you would like this conversation, wouldn't you? Sweep it under the rug. Pretend that nothing ever happened. Don't let the world know how incompetent you are. You can't even perform a task as simple as delivering a child safely into this world. Lily and my son weren't the first patients you've killed, were they?"

Michael swallowed hard. "I am very sorry for your loss. Unfortunately, childbirth is a dangerous event. Sometimes, the mother or the child or both do not survive. I wish I could have done more to save them. I tried everything. Again, you have my deepest sympathies."

"Your sympathies. Bah. I want nothing to do with them." The man spat again. "What I want is my wife and child back." Paul shoved Michael into the arms of the surrounding crowd. Whoever he landed on pushed him back to his feet.

Paul raised his already-booming voice. "Listen to me, good people of Somerville. If you know what's good for you, if you want to preserve the lives of those you love, don't allow this doctor to enter your homes. Have nothing to do with him."

A murmur rose through the crowd.

A whistle pierced the din as a police officer rushed toward the mob. He waved his nightstick, cutting the thick, humid air. "Break it up now, break it up. Nothing to see here. Come on, off with the lot of you. Back to business." The crowd dispersed, returning to their normal routines.

The policeman focused on Paul. "I should arrest you for disturbing the peace."

Michael stepped between the officer and Paul. "Please, sir, let him be. He is mourning his wife and son. He has enough grief in his life. Don't add to it."

The officer stared Michael straight in the eyes, his own brown ones narrow and hard. "Are you sure? Who knows what he might have done if I hadn't come along."

Michael nodded. "I'm sure. He meant no harm." His actions would do nothing to repair his very damaged, very sullied reputation, but this was the right thing to do. "Let him go."

"Get out of here, then, Gilliland. I'd better not hear of you bothering Dr. Wheaton ever again. Scram, before I change my mind."

Paul raced down the street and around the corner, out of sight.

Michael rubbed his throbbing temples. "Thank you, sir."

"Think nothing of it. You let me know if that man bothers you again."

"I will." Hiding in his office for the rest of the day sounded like a good plan to Michael. So he made his way down the street. Before he could enter, though, someone called to him.

"Dr. Wheaton, thank goodness I caught you here."

Michael glanced over his shoulder at Charley Robinson hurrying down the road in his direction. He rubbed his suddenly-chilled arms. "Is it Harriet?" He could only whisper the words.

Charley shook his head, his fair hair flying free. "No. Tommy."

"Tommy?"

"Same symptoms as Lizzie and all the others. Suddenly stricken with intense stomach pains and every other symptom. Dr. Beers is with him now, but I don't trust the man. I've never liked him, not from the moment he set foot in our home after Papa's death. I've heard the talk about him being a quack. He's there now, hovering over Tommy. Mama had to go to work, but Harriet is beside herself."

"Your mother doesn't want me there." Though Michael ached to run straight to the patient's bedside and work to save him, he restrained himself.

"I don't care. I want you there and so does Harriet. You let me worry about my mother. You just take care of my cousin. Please, do everything you can to save him."

Michael inhaled a fortifying breath. He'd failed Miss Robinson. He'd failed the Gilliland family. This time, would he fail Tommy?

Chapter Eleven

I hurried home from work as fast as I could."

Though Mrs. Robinson's face was flushed, she held herself erect and her words were high pitched. Michael rubbed Tommy's back as he retched into on old bucket. The poor boy struggled to empty his stomach, alternately being sick and screaming in pain. This seven-year-old was suffering more than any human being ever should, no matter their age.

During the brief interludes in between vomiting bouts, Harriet pressed cool compresses to Tommy's head. She'd set her mouth in a grim line.

"What is this man doing here?"

Busy caring for his very sick patient. Michael ignored Mrs. Robinson's shrill voice in his ear.

While Michael wiped Tommy's mouth, Charley took charge of his mother. "I came home from work to find my cousin in this horrid condition. Just like his father not more than a year ago. Like all the others. Your Dr. Beers is worthless."

Inside, Michael couldn't help but cheer.

The rotund physician who stood at the foot of the bed went as red as fireworks on the Fourth of July. Not good for a man of his advanced years.

"How dare you talk about my friend in such a manner? He's in the same room, you do realize." Mrs. Robinson's coloring almost matched that of the older doctor.

Harriet wrung the towel in a basin of water. "I, for one, realize that, and I don't care. At least Dr. Wheaton is doing something to aid Tommy."

Mrs. Robinson swung around to face Harriet, who sat on the other side of Tommy's bed. "Have you been following my instructions to the letter? Giving him the tea I left for him?"

Harriet glanced up, a dark wave of hair falling across her pale cheek. "I have. He's only been getting worse. I didn't ask for Dr. Wheaton. Charley did. But I'm terribly glad he's here."

"Dr. Beers, may I speak to you in the hall?" Mrs. Robinson opened the door and motioned for her friend to follow. He did her bidding.

Michael released a pent-up breath when the two of them exited. He gazed at Harriet. "I wonder what they had to say that was so secretive?"

She shrugged. "They're always huddled together, whispering about this and that. Who knows? And right now, I don't care about anything other than Tommy."

The little boy cried and moaned. "It hurts. It hurts. My stomach burns." He grabbed Michael by the forearm. "Am I going to die, Doctor? I don't want to die. I just want the hurt to go away."

"I'm going to do everything I can to help you get better." What more could he promise the child? Nothing. The bismuth phosphate, the tincture of nux vomica, the mustard and milk, none of it was alleviating the symptoms. In reality, if this illness ran its course in the same manner as the others, Tommy only had somewhere from a few hours to a few days to live.

"Mama and Daddy are in heaven, aren't they?" Tears rolled down Tommy's sunken cheeks. "Maybe I'll see them."

"Perhaps you will." This young boy's faith put Michael to shame.

"Why don't I sing to you for a while?" Harriet stroked Tommy's arm. "That might help you feel better."

"I like it when you sing."

"Good. And I know just the song." The clear notes of the hymn filled the room as Harriet sang.

Jesus loves me! He who died
Heaven's gates to open wide;
He will wash away my sin,
Let his little child come in.

Yes, Jesus loves me. Yes, Jesus loves me.
Yes, Jesus loves me. The Bible tells me so.

Jesus loves me! He will stay
Close beside me all the way;
If I love him when I die,
He will take me home on high.

Yes, Jesus loves me. Yes, Jesus loves me.
Yes, Jesus loves me. The Bible tells me so.

She hadn't yet finished the song when Tommy fell asleep. "Praise the Lord for that." Harriet's shoulders slumped.

Mrs. Robinson and Dr. Beers returned to the room. "Good. He's resting. I'll fix some more tea for when Tommy wakes up." Mrs. Robinson glared in Harriet's direction. "Dr. Beers can take it from here. Why don't you and Dr. Wheaton get some rest." It was a command rather than a request.

Harriet nodded. Michael trailed her and Charley out of the room and into the parlor. She stood in front of the dress form in the far corner, fingering the shimmering green material that now was taking shape as a skirt. Sewn in her favorite color, it was beautiful. "Are we going to lose him?" Though she didn't weep, her words were heavy with tears.

Charley embraced her, and she clung to him. Michael's chest tightened. His arms ached to hold her the way Charley did. Perhaps there was some kind of relationship between them. Perhaps she and Michael didn't have a friendship after all.

He turned to give them a moment. After a long while, Charley whispered something to Harriet that Michael couldn't pick out. With a few creaks of the floorboards, he disappeared into the kitchen.

At last, Harriet and Michael were alone in the room. All was quiet in the sickroom. The stove rattled in the kitchen.

Michael stepped closer to her. He couldn't help but stare at her lovely, worry-worn face. "I'd like to get some fresh air. Would you care to take a stroll with me?"

"I can't leave Tommy." She cast a glance in the direction of the boy's room. "He might need me."

"Your devotion to him is admirable."

"I've come to love him very much. If the worst happens, I don't know what I will do." Tears leaked from her closed eyes. "I'm so scared."

Without thinking, Michael drew her into his arms as he had longed to when Charley embraced her. Up close, she was so small, fragile, and vulnerable. She trembled from head to toe. Oh, how this had to be tearing her in two. "Shh, don't worry. Everything will be fine."

Yet isn't that what he'd promised Paul Gilliland, that nothing bad would happen to his wife and baby? Look how that turned out. He knew better than to make vows he couldn't keep, but he had to give her a measure of reassurance. Had to give himself a measure of reassurance that this wouldn't turn out the same way the other illnesses in this home had.

"Mrs. Robinson had some kind of fit this morning." She spoke into his chest, her voice sending his heart skittering.

"Really?" Was it like the other one? Had the woman lost her mind? He knew insanity. Had lived with it, seen it up close. There was nothing pretty about it.

"Yes. She even foamed at the mouth. And then, in this deep voice which said he was her late husband, she declared that Tommy would die. I've never been so petrified in my entire life."

"I can only imagine." Michael's arms broke out in gooseflesh even though the temperature in the apartment was like that of an oven. He was all too familiar with such bizarre behavior. All too familiar with people hearing voices. He tightened his grip on Harriet.

Each of the victims, at least according to Harriet, were in their right minds up until the times of their deaths. Mrs. Robinson was the one who appeared crazy. Perhaps they could take steps to getting her committed to the asylum. Unfortunately, he also was familiar with that process.

"Please, be careful."

"I'm so afraid, Michael. I don't know what's happening. Everything is so strange. Nothing is as it should be. What if Tommy dies? He's such a little boy. How can I comfort him when I'm so scared myself?"

At that moment, Willie burst through the door. Michael released his hold on Harriet and stepped away from her. Willie shot glances between the two of them. "You look like you've seen a ghost. Both of you."

Harriet rushed to him. "It's Tommy. He has the same illness as the rest of your family."

"No. No, please tell me this is a joke."

She shook her head. "He was sick when I went to wake him up this morning, and he's only been getting worse as they day has worn on. You have to come see him. He'll want to talk to you. You know how he looks up to you."

Willie started down the hall with Harriet in his wake. Before she got to Tommy's door, she stopped and turned to Michael. "Thank you. I appreciate everything you've done for us." For the first time that day, a genuine light shone in her cobalt-blue eyes.

"You're welcome. I'm happy to do whatever I can. I've. . ." He cleared his throat. "I've come to care a great deal about this family."

Harriet disappeared into the bedroom.

Michael turned to leave, his gaze sweeping the room. There on the ornate fireplace mantel sat an amber vial.

And a vase of dead flowers.

Michael sat across the paper-strewn desk from Chief Parkhurst. The man chewed on the end of an unlit cigar. A blue haze filled the smoky room. Parkhurst's was the only smoke not lit. "Another illness, you say?"

"Yes. This time, Mrs. Robinson's nephew. Both of his parents died of similar ailments, so Mrs. Robinson is raising him." Michael leaned forward, his weight on his knees. "Don't you find it strange there are so many deaths of the same sort in the same family? And such horrible deaths at that." He shuddered at the memory of the small child writhing in his bed.

Chief Parkhurst uncrossed his legs and steepled his fingers, tapping his bearded chin. "In your medical opinion, what do you make of it?"

Michael came to his feet and clenched the back of his chair. "I don't know. I can't put my finger on it, it's so baffling. The symptoms don't resemble anything I learned in school or in my practice. Though I've combed my medical books, I haven't come up with a firm diagnosis."

"You're sure."

Michael's mouth was dry. "Well, there is one thing, but it's so illogical and improbable." He croaked out the words, holding back the ones he didn't want to voice.

"You must feel strongly enough about it to be here. If you didn't have a hunch that some nefarious activity was taking place in the house on Holland Street, you would never have come to me. Especially after I told you not to return unless you have some hard proof."

Yes, the chief's laughter continued to ring in Michael's ears. "As far as definitive proof, that is still lacking."

"Then I don't know why you're standing in front of me."

"Don't you see? It's not a disease or a condition. Not this. No one catches this from someone else in the house. There are months between the deaths. And suddenly, another family member falls ill and inevitably dies. This is no coincidence."

"Now you really have my attention. Because you wouldn't be here if it were happenstance." Chief Parkhurst chewed harder on his cigar.

"I hate to say the words." If Michael did, he wouldn't be able to take them back. He might start something he couldn't stop. Yet the image of that young boy screaming as his stomach burned flashed in front of his eyes. Still, if he was wrong, the consequences to the Robinsons and to himself could be catastrophic.

"Spit it out, man." The chief crushed the cigar with his teeth.

Michael drew in a deep breath and held it for a second. "The symptoms each of the family members have displayed are consistent with poisoning."

Chief Parkhurst rocked backward. "I thought that might be what you would say. Yet you have no proof of this?"

"No." Michael bit his lower lip. "Just my medical knowledge. If I was forced to give a diagnosis, this is would be my conclusion."

"Have you consulted other physicians?"

"I have consulted with my mentor, Dr. White. He is baffled."

"Has he examined the boy?"

"No. Should he?"

"I think another opinion or two would be helpful. They might claim you have a bias against the family. If the diagnosis could be corroborated, it would build a stronger case."

"You don't think I'm crazy?" Michael didn't use that word lightly.

"Stranger things have been known to happen. I've been in the business for a long time. I've seen it all. Then again, there's always something new. Who do you think might be poisoning the family?"

Michael shook his head. "That, I couldn't say. It could be one of the sons or this strange doctor that visits the house almost every day. He's been present for all of the deaths, as far as I know. So has one of the members from the church who comes to pray for each victim soon before they pass."

"I'll open a case." Parkhurst drew a sheet of paper from his top desk drawer. "Until I have more proof, though, there's little I can do. So far, it's nothing more than a hunch on your part. I can't bring that to the district attorney. I'm going to need more evidence to proceed any further."

"I understand." Michael's shoulders sagged. Though his head got what Parkhurst was saying, his heart didn't. "I think I know who might be able to help us in that regard. I'll be in touch when I have more information." Michael reached to shake Parkhurst's hand.

Despite the urge to return to the Robinsons to check on Tommy's condition, Michael made himself go to Dr. White's office. The man claimed to be retired, but he continued to spend more time at work than at home. "Ah, young Dr. Wheaton. How good it is to see you again. I'm just returning from a difficult delivery. Been up all night."

The dark bags under the doctor's eyes testified to that fact. "I'm sorry. If this could wait, I would let it. However, there is another case at the Robinson home. A young boy is dying, and I think I've figured out why."

"Come on in, then." Dr. White entered the office, Michael scurrying close on his heels. As soon as they were inside the door, the older man turned to him. "What is this all about?"

"The young boy, the son of the woman's deceased sister and brother-in-law, has come down with the same symptoms. The exact same ones. The child is in sheer agony, and nothing I do or prescribe gives him any relief."

"And?" Dr. White tented his fingers.

"I've scoured my medical books, and there is only one conclusion I can come to. You may think me out of my mind, but I believe each of these people were victims of poisoning."

"Poisoning?" The doctor widened his hazel eyes.

"What else makes sense?"

"Perhaps food poisoning, but I don't think that's what you're referring to."

Michael strode to the window and stared at the Saturday shoppers rushing home with their packages to enjoy dinner with their families or an evening at the theater. Leading normal lives. "No, it's not." He whirled around. "I need your professional opinion."

"You want me to examine the child?" Dr. White raised his eyebrows.

"Yes, I do. If you wouldn't mind."

Dr. White heaved a sigh. "Do you have any idea who might be administering the poison?"

"A couple of people have the opportunity. As to motive, I have no idea."

"And the authorities?"

"They're the ones who suggested I consult with another physician to give the case more substance. There is Dr. Beers. I'm sure he wouldn't be of the same opinion as myself."

"Ah, I agree."

"He's in love with Mrs. Robinson, who, by the way, claims that her late husband visits her and tells her that certain family members are going to die. Charley shared with me how she even predicted that his uncle would fall ill. Not more than a handful of hours later, he was sick. He died almost exactly one year ago."

"This is pretty serious stuff. You do know you're treading in some dangerous territory."

"I know." As did his fluttering heart and clenching stomach. "But I also know that Tommy will not live if I do not act. If I fail, others may suffer the same fate."

Chapter Twelve

Dark shadows slanted across Tommy's bed, covering his face, his sunken eyes even more deep-set. Harriet sat on the bed beside him, dabbing his sweaty brow as he writhed, tangling himself in the sheets.

Mr. Smith had arrived not long ago. As he did during the final hours of Lizzie's illness, he laid hands on Tommy and whispered prayers for the child.

With each moan of pain, Harriet's heart cracked a little more. Because it was only a matter of time until she was without her precious boy. She'd stopped praying for his recovery. As much as the words stuck in her throat, she now prayed for Tommy's quick release from his pain.

Wasn't that what she would wish if she were in his situation? Or would she cling to this life, afraid of what lay ahead? She closed her eyes and tried to imagine heaven. The Bible said it would have streets of gold and a river of crystal. Everyone would have their own mansion. That was beautiful.

But what if she wasn't good enough to get there? What if God turned her away? She couldn't begin to imagine what hell was like.

Taking a sharp breath, she opened her eyes. Right now, her focus needed to be on Tommy. Soon, he would stand in front of the judgment seat. He was good and sweet enough that God would be forced to admit him to heaven.

"Oh Father, we pray that You would spare the life of Thomas Freeman." Mr. Smith's raised voice caught Harriet's attention. Even Tommy ceased his struggle. "We ask You to remove this awful curse from this family and spare them from further loss. Yet we ask not for our wills to be done, but Thine."

Mr. Smith lifted his eyes to heaven. "Lord, be merciful and gracious to this family." Then once more, he bowed his head and murmured his prayers.

Everyone else had gone to work as usual, as if a life wasn't slipping away from this world. Then again, the household needed the money. They couldn't afford for any of them to lose their jobs. So here Harriet sat in the now-quiet room, with the mantel clock in the parlor ticking off the minutes, each one closer to the time when Tommy's soul would fly away. In the moments when Tommy slept, she worked as hard as she could on the hat orders she had to fill.

Right now, Tommy was awake and alert. Harriet wrung out the cool cloth she'd been bathing him with. It was time for another pitcher of water. She gathered her supplies and headed toward the kitchen, but she didn't get very far.

Gracie stood in the doorway, her blue eyes large. "Miss Harriet?"

Harriet knelt to Gracie's level. "What is it, sweetie?"

"Is Tommy gonna die too? I heard Mr. Smith praying like he always does right before somebody dies."

How did one answer such a question? Harriet had seen many more years than Gracie's tender seven, but she didn't know how to break the news to the little girl. She brushed a red tendril from the child's round cheek. "He is going to see Jesus soon."

"The preacher says heaven is very pretty. And you never get sick there and you never cry. Will Tommy like it there?"

"I imagine he will. I've also heard that it is more wonderful than anything on earth. There's a crystal river and glimmering gold, and the sun always shines."

"I'm glad Tommy is getting to go to such a nice place."

A lump swelled in Harriet's throat. "Me too." If only she had the assurance she would end up there someday.

At a stirring behind Gracie, Harriet peered through her lashes. There stood Michael and another man. "Gracie, you didn't tell me we had visitors."

"Sorry."

"Don't be, honey. It's fine." Harriet rose. "Dr. Wheaton, it's good to see you again." Though she couldn't imagine why he'd taken yet another chance to come to the house.

"I only wish it were under different circumstances. I've brought Dr. White with me to examine Tommy and confirm my diagnosis."

Her heart skipped a beat. "Do you mean you think you know what's wrong with him? That you can cure him?" Just a moment ago, she'd had no hope. Now Michael held out a fragile thread.

"I'm not sure. Let's see Tommy and hear what Dr. White has to say, and we'll go from there."

"Thank you for coming, Dr. White." Harriet nodded in the man's direction. He stood a head above Michael, not a bit stooped, even though an abundance of gray hair crowned his head.

"I'm glad to be able to offer my opinion. Can you tell me something of the boy's illness?"

Harriet shared with him everything she could, how Tommy had fallen sick and what they'd been doing for him since then. Once he'd heard her account, the doctor shooed them all from the room, with the exception of Mr. Smith, who would not be moved, and shut himself inside with Tommy to examine him.

Harriet paced the parlor as she waited for the verdict. Were the hands on the clock even moving? She wandered to it to check. Yes, it continued its steady *tick tock*.

She walked to the green dress on the form. Last night, Mrs. Robinson had added the bodice. Working on the still-sleeveless dress gave her something to do while she sat vigil at her nephew's bedside. The creation was stunning. Whoever would get to wear it was a fortunate woman.

Michael came up behind her. "Waiting is the hardest part. Rest assured, Dr. White is well respected in the profession, and he's good at what he does. He was my mentor and continues to guide me."

She faced Michael. "I can't believe this is happening. It's like a nightmare that never ends. He's just a little boy to be suffering so much. I've watched several of his family members die. You'd think I'd be hardened to it by now, but it never gets easier."

"It's not supposed to." He touched her arm and warmed her from the outside in.

With him here, she managed to relax a little. She could face the inevitable. Tommy was so sick and so near death, there couldn't be much either doctor could do. A heaviness settled on her chest. She couldn't keep the promise she'd made to her very best, her one and only friend.

"Let me get you a cup of tea."

"That would be nice."

He returned in a few moments with a warm cup. The flowery fragrance drifted to her in the steam. Though sweet smelling, her stomach churned. She lifted the cup to her mouth and sipped, almost burning her tongue. "That's rather hot. I'll have to let it cool." She set it on the octagonal pedestal window table.

"I didn't realize it was that warm. I poured it from the pot on the stove."

"Oh, that's the special pot just for Tommy. When it cools, I'll see if I can get him to drink some of it." The steam swirling against the black curtains at the window mesmerized her. Was that like Tommy's soul flying to paradise? "What is your preliminary diagnosis?"

He scrubbed his narrow face. "I'm not sure how to say it. You'll think me mad."

"Just tell me. I doubt you're crazy."

She stared at him, his face white, his features pinched. "There are some who would disagree with you. Through all my research and consultations, the symptoms point to only one possibility. I believe. . ." He cleared his throat. "I believe Tommy has been poisoned."

Harriet stumbled backward, knocking the tea from the table, the cup crashing to the rug. "Did you say poisoned?"

"I did."

"On purpose?"

"Yes."

"But—but that's impossible. No one would want to hurt such a sweet little boy." She clutched her throat. "No. I can't believe it. And what about the others? So many shared the same sickness."

"It's very likely they were also poisoned."

Harriet's breath came in short gasps, and the world around her spun. "You're right. I think you're mad. Completely out of your right mind. There is no way someone could do this. Who? Mrs. Robinson? She would never hurt Lizzie. Lizzie was her world. Charley? No, he had a very close relationship to his uncle. And not Willie. He reads to Tommy many nights before bed. They have a special bond."

Like a thunderbolt, a terrible thought hit her. "You don't think I had anything to do with this, do you?" She grasped for something, anything to support her but found only air. She crouched against the wall, the rug at her feet wet with the tea.

Michael squatted beside her. "Of course not. You've not been with the family that long. I think I know you well enough to know you would never do such a thing."

"And neither would anyone else. I can't believe such a thought would even cross your mind."

Tommy's door creaked open and clicked shut. The floorboard underneath Dr. White's feet squeaked as he strode to the parlor. His pallor was almost yellow.

He nodded once.

Harriet clenched her fists. "No. I won't allow you to accuse anyone in this house of such a crime." She raised her voice and turned her venom on Michael. "You couldn't come up with any other explanation, and because Mrs. Robinson has been unkind to you, you made this up to ruin her."

"Harriet, that's not true at all."

"I want you out of here. Now. The only way I'll ever allow you back in is if you come armed with an apology." She pointed toward the stairs. "Leave."

They did as she bid.

Once they had left, she fell to her knees and covered her face as soul-ripping sobs tore from her. Lizzie, gone because someone killed her? Tommy about to die at someone's hand? No. No, she couldn't even entertain the possibility.

Get out of the house.

She plugged her ears.

Get out of the house.

She was going as crazy as Mrs. Robinson.

Releasing a pent-up breath and steeling his shoulders, Michael stepped from the carriage as it pulled to a halt in front of the tan brick building, white stone columns holding up the small front porch, a multitude of windows overlooking the lawn. A fierce, hot wind greeted him, almost tearing his bowler hat from his head. He removed it and spun it around. Anything to avoid going inside.

There was no sign to name this place, but everyone in Belmont knew what it was.

Everyone in Somerville had known it too, when it had been located there.

The screams pouring from the building were more informative than any sign ever could be.

The McLean Asylum for the Insane.

He licked his cracked lips and, holding himself as straight and tall as possible, strode into the building. A young woman, not more than eighteen or twenty, wearing a striped blue gown and a full white apron, greeted him. "Dr. Wheaton, how good to see you. It's strange to use that title with you."

"There is no need for titles, Amy. Please, call me Michael, as always."

A small smile lit her rather plain, bland face. "I think I saw her in the dayroom not too long ago. If you'd like, you can go up."

"Thank you." Amy swept down the hall and around the corner, the keys at her waist clanging with her movements. From above him, a man screeched like a banshee. The grating noise rang in Michael's ears, and he scrunched his eyes shut, as if that would halt the commotion.

This was the reason the boys at school teased him every day. This was the reason he was determined to rise above them. And the reason it made Tommy's diagnosis all the more difficult to pronounce.

Because people would believe him to be a lunatic to think that. He shook the thoughts from his head and once again held himself erect. He climbed the stairs to the third floor. The wind whistled through the drafty panes, and tree branches scraped against the glass. He hurried his steps.

The large number of oaks and maples surrounding the building shut out the bright summer day. The shadowed room was dim, the walls painted a ghostly gray. In scattered chairs and at various tables, the patients sat. Some of them hummed to themselves. Some of them talked to themselves. Some of them rocked themselves.

There, in the corner, in a straight chair, there she was. As always, at the sight of her, a lump formed in Michael's throat. The young, vibrant, happy woman he had known had disappeared.

Stringy gray hair hung about her face. Her green eyes, so much like his own, stared straight ahead. Vacant. Empty. Like her spirit. Like his life without her.

In the opposite corner, a hairy man moaned and pounded his head with his fists. An older woman sat at a table, pulling out what little blond hair she had left on her head. She laid each strand out in front of her, straight as a Sunday saint.

On unsteady feet, he moved toward the woman in the corner. As always, she didn't move to the left or to the right. Her eyes showed no sign of recognition. No spark in them at all. She'd become nothing more than an empty, hollow shell.

He knelt in front of her and held her by her icy cold hands. "Hello, Mama."

She removed herself from his grasp. When he touched her cheek, she finally turned her attention to him. No smile graced her lips. She spoke no kind words. No words at all. She simply patted his head.

Oh, but that gesture was everything, a small glimmer of the past, when she used to pat his head, stroke his hair, and tell him how much she loved him. He needed to believe that's what this gesture still meant.

"I love you too, Mama. I miss you so much."

She continued to stroke his head, much like she would a dog. Perhaps it calmed her and comforted her in the same way it did him.

"I'm working on a difficult case. I wish you could advise me what to do."

She gave a small sigh. Had she, in her own way, heard and understood? Was she so locked inside herself she couldn't express what she was thinking and feeling? How his heart ached for her. Longed for her to return to him.

"Dr. White has been good to me, though. He's helped me out. It's just that, if I stick to what I believe to be true, it might cost me my dream of practicing medicine. At best, I'd have to leave here and go West to a place where they've never heard of me."

Mama whimpered.

He rubbed her knee. "Don't worry. I'm not going anywhere. I could never leave you. Coming here and seeing you each week is what I look forward to the most." His words were half truthful, anyway.

He did have an obligation to her. He would never walk away from her. From now until one of them died, he would come each week and speak to her of the normal world outside the asylum walls.

"I have to tell you about this woman I met."

Her patting ceased. He had her interest.

"She's very lovely with the blackest hair you've ever seen and the bluest eyes. I can't really describe them except to say they're beautiful. Even more important than that, she's sweet and gentle and caring."

Mama wriggled in her chair.

He couldn't help his grin. "You want to hear more about her. Oh, there is so much more to tell." And so he shared with her everything about Harriet. The words rushed out of his mouth, like water over a rapids.

What was this warmth that consumed him when he spoke of her? What was this lightness in his heart that he hadn't had since they'd brought Mama to this awful place?

All too soon, he had to leave. "I have to get back to my work, but I'll return next week. You wait for me. I'll be here."

Someday, if he continued to see Harriet, he would have to tell her about his mother. Of course, since Harriet had kicked him out, she may never want to see him again. If she did, how would she react when he revealed the truth about his mother? He prayed it would be without revulsion.

Unfortunately, that was how most of the world saw her. And why most of the world shunned him.

Chapter Thirteen

Silence roared in the apartment where Harriet kept her vigil. The heaviness of it restricted her breathing and filled her ears.

On the other side of the bed, Mr. Smith, the Robinsons' friend from church, stood laying his hands on Tommy and praying for him.

Harriet stared at Tommy. Afraid if she took her eyes from him, his heart might stop. With an unrivaled intensity, she counted each shallow rise and fall of the little boy's chest. His cold hand, clasped in Harriet's own, twitched.

Leaning over him, she kissed his damp forehead and whispered to him. "Don't worry, Tommy. If it's time for you to go, you go. Heaven is a beautiful place, and you'll be so very happy there. Jesus is waiting for you."

Mr. Smith nodded. "Miss Peters is right."

Going to heaven would be the only way the dear boy would escape his agony. Though she had vowed to Lizzie to watch out for him, in the end, she hadn't been able to protect him.

The bed beside Harriet creaked and bent under Charley's weight. She hadn't even heard him come in.

"How is he doing?"

"Not well. It's only a matter of time. I can't even get him to drink any tea."

Charley shook his head, his hair a shade lighter than his brother's straight locks. "Such a shame. Just seven. Younger than Emma's ten years. And Tommy is smart too. Who knows what he could have been? Maybe a doctor or a lawyer or even president. His potential ripped away from him." He gave Harriet a side hug.

She nudged him in the ribs and stared at him, a pock mark by his right eyebrow. "Can you keep a secret?" She whispered in his ear so Mr. Smith wouldn't hear.

"Of course. You know you can trust me."

She could. He was a good, hardworking man, active in his church. Of all the people in this house, she trusted him the most. She pulled him from the room, leaving Tommy with Mr. Smith. "Dr. Wheaton was here earlier, and he brought another doctor with him. They agree on a diagnosis."

Charley stood up straighter. "What is it? Why aren't they here helping Tommy?"

"Because I threw them out of the house."

"Why would you do such a thing?"

Harriet fought against the tears that threatened to fall. "They think someone is poisoning Tommy. And that they poisoned all the others."

Thunder filled Charley's face. "That's impossible. No one would do such a thing. And I suppose they have a suspect?"

"They didn't mention anyone."

Charley grabbed her by her upper arms, his hold fast and firm. "What if they go to the police?"

"I never even thought about that." Her breath hitched. "I'm sorry, I'm so sorry."

"What do you mean?" Charley whispered the words. "Was it you?"

She wrenched herself free from his grasp. "Of course not. How could you accuse me of such a thing? I'm just sorry I ever brought Dr. Wheaton into this home. He's done nothing but cause trouble for the family. Now this."

"Sweet woman, it's not your fault. You had no idea what he was like. A lion in dog's clothing."

His interpretation of the cliché brought a smile to her face, a rare occasion these days. "Still, I'm sorry for whatever problems I brought. I would understand if you would like me to leave."

"Never. You know I could never ask you to go. I could never do without you, Harriet. I, we've come to depend on you. You're filling that hole in my heart Lizzie left. Another sister. We couldn't survive without you. Most of all, me. And think about Gracie. If Tommy dies. . ."

"When. There's nothing Dr. Beers can do. Even Dr. Wheaton is helpless, despite his supposed diagnosis. He claims it's too late. We're going to lose Tommy. This dear boy is going to be in heaven sooner rather than later."

Charley's Adam's apple bobbed. "When Tommy. . ." He drew in a deep breath. "When Tommy slips away, Gracie will need you more than ever. That poor girl has lost almost everyone she's ever loved. She doesn't even remember Papa. We'll all need you in the days and weeks to come."

"Thank you, Charley. You're kind to say so."

From the hall, Harriet peered into the bedroom where Tommy stirred on the mattress. Charley and Harriet returned to his side.

She adjusted the blanket around his bony shoulders. "I'm here, Tommy. I'm not going to leave you." She kissed his cool forehead. His body was shutting down.

His eyelids fluttered, but he didn't awaken. If possible, his breathing slowed and grew shallower. He twisted and writhed, much like Harriet's stomach.

"Shh, quiet now. Just lie still."

Tears slipped from Tommy's eyes and slid down his face. "It hurts."

"I know, sweetie, I know." If only there was a powder or an elixir they might give him to ease his suffering. "Perhaps some tea?"

"No! No!" Despite his weakened condition, he managed to force the words out with a great deal of vehemence.

Not only did his moans of pain pierce Harriet's eardrums, but they pierced her heart and soul. No child should have to endure such suffering. No one should. If only she could stop it.

What if Michael was right? What if someone had inflicted this agony on a young child on purpose? No, it was impossible. No one could be so cruel, so heartless, so ruthless to a young person. One who had never done any of them any wrong.

"Lay down with me, Miss Harriet." Tommy reached out for her.

Each night before bed, he liked it when she lay beside him and read a book. Perhaps it was a ritual he and his mother had shared years ago before she passed away. Whatever the case, she wouldn't deny him anything at this point. After slipping off her shoes, she stretched out beside him. She motioned for Charley to do the same, which he did. They sandwiched the child between them. He quieted.

"Charley and I are here. You aren't alone. We won't leave you by yourself."

"I see Papa."

Mr. Smith remained on vigil at the bedside, never ceasing in his prayers.

Harriet squeezed her eyes shut. The end was coming now. Tommy was slipping away from them. She had promised Lizzie she would take care of this little boy. What a miserable failure she was. "I've let you down, my dear friend. I'm so sorry."

"Gold. Crystal. Gems. Oh, it's so beautiful."

She gathered Tommy to herself, as if that might keep him with her.

"Mama. There's Mama." With a shudder, Tommy breathed his last.

For the longest time, Charley and Harriet lay beside Tommy's body. Little by little, his skin cooled.

Mr. Smith slipped from the room. Charley was the first one up. He came around the bed to Harriet and took her by the hand. "There's nothing more we can do."

"He's gone, then?"

Harriet peered up. Mrs. Robinson stood in the doorway, her arms akimbo.

Charley approached his mother and embraced her. "Yes, Mama, he's gone. I'm so sorry."

"At least his shirt is finished. Just in time for it to be his burial shroud."

"We're going to miss him. The house won't be the same."

No, it wouldn't. It never would be. First Lizzie, now Tommy. Harriet's world was shattering.

Willie came behind his mother. Though his mouth was turned down, he nodded. "For the best, really. He hasn't been well for a while. He was all alone in the world too."

Except that he hadn't been alone. Not really. He had his aunt and cousins and her. So what did Willie mean by that comment?

Harriet slipped on her shoes. After she laced them, she glanced up. Charley still held onto his mother. What he couldn't see was that one corner of her mouth tipped up.

Harriet's stomach convulsed. She had dismissed Michael's claims as ludicrous. Impossible. Crazy.

But both Willie and Mrs. Robinson were behaving very strangely for having lost yet another family member.

What if Michael's accusations held a kernel of truth?

A woman, her face thick with rouge and lip color, her ample bosom much too exposed, her ankle and more showing, sat slumped on a wooden bench as Michael entered the Somerville police station. The noxious odors of alcohol and cheap perfume sent bile rising into this throat.

He shouldn't have to be here.

Willie had come by on his way to the undertaker to let Michael know that Tommy had passed away. At least the child's suffering had come to a merciful end. His suffering, though, was needless. Inflicted on him by someone else. Quite probably someone in the same household.

Michael shuddered. If they didn't stop this madness, who would be the next victim? Harriet? He hugged himself to ward off the unseasonal chill.

He had to ensure that there were no more victims. Including the beautiful woman he couldn't shake from his mind as he made his way to the back of the large, open room. He focused his attention on the bruised and battered wood floors that squeaked underneath his feet. He didn't gaze up until he stood in front of a desk almost as worn as the floors.

Chief Parkhurst rose from his chair. "Dr. Wheaton. I wasn't expecting to see you so soon again." He reached to shake Michael's hand.

Michael bit the inside of his lip. "Tommy Freeman died earlier this evening."

The detective deflated. "That's terrible." He stroked his beard.

"Before he passed away, I brought a colleague of mine, my mentor, Dr. White, to confer with me on Tommy's case. He conducted a thorough examination of the boy and came to the same conclusion. Poisoning. There's no doubt about it."

"Any physical proof?"

"No, but I do understand there is a professor at Harvard University who is able to determine if there is poison in the system. We need either the contents of the stomach or the stomach itself."

"Did you witness anyone poisoning the boy?"

Michael slammed his fists on the desk. "Do you think they would be stupid enough to commit their dirty deed in front of a doctor? All I ever saw given to the boy was tea."

"Who administered it?"

"Several of the people in the household, including Mrs. Robinson and Miss Peters."

"So there are at least two suspects."

Michael puffed out a breath. "No. Not Miss Peters. She would never do such a terrible thing."

"I can see it written all over your face." Parkhurst nodded and leaned back in his chair. "You harbor feelings for Miss Peters. I'm going to give you a warning. Don't allow this to cloud your judgment when it comes to the young lady. Many women have used their wiles to fool many men. Started in the Garden of Eden."

Michael couldn't allow the possibility into his mind. "She couldn't be part of this. She didn't move into the house until after

Miss Lizzie Robinson's death."

"I recall you telling me she attended to the young lady during her illness."

"That's true but not any of the others. Maybe Mr. Freeman, but that's all."

Parkhurst rubbed his bloodshot eyes. "Unfortunately, I can't do much more about it until I have some conclusive evidence. Some physical proof there has been a crime committed. Otherwise, it's nothing more than a strange and unfortunate set of circumstances. One-in-a-million odds."

"More than that, I would say." Michael resisted the urge to pull out his hair. "This time, I have to have enough for an arrest. Another doctor concurs with my diagnosis. We have a way to test for the poison. Get Tommy's stomach from the undertaker, and let's get it tested."

"It's not that simple. I'd need a warrant from a judge."

"Then procure it." Michael roared the words. The entire station quieted.

"Trust me, I'll do my best. Without solid evidence, an eyewitness, it won't be easy."

Michael leaned over, nose to nose with the chief. "This is ridiculous. Without evidence, you can't get the warrant, but without the warrant, we can't get the evidence."

"I'll do everything in my power to convince the judge to issue that warrant. That's the best I can offer you at this point. You're sure this Harvard man can do what you say he can?"

"He's well-known in the field."

"I'll do all that is possible on my end. The more you can snoop around there, the better. Find me something concrete."

"Both Mrs. Robinson and Miss Peters have banned me from the house. I don't know that there is much more I can do."

"You're a smart man, Dr. Wheaton. You can figure it out."

The problem was, he hadn't figured out what was going on with Tommy until it was too late. The boy had died. Perhaps Paul

Gilliland and the others in the crowd were right. He was worthless. Useless.

The childhood taunts rang in his ears. Crazy. Loony. Out of his mind.

The hatred smoldered in his chest, though he worked to overcome it.

He'd proved the bullies wrong by becoming a physician. That was the easy part. Saving lives was so much harder. Something he was not good at.

Maybe they'd been right all along.

A misty fog hung just over the headstones littering the graveyard at Garden Cemetery. The humidity clung to Michael, wrapping itself around him. He wiped the sweat from his brow. Might be from the weather or might be from being here at Tommy's funeral.

He didn't approach the mourners but hung back a ways, among the other markers, and leaned against a large maple tree. He wouldn't be welcome, would only cause a disturbance. This time should be about Tommy and remembering his brief life and grieving his tragic death.

No doubt about it, the family moved to the burial rather fast, a mere day after his passing. There hadn't even been a wake for Thomas. Just this hasty, simple graveside service as the boy was laid to rest beside his parents.

An entire family dead.

The pastor, in his flowing black robe, a Bible in his hand, stood at the head of a small group, each of them also dressed in black, surrounding a child-sized hole in the ground. Both Mrs. Robinson and Harriet pressed black-edged handkerchiefs to their eyes. Gracie clung to Harriet's skirts. Dr. Beers, Charley, and Willie stood behind them.

One of those gathered around the pine coffin was the one who had put that little boy in the box.

Though he had no proof, he would stake his life on it. And pray that discovering the truth wouldn't cost his life or anyone else's.

The women stepped forward, each dropping in a handful of earth. Then came the men, including Dr. Beers. Strange, because he wasn't even officially part of the family. He'd been loitering around the apartment on Holland Street, even though Harriet had told him that Mrs. Robinson had turned down every one of his many marriage proposals. Why didn't he grow discouraged and leave?

The group bowed their heads, and Michael said his own prayer for comfort for those left behind. He added a petition for the capture of the person responsible.

So ended the brief service. The pastor greeted each of the attendees, and then the group scattered. Michael squared his shoulders and approached Harriet.

Even through the dark veil covering her face, he didn't miss her glare. "I came to pay my respects and convey my deepest sympathies to you and to Tommy's family."

"Thank you." Harriet's words were polite but clipped. "I'm surprised you dare to show your face."

"Despite what you think of me, I don't hold any ill will toward you or the Robinsons. My concern is for the well-being of the family members. I don't want to see any others come to the same end. Don't you think it's time for this rash of deaths to cease?"

Harriet blew out a breath, her veil moving with the air. "I would like nothing more than to have this family enjoy health and happiness for many years to come. I don't want any others to suffer the way Lizzie and Tommy have."

Chief Parkhurst warned him not to allow his feelings to cloud his judgment, but his whole being screamed that this woman had nothing to do with the deaths. "Then I need your help."

She glanced over her shoulder where Dr. Beers led a weeping Mrs. Robinson from Tommy's final resting place. "I'm not sure. I'm not convinced that this is, well, what you say it is."

"You don't have to do much."

"I shouldn't even be seen speaking with you. I told you to leave us alone and never bother us again, remember?"

"All too well."

A tiny grin brightened her otherwise grim face.

"Think about Tommy. And Lizzie. And all the others. Do you want to see anyone else succumb in the same agonizing manner?"

She blanched. "Of course not."

"Then I'm going to need your help."

"You've gotten the police involved, haven't you?"

He should have known he couldn't get anything by her. There was no need in lying to her. Sooner or later, she was bound to find out. "Yes."

"When can I expect to be arrested?"

"None of you is in imminent danger of being taken into custody. I don't believe they even have plans to question anyone. They need proof."

"Of what?"

"Poisoning. And of someone administering that poison."

"How am I supposed to get that?"

"If one of the others falls ill, we'd need a sample of either the stomach contents or the stomach itself."

Even under her veil, her pale face turned rather green. "I don't know about that."

"In order to prevent another family member perishing in this same way, it must be done. At the very least, get in touch with me immediately so I can get involved."

With long, purposeful strides, Mrs. Robinson marched toward Harriet and Michael. "I'm surprised you had the fortitude to show up here. This is a private occasion. As you can see, just as I predicted, we have lost another family member. We would ask that you respect our wishes and leave us alone. Come along, Harriet. I'm going to have to lean on you now more than ever."

Michael couldn't release Harriet before he had her assurance that she was on his side and would be on the lookout for anything out of sorts. "I'll see Miss Peters home shortly."

"I'm in great need of her at present. I'm sure you understand. Gracie is quite distraught at the loss of her cousin, as am I. We're all feeling this keenly. Now is the time for us to draw closer as a family." Mrs. Robinson tugged Harriet by the arm.

Harriet had no choice but to go with Mrs. Robinson. Had the woman overheard any of their conversation? Did she know that Michael's suspicions were growing?

"Of course. I understand. Please, accept my deepest sympathies. I'll keep your entire family in my prayers. May God provide each of you great comfort in this trying time."

"Thank you, Dr. Wheaton. Now we really must be going." She tugged harder on Harriet and pulled her away. They beat a hasty retreat, Harriet never so much as glancing over her shoulder.

A stiff wind picked up, blowing away the morning mist, almost knocking Michael's hat from his head. He grabbed for it and twirled it in his hands as he made his way to young Tommy's final resting place.

He stared at the mound of dirt the gravediggers had already used to cover the casket.

Why did it have to end like this? What motivation would anyone have to commit such a heinous act? He stretched the kinks out of his neck.

He must have stood there for quite some time, because the sun was high overhead when he gazed up. Sweat trickled down his back. Parkhurst approached. "You are a tough man to locate."

"I think I lost track of time. As you can see, they've already buried the boy. Curious, isn't it, that they did it so fast?"

"If there isn't any other family to mourn him, it isn't that out of the ordinary."

Michael turned to the detective. "So you think I'm making more of this than there is?"

"I didn't say that. Add everything up, and you can come to some pretty crazy conclusions."

"Why did you track me down?"

"I went to the judge this morning to try to get an order to send Tommy's stomach to this expert for analysis."

Some of the tension drained from Michael's body. "That's good news."

Parkhurst shook his head. "No, it isn't. He denied my request. Now, with the boy buried, we would also need an order to exhume the body. I'll keep investigating, and you keep your eyes open. We'll see what we can come up with."

"I asked Miss Peters to help me."

The detective removed his black-billed blue hat, slicked back his hair, and replaced his cap. "I wish you hadn't done that. You don't know that she's not involved in the crimes. You may have tipped her off and sunk the case before we really got it afloat."

"Sir, I know she's not the perpetrator."

"No, you don't. Whoever is doing this is good. Sneaky. Underhanded. And dangerous."

Michael sucked in a breath. If the perpetrator of these crimes discovered Harriet snooping around, getting close to the truth, he may have just doomed her to death.

Chapter Fourteen

And that's the end." Harriet shut the book she'd been reading to Gracie and cuddled the child close to her heart. Though old enough to not be sucking her thumb anymore, Harriet allowed her the habit. The poor girl had been through so much in the past few months, she needed the comfort—one Harriet wasn't about to deny her.

She rocked the girl and sang into her hair, happy songs like *I See the Moon.*

I see the moon, the moon sees me
shining through the leaves of the old oak tree.
Oh, let the light that shines on me
shine on the one I love.

Over the mountain, over the sea,
back where my heart is longing to be.
Oh, let the light that shines on me
shine on the one I love.

I hear the lark, the lark hears me
singing from the leaves of the old oak tree.
Oh, let the lark that sings to me
sing to the one I love.

Over the mountains, over the sea
back where my heart is longing to be.
Oh, let the lark that sings to me
sing to the one I love.

Did life get any sweeter than with a child in your lap?

At last, Gracie's eyes fluttered shut, and Harriet tucked her into bed, kissing the child's smooth brow. Perhaps someday, the Lord would bless her with a child much like this one.

A picture of a little boy with dark hazel eyes and dark hair and a long face flashed through her mind.

An image that very much resembled Michael.

Why on earth would she think of that? Especially considering what he believed someone in the family or associated with the family was doing.

Still, this little niggle pricked the back of her conscience. Was Michael on to something? Could it be that someone was poisoning the members of the Robinson family one by one? But who? And why?

All of these questions brought a tremendous pounding behind Harriet's left eye.

At the burial, she hadn't had a chance to give Michael her answer to his question about being on the lookout for suspicious activity before Mrs. Robinson had pulled her away. Almost like she didn't want Harriet speaking to him.

No, that was ridiculous. Now Michael's accusations were seeping into her brain and making her think and believe stories that couldn't possibly be true. She refused to live her life always looking over her shoulder, always suspecting or being on the watch for the worst in the people around her.

That was no way to behave, and it was no way to treat these people who had been nothing but kind to her.

If Michael asked her, she would turn him down in a heartbeat.

Mrs. Robinson mourned Tommy's loss with all her heart. True, she had placed much of the burden of looking after the boy on Lizzie and then on Harriet, but that was only because her own grief was so strong. Right?

Whatever the case, Harriet needed headache powders, or she would never be able to sleep tonight. Though she had already bid

Mrs. Robinson, Dr. Beers, and Willie good night, she crept down the hall and back to the parlor.

When she entered the room, the three of them were huddled together by the small, octagonal parlor table, so engrossed in their conversation that none of them paid her any attention as she moved across the room.

"It's just like I told you." Mrs. Robinson's words were low and intense, even as her needle flew through the puddle of green fabric on her lap. The dress was missing from the form in the room's corner.

"And what are you going to do about it?" Dr. Beers also kept his voice quiet.

"I'm going to have to pressure him."

"I don't know if that's such a good idea." Willie didn't keep his voice quite as low.

"Why not? You know what straits I'm in."

"I'm well aware of them, dear lady." Dr. Beers cleared his throat. If you would marry me—"

Mrs. Robinson held up her hand to halt Dr. Beers midsentence. "I do wish you would stop asking me. I have given you my answer a thousand times, and a thousand times, it's been the same."

"One can always hope that the thousand and first time is the charm." A dimple lit his sagging, fleshy cheek.

"You are much too old for me. Besides, I have more pressing issues, and you know it."

"I've given you my best suggestion."

Willie straightened. "I agree with Dr. Beers. You're going to have to speak to Mr. Bugbee and explain all this to him."

Wasn't that the man from the Order of Pilgrim Fathers? Harriet attempted to slip out of the room and into the kitchen without disturbing their conversation, but her toe caught on the edge of the bright red and blue throw rug in the middle of the floor. She fell with a thud.

Pain sliced through her knee. Mrs. Robinson gasped.

Willie jumped from his chair. "What in tarnation are you doing?" He stood over her, his fair face flushed.

"I didn't want to interrupt your conversation, but I needed some headache powders. Though I was trying to be as quiet as possible, I tripped on the rug. And bruised my knee, I'm afraid."

"More like eavesdropping, wasn't it?" Mrs. Robinson sidled next to her doctor friend who now stood beside Willie.

"No, not at all. I would never do that." Though wasn't that just what she was doing? "I apologize. Next time, I will be sure to make my presence known."

"Please do." The red in Mrs. Robinson's face now matched that in Dr. Beers's. Willie's face remained as implacable as ever.

Harriet scrambled to her feet, though she winced as she put weight on her right leg. Those powders had better work on more than her head. "Again, my apologies. I'll get that medicine and then be off to bed. I'm going to take Gracie to the shop with me tomorrow to get some work done."

Mrs. Robinson frowned. "I don't want Gracie going out tomorrow."

"May I ask why not? She's been cooped up since Tommy's death. The weather has been so fine, I thought it would be good for her to get out and get some fresh air."

"I would prefer that the two of you stay home as much as possible. And limit contact with outsiders."

Harriet furrowed her brow. "Whatever for?"

"How do we know where Lizzie and Tommy and the others contracted their illnesses? I've already suffered so much." A tear trickled down Mrs. Robinson's cheek, and Dr. Beers handed her a pressed handkerchief. "I couldn't bear it if another one of my children fell sick."

"There, there, my dear." Dr. Beers patted Mrs. Robinson's shoulder before focusing his attention on Harriet. "It's under my advisement that Mrs. Robinson makes this request. Until we can pin down the source of this mysterious ailment, it's best that you and

Gracie do not go out."

"What about the rest of you?"

Mrs. Robinson shook her head, a strand of hair coming loose from the severe bun she kept it in. "We must eat, and so we must go to work."

Willie nodded. "You must agree, Harriet. We have no other choice."

"How about my job? The shop I've worked so long and hard for? I can't let that go. I refuse."

"Please, dear, try to see it from my point of view. You can work from home while caring for Gracie. I don't have that luxury."

Was Mrs. Robinson jealous of Harriet? "My shop is everything to me."

"And so is my daughter. I'll do what I have to in order to protect her."

"I will do whatever I have to in order to keep my business."

As the hot, late-afternoon sun almost blinded Michael, he paced in front of Harriet's hat shop. More than a week had gone by since Tommy's burial, and he hadn't seen her at her place of business the entire time. The door remained locked. He peeked through the large window into the dark room. A note was posted on the glass informing clients that Miss Peters was out due to a family emergency and giving the address of the house on Holland Street where she might be contacted.

He stretched. True, Harriet and the Robinsons were in mourning, but she'd shared with him Mrs. Robinson's financial difficulties, so it would only make sense that she would come by the millinery. Harriet had told him the family relied on her income.

Still, no sign of her. Here it was, late in the day on Saturday, and the shop remained shuttered. He again peered in the window, once sparkling clean, now rather dirty. Nothing inside had been disturbed. The ribbons and hat forms and even the scissors sat in the same places they had occupied all week.

The clanging of the horse car bell pulled Michael from his musings. The horse slowed as the driver reined the large black animal to a stop at the corner. A young man with blond hair jumped from the car. With a crack of the reins, the horse car moved forward again.

Ah, it was Charley Robinson who had alighted just down the street. Good. Perhaps now Michael would get the answers to the questions that had plagued him all week.

As Charley approached, Michael lifted his bowler hat in greeting. "Hello there." He held his breath in anticipation of the other man's reaction. Did he have the same attitude toward Michael as did the rest of his family?

A wide grin crossed Charley's face. "Dr. Wheaton. It's good to see you."

Michael released his pent-up breath and shook Charley's large hand. "I didn't get a chance to express my condolences to you on the loss of your cousin."

A shadow crossed Charley's face, and it had nothing to do with the small clouds passing in front of the sun. "I can't believe they are all gone. All of my mother's sister's family now lie in Garden Cemetery."

"I understand from Miss Peters that you were very close to your uncle."

Charley nodded. "I was. We spent much time talking to each other. In fact, we enjoyed each other's company at a church social the evening before his sickness. The next day, he became ill. Just like Lizzie and Tommy, it was so sudden. Every bit of it. Except that in the week or so before he got sick, Mama predicted he would. She even told him to go visit his mother, as it might be the last time he would see her. And it was." The young man scuffed his heavy work boot on the walk.

"I wish there was more I could have done for young Tommy. And Lizzie."

"We know you tried your best. You have to forgive Mama for not behaving in the most cordial manner. All the grief and tragedy hasn't been easy on her. From the time she was a young girl in Ireland, she's lost almost everyone she loves. With Papa gone, she bears such a burden for the family's well-being. Willie and I shoulder as much as we can, but it's been a heavy cross for her."

"I understand." Michael shifted his weight from one foot to the other. "And how is Miss Peters faring?"

Charley sighed. "As well as can be expected."

"I had been hoping to run into her at some point this week. As you can see, it's Saturday afternoon, and she isn't here."

"No. Mama and Dr. Beers both want her to stay inside with Gracie. They're afraid of my sister contracting whatever Tommy had."

Michael chewed on his upper lip. "I can understand your mother's concern, but as for Dr. Beers, that doesn't make sense. Rather, fresh air, away from the stale odors of the sickness, would be my prescription. Especially given the fine July weather we've been enjoying. Winter and the time for staying inside will come soon enough."

Charley shrugged. "Perhaps you have a point, but you know how much Mama relies on Dr. Beers. He has been good to our family and has been there for us in each time of crisis. Unfortunately, there have been many of those."

"Unfortunately." Michael loosened his cranberry-red cravat. "What brings you by? This isn't on your way home from work."

"Harriet asked me to stop at the store and bring a few supplies for her. She's struggling to keep the clientele she's worked so hard to build. She has sacrificed a great deal to help our family. Without her, I don't know what we would do."

"She is a gem."

"We do treasure her."

"Would you mind delivering a note to her for me? I'll write it while you gather the supplies she has requested."

"That should be fine."

"Just make sure your mother doesn't discover the letter."

Charley laughed. "Does she intimidate you, sir?"

"Just a slight bit." Michael slapped Charley on the back. "You're a good chap."

"No matter what Mama or Dr. Beers says about you, I would agree you are too."

"That means a great deal." Michael spun toward his office, then toward Charley once again. "Would you do me one more favor?"

"If I can." He dug the key from the pocket of his work pants and slipped it into the shop's lock.

"If anyone else in the house, anyone at all, comes down with the same or similar symptoms, would you send for me at once?"

"Even knowing how Mama feels about you?"

Michael nodded.

Charley paused, the key remaining in the lock. "I'm aware of your suspicions."

Harriet had told him? She shouldn't have done that. He should never have confided in her. "Nothing is definitive." Michael wasn't about to elaborate. Not that he suspected the kind young man, but because he didn't want to put anyone else in the home in danger as he feared he had possibly already done with Harriet. "That's why I need to know as soon as the next person falls ill. If anyone does. I've already asked the same of Harriet, but if she would be the one to get sick, I must know as quickly as possible. Time is of the essence."

"I'll do my best."

"Thank you." Michael hurried away to write the note to Harriet. Though his mind raced with a thousand thoughts to share with her, when it came time to put pen to paper, he couldn't form a single letter. He tapped his pen against his wood desk then made a couple of false starts, crumpling the paper and tossing it into the trash bin each time.

"Ugh." He pushed his chair backward and completed several circuits around his office, finally stopping and pressing his closed eyes, as if that would make the words come.

It actually worked. He returned to his desk and composed the letter in the matter of a few minutes. He dusted it dry and sealed it with a wax seal. He wasn't about to take any chances with the missive falling into the wrong hands.

In a flash, he returned to Harriet's shop to find Charley exiting with a large basket full of items.

"I'm afraid people are going to be staring at me on the horse car." He grinned.

"I'm afraid you're right about that." Michael tucked the note among the frippery overflowing from the basket. "Thank you. Let me know if there is anything I can do for your family."

"Right now, we appreciate your prayers. I will let you know right away if anyone else in the house falls ill."

Michael prayed he would never get that message.

Chapter Fifteen

As Harriet went about stripping the sheets from the beds, she felt for the piece of paper in her skirt's pocket. The words penned on it brought a smile to her face. She didn't even need to look at it to know what it said. For as many times as she had read it, she had it committed to memory.

She whispered the message, even though only she and Gracie were home. "My dear Harriet, I know you may not believe me or even trust me, but I only have your best interest at heart. My concern is for your well-being and the health of all in the Robinson household. I am sorry to have caused you distress. Though you may not agree with me on a certain issue, I would very much like the chance to make amends for myself. Mrs. Robinson will not allow me at the house, but if there is a time when she will be out, perhaps at work, I would like to come calling. Sincerely, Michael Wheaton."

"What are you talking about?"

At the sound of Gracie's voice, Harriet jumped a mile, her heart hammering against her ribs. "Goodness, sweetie, you just about scared the stuffing out of me."

A frown crossed the child's face. "I'm sorry."

Harriet knelt beside her. "No, I'm the one who should apologize. You didn't mean to sneak up on me. I was thinking about something else and never heard you. It wasn't your fault at all." She brushed a strand of light red hair away from the girl's thin face and gathered her close.

"Harriet, Harriet, where are you?" Mrs. Robinson's strident voice pierced through the house's stillness.

Harriet kissed Gracie's forehead before releasing her.

"What are you doing?" Mrs. Robinson stood in the bedroom's doorway.

"Apologizing for scolding Gracie and showing her a little affection." Which is more than Harriet could say for Mrs. Robinson lately. Starting with Lizzie's death and only getting worse with Tommy's, the woman withdrew more and more from her children.

"Stop mollycoddling her. If you scolded her, I'm sure it was for a good reason. She shouldn't be bothering you when you have work to do."

"She wasn't, I can assure you. Just a little misunderstanding."

"Well, whatever you're doing in here, I need you to stop. Come and clean the parlor. Mr. Bugbee from the insurance agency is stopping by this evening. The place is positively covered in such a thick layer of dust, I doubt we'll ever find the furniture underneath it."

That was the furthest thing from the truth. Harriet had dusted in there yesterday. Without the ability to go to her shop, she was losing clientele at an alarming rate. Nowadays, she had little hat-making work to occupy her time. Gracie didn't require much care, just some attention every now and again.

"Mama." Gracie tugged on her mother's skirts. "Can I please go to Fran's house? I haven't seen her in a long time, and I want to play dolls."

"Harriet can play with you after she finishes straightening the other room and getting supper going."

"I don't want Harriet." Gracie stomped her foot. "I want Fran."

"Well you can't have her, so that's the end of that. I don't want to hear another word about it. Do you understand me?"

At Mrs. Robinson's words, Harriet sucked in a breath. Gracie only wanted to be allowed to play. No one in the area was sick. They would know if someone had similar symptoms to Lizzie and Tommy. "Surely she can go out for a short time, just to see her friends. She's been cooped up for days on end. I need to go to my shop, anyway. It will be good for both of us to be out."

Mrs. Robinson pursed her lips, and she stepped closer to Harriet.

"I am Gracie's mother. It is my job to protect her. If Dr. Beers says it is best for everyone to stay as close to home as possible, then that is what I ask you to do."

"You have a better chance of bringing home a sickness from where you work than Gracie does going two houses down the street to spend some time with her friend or from coming to my shop with me."

"This discussion is over. Gracie, you go to the kitchen." The girl scurried to comply. "And you, Miss Peters, get to work. After all I do for you, the least you can do is to help out every now and again."

"I pay for my own food and ask for nothing for the work I do in caring for Gracie and the house. I have to go to my shop. I have appointments with clients I plan on keeping, or else there will be nothing left of the millinery."

"What is more important? A few women's hats or this family?"

"Both are of equal importance to me. If you can't respect that, I will have to leave."

"No." In a split second, Mrs. Robinson changed her tone. "Goodness knows what Gracie would do without you. It may well be the end of her. Losing you will be another death to her, one more in a long string of them. If you want that on your hands, that's up to you." Mrs. Robinson flounced from Harriet's room.

A moment later, Willie entered. "What was that all about? Upsetting Mama again?"

"Nothing. Just a misunderstanding between your mother and me. We'll smooth it over in no time."

"You told me you wouldn't argue with her."

"I know. But..."

"What?"

Harriet sighed. "Nothing." She bit her lip. "I'm having a bad day, that's all."

"Don't upset her. You promised. I'm going to hold you to it."

"I'll do my best. I'm not perfect, Willie. That's all I can say. I will try to work it out with her." Though it took everything inside her to keep from packing her bags and fleeing to the peace and safety of her little space above her shop.

"You'd better." With a glare, he left the room. A moment later, his door slammed. He would likely remain there the rest of the evening, save for supper time. When he was home, he didn't join the family in the parlor in the evenings, preferring to lock himself in the room he shared with Charley.

The kitchen door slammed shut, and Gracie raced to Harriet. "Mama says you might leave. Please, please don't go. Lizzie went away and Tommy too. I don't want you to not be here."

Harriet's heart constricted. How could she walk away from the little girl? She loved her so much. She had promised Lizzie. "Don't worry, sweetheart. Your mama and I will work this out. If nothing else, I will come here during the day with you and sleep at my shop when your mother comes home from work."

Gracie hugged her legs.

The gesture only tore at Harriet. For this precious girl, she would try to stay. For now. For a little while.

Well, the sheets would have to wait. She'd better get started on the parlor, though there wasn't much dust to brush away. Gracie had been drawing on her slate for most of the afternoon. Her dolls were in the room the two of them shared. Harriet stood in the middle of the parlor, her arms crossed. She'd move a few items around and sweep the already-clean floor.

As soon as she finished that chore, Mr. Bugbee arrived. Mrs. Robinson hustled him inside and up the stairs, throwing a pointed glare at Harriet. "Is supper going? We don't want to wait all night for it."

With a sigh, Harriet strode to the kitchen where Gracie sat with her slate. Harriet pulled out the flour and lard to start a batch of biscuits. Another headache was coming, the back of her neck aching. At least it wasn't her stomach.

They didn't have much flour left or much sugar or salt for that matter. At some point, they would need more food. Harriet would have to leave the house to shop.

"I have to use the privy." Gracie set aside her chalk and clapped her hands to rid them of the dust.

"Go ahead."

As the child exited, the door swung open. Voices floated in from the other room.

The first was Dr. Beers. "You'd better give Mrs. Robinson what she asks for soon. She needs that money."

"Please, Mr. Bugbee, we're in financial distress." That was Mrs. Robinson. Then the door closed, and Harriet couldn't catch any more of the conversation.

Why did everything have to be about money with Mrs. Robinson? All four adults in the household were employed. Harriet's presence was no strain at all on the family budget. True, between paying the rent on her shop and the money she sent home to her family, there wasn't much left, but she paid for everything she used and then some.

The pain in her neck spread to her head and exploded into a thousand different colors in front of her eyes.

Why was it so dark? Harriet struggled to open her eyes, but even that small movement sent shards of pain slashing through her head. Her stomach roiled and churned. She couldn't get sick, because she would never be able to move her head enough.

"Harriet? Harriet?" The deep male voice came from a distance. Like he was calling from the next block. Still, it resonated with her.

"Um."

"You need to open your eyes."

Even though she didn't understand why she had to do so, she worked to comply, managing to raise one eyelid. Even the dim light that filtered through was much too bright.

"Now the other one."

With a bit of effort, she got both lids opened. Willie stood over her, his expression neutral. As unreadable as ever. The light burned her eyes. "What happened?"

"I don't know. I came into the kitchen and found you lying on the floor." He bent closer. "Do you remember anything?"

She tried to shake her head, but that only sent her stomach into convulsions. She bit back the foul taste. "Nothing. I had a headache. Then such bright lights flashed in front of me, like a kaleidoscope, before everything went dark."

"Can you get up?" Though he asked the question, he didn't offer his assistance.

Little by little, she pushed herself to a sitting position. The world spun as it had when she was a small girl twirling in the grass. She grasped the leg of a chair beside the kitchen table to steady herself. "If I give it a minute, I think I'll be fine."

"For a while there, I thought we'd have to call the undertaker again."

What an odd comment. What did he mean by that? "No, I don't plan on going anywhere, though I can't imagine why I fainted, if that's what happened. The bright lights are bizarre." She rubbed the back of her head and discovered a large bump right in the middle of it.

Had someone hit her over the head, trying to get rid of her as they had the others? No, it didn't make sense. The others were poisoned. But maybe the perpetrator couldn't get the poison. Maybe they wanted a swifter death this time.

She shuddered, then worked to control her emotions in front of Willie. It wouldn't do to let him see the thoughts running through her head. Though it was strange he was the one who found her.

Oh, this headache or blow or whatever it was muddled her thoughts. She was seeing things where there weren't things to be seen. She would have to ask Michael about it. And about this bump on her head.

Willie continued to hover over her, staring at her. She needed to get fully upright so he would go away.

Though the pain in her head increased, she pulled herself to her feet. Once steady, she flashed him a wide grin. "See, right as rain."

"Well, at least I don't have to go out again tonight. I'm too tired to be chasing all over town." He left the kitchen. Harriet could do nothing but gaze at the closed door, her mouth open.

She felt for the note in her pocket. No paper crumpled under her hand. To be sure, she turned the pocket inside out.

Nothing.

Where had it gone? She scanned the kitchen floor, but there was no note. She turned her other pocket around, but no piece of paper fell out. Had she left it somewhere? Perhaps in the bedroom. What if it had fallen out in the parlor?

Her knees knocked as she stumbled toward the counter to continue dinner preparations. There was nothing she could do right now to look for the note. Mrs. Robinson and Dr. Beers were holed up in the parlor with the insurance man. She had to cross through it to reach the bedrooms.

Dear Lord, don't let them find it.

Only Charley knew about it. She could trust him. She especially couldn't allow the note to fall into Mrs. Robinson's hands. That would anger her to no end. They'd had one argument already tonight. Harriet popped the biscuits into the oven.

She had to search for the letter right now, even if she had to turn the place upside down. Even if she had to interrupt the meeting taking place in the other room. She pushed the door open as Mr. Bugbee rose to his feet. "I'm sorry I couldn't give you better news, Mrs. Robinson. These things take time to sort out. I understand your circumstances. Perhaps in the meantime your church would be able to assist you. I will do my best to expedite your case, but as I said, there have been some holdups."

"Yet you won't tell me what they are."

"I'm afraid I can't." Mr. Bugbee rubbed his arms as if chilled, even though the western sunshine slanted through the windows and baked the apartment.

"Excuse me, please. So sorry for intruding." As fast as her

still-throbbing head would allow, Harriet rushed through the parlor, glancing for the missing note, and scurried down the hallway to the bedroom. She lifted the crumpled sheet from the bed, but nothing fell from the folds. Where could it have gone? It had to be here somewhere. It didn't disappear into thin air, though that would be preferable to either Mrs. Robinson or Dr. Beers finding it.

Light steps sounded in the hall. Mrs. Robinson, most likely. Harriet set to fixing the sheets.

"Busy at work, I see?"

"Of course."

"From now on, please do not intrude on my private meetings."

"I never meant to interrupt you. With dinner going, I thought I would straighten this room and get it ready for Gracie tonight." If only the world would stop this crazy twirling about.

"If you didn't lollygag, you wouldn't be dealing with the beds at this time of day."

Harriet's shoulders sagged. "To tell the truth, I'm looking for something."

"What might that be?"

"It's nothing important, really." She gave a half-hearted laugh. "I'm sure it will turn up at some point. It has to be somewhere in the house. So silly of me to misplace it. You have enough going on. I won't trouble you."

"How kind and thoughtful of you." Mrs. Robinson reached into her pocket and withdrew a piece of paper. "Is this what you're looking for?"

Chapter Sixteen

Never in his life had Michael been so happy to see his little office and apartment. He'd been up most of the night and all day attending a difficult birth. Both the child and the mother would live, praise the Lord. This time, anyway. He yawned. Even though it wasn't yet suppertime, his soft, clean bed called to him.

He wouldn't be able to resist its siren song. Too tired to even change out of his clothes, he climbed the steep, narrow, creaky stairs to his single-roomed living quarters and flopped on the bed. All he'd have to do was count to ten, and he'd be asleep.

Before he had a chance to close his eyes, though, someone pounded on the door downstairs. Couldn't he even get a couple hours of rest? With a great deal of effort, he pulled himself from his comfortable mattress and stumbled down the stairs.

When he answered the door, a man stood on his step, his dark eyes wide and wild, his even darker hair mussed. His chest heaved. "Please, please, ye have to be coming right now."

"Take a deep breath." The man had such a deep Irish accent, Michael wouldn't be able to understand what was wrong if he didn't calm down. The man followed his commands. "Good. Now, tell me what the trouble is."

"It's me son. Just a wee little lad. Me wife found him. He'd been eating the rat poison."

Dear God, not a child. Sometimes immigrants didn't understand the dangers of the poison. They only wanted to be rid of the rats that infested the crowded tenements.

They had no time to lose.

Michael picked up the bag he had dropped beside the door and stepped outside. "How far?"

"If we're running, ten minutes."

The two men tore down the street, Michael commanding his legs to pump faster than they ever had before. Still, he couldn't match the pace of the frantic father. Every now and then, the man turned and urged Michael forward.

For that little boy, he had to race as if the devil himself were after him.

Those blocks had never been longer, the run had never been farther, but at last they came to the brick building, windows cracked, stoop sagging, laundry strung from building to building in this section of town teeming with humanity. With no grass, kids played in the muddy road.

The father entered, and Michael followed, taking the steps to the third floor two by two. Three small children, their faces dirty, snot running from their noses, peered at their brother who lay on a large, lumpy bed. Their heavily pregnant mother leaned over her young son. He couldn't be more than a year old.

The little boy with hair that matched his father's writhed on the filthy mattress. The stomach-churning odor of vomit mixed with urine hung over the place.

"Doc's here."

The woman turned, her lips pinched, her mouth turned down. "I'd only been sleeping a wee bit." A few crystal tears slid down her olive-toned cheeks. "Ye have to be helping him. Me boy. How could I have done this to him?"

Michael didn't have time to ease the woman's conscience. Not now. He pushed by her to the child's bedside. The little one thrashed and moaned. He turned to the mother. "Get clean sheets. And a glass of water. Start some broth."

While the mother lumbered off to carry out his requests, Michael examined the child. Already, his pulse was weak and thready. When he pushed on the boy's stomach, he screamed in agony. The symptoms were consistent with rat poisoning.

Michael would give him some bismuth phosphate, what little good it would do at this point. The best they could do for him was keep him hydrated and pray.

The father hovered over the bed, pacing the small room, paying no attention to his other three children who stood with their thumbs in their mouths. At last, the mother returned with the water and handed the glass to Michael. "Broth's on."

"Good." While he tended to the boy, he needed the parents to stay busy, to keep their minds occupied. "Get some water boiling. And take the others from the room."

Both parents exited, the father shooing his kids out ahead of him.

Once they were gone and the door shut, Michael sat on the bed beside the boy. He hadn't even taken the time to ask his parents what the child's name was. He mixed the bismuth phosphate into the glass, stroked the child's arm, and whispered to him. "Come on, take a little sip."

The boy stared at Michael with glassy eyes.

"Just a small drink. Can you do that for me?"

"Owie! Owie!" He clutched his stomach and was sick again.

While vomiting was good for getting rid of the poison, too much of the toxin might already be in the child's system. There was no telling if he would survive or not. It didn't take much to kill one so small.

The hours dragged on. For a time, the boy slept. During that period, his mother crept into the room. "How is he doing?"

"Do you know how much poison he ate?"

She shook her head, several curls escaping their pins. "I dunno. He was supposed to be sleeping next to me." She rubbed her belly. "This one has me more tired than the others. Then me oldest was running and getting me, saying Samuel got into the poison."

Samuel. Poor boy.

His mother covered her face. "This is all me fault. If I hadn't been sleeping, if I had been keeping the poison up higher—"

"Let's worry about Samuel right now."

She went to her son's bedside. "Oh, my wee one. I'm ever so sorry about this, I am. Please, please, don't die. I cannot be losing you."

Samuel's eyes flicked open. "Mama." His voice was weak, strained. He was losing the battle.

Michael went to the door and motioned for the father to come in. He knelt before his little boy. "Samuel, we're here. We love you."

Samuel patted his mother's hand. A shuddering breath. Then his soul flew heavenward.

Mrs. Robinson stood in front of Harriet, so close the odor of garlic coming from her was almost overpowering. "Is this what you were looking for?"

Dr. Beers peered at Harriet from behind Mrs. Robinson's shoulder and shook his head. "I'm disappointed in you, Miss Peters."

"Give it to me now." Harriet reached to snatch away the note.

Mrs. Robinson yanked it behind her back. "I don't think so. We gave strict instructions that you and Gracie were not to leave the house and no one was to come in."

"You have him here all the time." Harriet glanced over Mrs. Robinson's shoulder to the old man behind her.

If possible, the woman's face reddened further. "He is a doctor and has every right to be here, an invited guest in *my* home."

"Dr. Wheaton is my invited guest. I'm an adult and a contributing member of this household. Trite as it sounds, this is a free country. I should be allowed to see who I want to see."

"Not when it puts me and my children at risk. I forbid it. If I have to, I will hire someone to come and watch you."

Harriet gave a single-note laugh. "I heard about your money troubles. You don't have the cash on hand to do so. I don't have to stay here. I'm going back to my shop and home. Lizzie made me promise to take care of Tommy and Gracie. I failed Tommy. I will be here every day to watch Gracie, from the time you leave for work until the time you arrive home. After that, you're on your own."

Mrs. Robinson's countenance softened, and she grabbed Harriet's arm. "Please, don't do that to me. To my daughter. We need you. We would be in a desperate way without you. Don't go. I beg you not to leave. It would crush Gracie's heart. She's had too much loss already."

Mama had always accused Harriet of being too soft, of caring too much for others. The image of Lizzie in bed, agony gripping her, the promise Harriet had made, all came rushing back. How could she leave Gracie? She had vowed to protect Tommy, and she'd been a miserable failure. What would happen to Lizzie's only remaining sister if Harriet left?

If someone in the house was poisoning family members, including children, Gracie wasn't safe. Could she even trust Gracie to the care of someone else in the evening? A picture of Charley on her doorstep in the middle of the night, calling for Harriet to nurse Gracie, flashed in front of her.

Was there another way? A plan in which she took the child from the home to protect her? No. Impossible. Mrs. Robinson would know right away who had taken Gracie. Harriet might even be brought up on charges of kidnapping.

She had little choice.

A crushing load pressed on Harriet's chest. She couldn't walk away, but she couldn't stay here under these conditions. Her head throbbed all the harder. If she left and something happened to Gracie, Harriet would never forgive herself. That was the bottom line.

She'd made a vow she had to keep, no matter what the circumstances. Even if it cost her everything. This time, she wouldn't fail.

"Fine. I'll stay. On the condition that Dr. Wheaton be allowed to visit me. If you don't want to see him, he can come during the day."

Mrs. Robinson shook her head, quite vehement. "It wouldn't be proper for him to be here with you alone, unchaperoned. What would people think about you? About me? We're church-going people. No, I can't have tongues wagging about me behind my back.

Or about you. I'd hate to see your reputation ruined."

Dr. Beers stepped around Mrs. Robinson. "Think of the contamination he might bring. It's my belief that somehow, poison from one of the factories came into the house and sickened the family. Dr. Wheaton, good man though he is, works in the slums, among those employed in the factories. He carries poison with him wherever he goes. No, he can't be allowed in here. I don't treat patients anymore. No factory dust on me."

Harriet glanced from Mrs. Robinson to Dr. Beers and back to Mrs. Robinson. Could one of them be the person poisoning the family? How could she trust them? Should she?

Her tired brain hurt from the effort of thinking. Lizzie's words continued to ring in her ears. *"Promise me, Harriet. Take care of Tommy and Gracie."*

No matter the consequences, that was what she must do. She had done it for her own brothers and sisters. She would do it now for Lizzie's sake. And Gracie's. Only for them. "I will stay. But you must return the note to me."

Mrs. Robinson sighed but held out the piece of paper.

What they didn't know was that Harriet had no intention of preventing Michael from entering the house.

Mrs. Robinson pulled a handkerchief from her skirt pocket and dabbed at nonexistent tears. "You must promise not to go out. You must promise to stay inside and keep anything bad from happening to my sweet girl. Only those who live here are to come and go. No one else. I couldn't bear it if I lost my only surviving daughter. Please."

Harriet puffed out her cheeks. If she stayed and agreed to Mrs. Robinson's terms and someone else in the household fell ill, she could be reasonably certain that the murderer lived in the house. "What are you going to do when school begins again? Are you going to keep Gracie at home?"

Mrs. Robinson sighed. "I don't know. Right now, I'm mourning the loss of my nephew. I'm barely managing to keep this family from sinking into poverty. Going to school is a bridge we're going to have to cross when we get to it."

Gracie entered from the bedroom. "Is it time for supper yet? I'm hungry."

"Oh, the biscuits." Mrs. Robinson wouldn't be happy if Harriet wasted food. She hurried to the kitchen and pulled the pan from the oven just in time. As she turned to place them on the table to cool, she almost bumped into Mrs. Robinson.

"I know how difficult it must be for you to remain inside, especially in the summer. But it's for the best. Think of my daughter, of my sons, of yourself. This family couldn't stand another loss. If anything happened to any of you, they might as well bury me in the ground too."

Harriet scooted around Mrs. Robinson and placed the hot pan on the table. "I understand. You're looking out for the welfare of your family. I haven't forgotten my promise to Lizzie. Gracie has become like a little sister to me. I'll do what I have to in order to keep her happy and well."

"Thank you, thank you. You can't imagine how much that means to me. You are an angel sent from God to watch over us. I know it. I feel it in my bones. May He bless you, child."

Get out of the house. Get out while you can.

Harriet covered her ears but couldn't silence the voices in her head.

Chapter Seventeen

"Miss Harriet, can we have a tea party?" Gracie gazed at Harriet, her blue eyes wide and pleading.

Harriet wiped away a trickle of sweat that rolled down the side of her face. The fierce late-summer sun beat on the second story of the home. Even with the windows wide open, the air pressed on Harriet's chest. Drawing a deep breath was difficult. How wonderful it would be to get some fresh air. To allow the wind to blow across her skin the way it did the leaves that trembled in the poplar tree outside the parlor window.

At least playing tea party was a quiet activity that wouldn't require much exertion. They wouldn't get overheated. "Of course, sweetie. Why don't you get your tea set, and I'll grab some of those oatmeal cookies we made this morning."

Gracie gave a small squeal and pranced down the hall to her room. That was the most life Harriet had seen in her in days. Maybe even weeks. No child should be cooped up in a stifling apartment all summer. Though not all in this house or even in the larger world agreed with her, she was of the mind that fresh air was good for the body and the soul.

Once in the kitchen, she loaded a plate with the soft, cinnamon-and-raisin cookies she and Gracie had slaved over together earlier. Gracie met her in there with the delicate, pink-flowered china teapot that Harriet filled with water from the pump.

Just as they settled at the octagonal parlor table in the main room, a faint knock came from the door downstairs. Perhaps one of the church ladies had come with a loaf of bread or a pot of soup. Many had stopped by since Tommy's death with such condolence offerings.

Too bad Mrs. Robinson forbade Harriet from offering refresh-ment to any of the visitors. With a sigh, Harriet stood. "I'll be right back."

"Take a cookie for whoever's at the door." Gracie held one out.

"That is very kind of you." Harriet took the treat and made her way downstairs. At least she could offer the caller something other than expressions of thanksgiving.

A small gust of wind could have blown her over when she opened the door. "Michael." She worked to keep the note of sur-prise from her voice. "How nice to see you."

She glanced up and down the street to be sure Mrs. Robinson wasn't lurking around the corner. You never knew.

He gave a lusty laugh, one that tickled her chest. "Do you think she might be spying on you?"

"I wouldn't put it past her."

"Did you receive my note?"

"I did. I'm sorry I didn't reply. I haven't had much of a chance. Mrs. Robinson discovered it, and to say that she and Dr. Beers weren't happy about it is an understatement. Not to mention that around that time, I experienced some kind of fainting spell which left me with a bump on the head."

"That's too bad. Are you quite recovered? Would you like me to examine you?"

"No, I'm fine. Willie found me."

Michael studied her. Hard.

"I'd had a headache earlier and was overcome. I'm sure it's noth-ing more." At least, she had convinced herself of it. No one in the house would ever want to hurt her.

"If you're sure."

"I am."

"I never meant for the note to cause trouble. I. . . Well, I've missed you. You haven't been to the shop for a while."

"I've been from time to time. Not much, though. They prefer I stay inside with Gracie out of fear of contamination. I've been taking orders for my hats through the mail."

He wrinkled his forehead.

"They believe that somehow, whatever is making the family sick has been brought in from outside. Mrs. Robinson and the boys have to work, but otherwise, no one but Dr. Beers is to come and go."

"Funny that he would be allowed access to the house and no one else."

"That's what I think."

"So I gather by the fact that you haven't thrown me out on my ear that you've softened your stance on me."

"Being alone all day with no one other than Gracie for company has given me a good deal of time to think. While I still believe your assumptions are preposterous, I don't have any other explanation for the illnesses that have plagued this family. I will grant you that these deaths are not natural ones."

"I'm happy you've come to that conclusion."

"When I was growing up, taking care of my younger brothers and sisters, we often accompanied the pastor's wife as she made calls on families with sicknesses. An activity to keep the little ones from under Mama's feet. We played outside with the family's children, but from time to time, I would go in. I've watched people die before. I know what it should be like. And what it shouldn't be."

She stepped onto the porch, and he leaned against one of the fluted columns. "Am I to assume, then, that you won't be inviting me in?"

"I'm afraid not." Heat bloomed in her cheeks, and it had nothing to do with the weather. She glanced at her hand. Oh, she still held the cookie. She offered it to him. "Gracie thought whoever had come to call would like a treat. We were about to have a tea party."

He accepted the cookie with a polite nod. "My apologies for interrupting you."

"Not at all. Gracie would love to see you, I'm sure."

"How is she?"

"Perfectly fine. No symptoms at all. Then again, usually

several months go by between outbreaks of the illness. Right now, I'm holding my breath, waiting to see if another family member falls ill."

"I'm glad to hear she's well."

"I can't tell you how wonderful the breeze and even the sun feel on my face. We've spent far too much time inside."

"That's no way for anyone to spend a summer, especially a child. Would it be out of line for you to have your tea party on the porch? We can tell Gracie it's a secret game. Whoever tells about our fun, loses."

She stepped to the porch rail and leaned over, allowing her arms, bare where she had rolled up her sleeves, to drink in the sun. "I don't see how there could be anything wrong with that plan." With footsteps lighter than they had been in weeks, Harriet skipped upstairs, got Gracie and the tea party paraphernalia, and was back on the porch in a flash. The old man in the downstairs apartment was likely snoozing away the afternoon.

Once she had Gracie settled with her dolls and pouring tea for them, Harriet leaned against the column beside Michael. "I'm so glad you came."

He shifted his weight from foot to foot. "Like I said, I've missed you."

A slight flutter flitted through Harriet's body. No one had ever expressed that sentiment to her before. "I've missed you too."

"You don't look happy. I see a sadness and a worry in you that wasn't there before."

She swallowed hard. "I've lost maybe three-quarters of my clients. My business is dying. For the past year or so, I've put everything I have into it. Before Lizzie died, I was making a name for myself. Things were going well. I believed I was going to be successful. And now..."

Michael rubbed her hand.

She blew out a breath. "Now I'm on the verge of losing it all. But I can't give up on Gracie. I'm in an impossible situation. Because of what you told me, I'm scared to leave her alone. She needs me more than ever. Who knows what will happen if I'm not here to watch her?" Though she wiped her eyes, she couldn't stop the tears.

Michael touched her cheek, the gesture more intimate than an embrace. "You don't have to do this. Gracie isn't your child, your sister, or any kind of relation."

How could he even think such a thing? "I love her. It would be wrong to walk away from her and leave her in harm's way."

"You are a woman of incredible character. Are you willing to do this even if it costs you the millinery?"

Could she give up that dream? What if she had to?

Gracie pranced up to them, a cup in her hand, a wide smile on her face. "Would you care for some tea, sir?"

Michael bowed, his face serious, though his lips twitched. "Thank you very much, kind lady." He grasped the cup and made a big deal of sipping from it.

Gazing at him, Gracie beamed.

Harriet had her answer. Even if she had to lose her shop, Gracie's life was worth saving, the same as every other life.

Once Michael had emptied his cup and handed it to Gracie, she returned to the far end of the porch to play with her dolls.

He turned his attention to Harriet. "I have to tell you about a case I was called on earlier this week."

She nodded for him to continue.

"A little boy died."

"That's awful." Too many people lost children. She prayed that someday there would be better medicine to help more little ones survive.

"He died of rat poisoning."

"Oh, that's terrible."

"His symptoms were the same as Miss Robinson's and Tommy's. To the letter. So they either died of rat poisoning or arsenic poisoning. That's what's found in the rat killer."

"How tragic. But I never saw Tommy anywhere near the rat

poison, and of course, Lizzie knew better than to touch the stuff."

She could have recited the next words from Michael's lips. "I don't think they ingested it on their own. They had help."

Though her mind railed against the thought and her heart told her it couldn't be, she could no longer deny what smacked her in the face. Identical symptoms, Michael said. Identical to consuming rat poison. "But who would do such a thing?"

"Who do you think?" His voice cracked on the last word.

Harriet rubbed her eyes. "I don't know. I just don't know."

"Don't know or don't want to admit it?" He leaned closer to her, so close she picked out the gold flecks in his hazel eyes.

Her breath hitched. "Maybe a little of both."

Now he grabbed her by both forearms. In the distance, lightning flashed and a low rumble of thunder shook the porch under her feet. "What have you noticed that has been unusual? Anything out of the ordinary. Any small detail might help. Might be enough for the police to break open their investigation. I don't want to put you in danger, but you're on the inside. You see and hear all that goes on."

"Maybe not all. They are away from the house for the better part of the day."

"You see and hear more than anyone else."

There was that strange event when she either fainted or was knocked over the head. To this day, she couldn't determine what had happened. Though she had told him a little about the episode before, she now shared the details with Michael. "Do you think that might have something to do with the case?"

"It would have been easier for me to determine immediately after it happened. Charley or Willie should have come for me."

"Willie was home at the time."

"He could have hit you."

"But why?" As soon as the words slipped by her lips, though, she knew. Though never the warmest person, he had been cooler since she rebuffed him. Wasn't he the one standing over her when she came to? Hadn't he been hovering in the doorway each time a family member fell ill? Then again, he was so gentle and kind to Gracie. Had been with Tommy too.

"What are you thinking?" Michael's voice, though low, was firm and sure. Probing.

"He had opportunity. He was around when the others got sick. But he was so nice to Tommy, and he does care about Gracie."

"Have you ever heard the expression about a wolf in sheep's clothing?"

"He doesn't strike me as the sort to do such a thing. Just because he's quiet and reserved doesn't mean he's a killer. He might have been near Lizzie and Tommy when they were ill because he was concerned about them."

Michael blew out a breath. "Okay. Let's put him aside for the time being. What about Charley?"

"Never. Never, never, never. He was with his uncle the day he got sick. They walked to work together. They even ate the same breakfast, or so Lizzie told me."

"That sounds suspicious. They ate the same food, but only Mr. Freeman fell ill."

No, it couldn't possibly be Charley. He was so sweet and compassionate. Always good to her and all his family members. The hardest working of the bunch. "No. I refuse to believe it."

"Refusing to believe it doesn't mean it's not true."

"He would be the very last one I would suspect." The darkening sky lit up like Independence Day and the thunder boomed ever closer. Gracie scurried to Harriet and hid in her skirts, whimpering. "Hush now. Everything will be fine. I'm here. Nothing's going to hurt you."

But she'd made the same promise to Tommy, and she hadn't protected him. "I guess that leaves Mrs. Robinson and Dr. Beers."

"Anything about them?"

"They're the ones not wanting me to leave the house. They have both been present from the very first strange death, that of Mr.

Robinson. Mrs. Robinson has been so faithful in tending to her sick family members, though. So dedicated and caring. She hates to go to work when any of them are ill. What would a good, church-going woman have to gain from this?"

The thought struck her as sure as a stroke of lightning. The insurance money! Mrs. Robinson had much to gain. Harriet couldn't stifle the little gasp that escaped her.

"What is it?" Michael searched her face with an intensity that set her back a step.

She pulled from his firm grasp and hugged Gracie all the tighter. Fat raindrops pelted the porch's roof. The trees blew almost sideways in the sudden gust of wind. In the breeze, her skirts wrapped around her legs.

"You know, don't you?" Michael had to almost shout to be heard above the constant roll of thunder.

She shook her head as hard as she could. Such thoughts were ungrateful. Unkind. And had to be untrue. Another flash of lightning blinded Harriet. An immediate boom rocked the house. Gracie screamed.

"Tell me. You have to tell me. Now. Before anyone else gets hurt," Michael shouted at her.

Harriet shook her head again and gazed at Gracie. She couldn't say the words in front of the child. She was an innocent and didn't need to hear the thoughts racing through Harriet's brain.

Harriet opened the door and ushered Gracie inside. "Go upstairs and find a book to read. I don't want you to get wet and catch your death."

"Will you come with me?" Her eyes were round in her thin face.

"In a minute. Before you know it, I'll be there. Don't worry. The worst of the storm is almost over. Soon it will move on. There's nothing to worry about."

Gracie gave a single nod and plodded up a couple of stairs. Another bright flash. Another resounding boom. Gracie dashed back to the security of Harriet's arms. She needed Harriet.

"I can't talk now." She covered Gracie's ears and whispered, "Can we meet? Tomorrow night at the church on Highland Avenue?"

"When?"

"Midnight."

As Michael nodded and left, her heart thumped in rhythm to the tree branch grating against the window.

Because she did know something.

Chapter Eighteen

The clink of silverware against china plates provided the backdrop to the conversation swirling around Michael as he sat at a table with his colleagues for their bi-monthly meeting. The hotel dining room was full today and buzzing. As was Michael's head.

"Dr. Wheaton. Dr. Wheaton. Hello."

Michael startled. "I'm sorry." He turned his attention to the rail-thin young doctor, Herb Fraser, to his right. "Did you say something?"

Herb clucked his tongue and shook his blond head. "A lot of something. What's been going on with you? Still that case, the poisoning one?"

Two weeks ago Michael had been foolish enough to seek advice from Herb about the Robinsons' mysterious illnesses. "I'm more convinced than ever that someone in that house is feeding arsenic to the victims."

Herb raised one eyebrow. "Arsenic now? And victims?"

Michael worked to control his breathing, to not allow Herb's mocking words to stab him. "Last week, I watched a little boy, just a year old, die from ingesting rat poison. Same symptoms as the two people I treated at the other home. Horrible stomach pain, vomiting, agonizing death while I could do little to nothing."

Herb leaned over to the man beside him. "Michael is a police investigator now. Seeing things that aren't there. Dr. Beers told me about the family and Dr. Wheaton's hypothesis. Dr. Beers, however, believes the illnesses stem from poisons being brought into the home from the workplaces of some of the residents."

Michael dropped his fork to his plate. "Is that what he said?" He couldn't believe it. Dr. Beers continued to stick to that story. He was so convinced it was outside contaminates and refused to believe—or perhaps admit—that it could be anything else. "If the poison was from an outside source, everyone in the house and in the city would be sick. You don't hear of any other families in any of those factories having so many members dying such deaths. Come on. Open your eyes. There's no doubt in my mind." He raised his voice with each word. "Someone in that house is killing their family members."

All conversation ceased, and a tense silence settled over the room. He didn't have to peer around to know that everyone stared at him.

For a moment, he wasn't a qualified doctor treating patients all over the Boston area. He was an eight-year-old boy in the school play yard, the bigger boys taunting him for his crazy mother. The one in the insane asylum no one talked about but everyone knew about. All these years later, the taunts haunted him. *Cuckoo. Cuckoo.*

The words hadn't been creative, but they'd found their mark. No matter how hard he worked in school, no matter how polite he was, no matter how much he did to help others, he never could overcome those early humiliating days. Grandpop, the man who had raised him, said to ignore them. But how could he when those jests followed him everywhere? Not even becoming a doctor, proving everyone wrong, proving he wasn't insane like his mother, not even that was enough.

Now this. Could he ever live it down? What if he was wrong and the poison was coming into the house through clothing or shoes? But it didn't make sense. If that were the case, everyone would be sick at the same time. This was one-by-one, spaced out over the course of years.

He pushed his chair back and came to his feet. "If you'll excuse me, gentlemen, I have an appointment I must get to." An appointment with himself, but no one need know that.

The four men with him gave curt nods, and resumed their conversation as if he had never been there.

As he made his way to the horse car stop to catch a ride home, he worked to forget about the incident in the dining room. He shouldn't have raised his voice the way he had. He shouldn't have given those other doctors the satisfaction of flustering him. Those days were behind him.

Then again, if he was wrong and there was no evil activity at the Robinson home, he had gone and ruined his reputation and the family's for nothing. But there was something wrong. Deep down in his bones, he couldn't shake the feeling there was.

What brought a smile to his face was the reminder that he would see Harriet tonight. He prayed he hadn't put her in jeopardy by asking her to dig around and see what she could find out. If anything happened to her, he would never forgive himself.

What did she know? What insight could she shed on the case? Perhaps she did hold the key to rescuing everyone else in the house.

Including herself.

He came to the stop at the bustling corner, women dragging their children by the hands, couples strolling together, an old woman tottering on a cane. While he waited, he paced, unable to stand still for even a moment.

Midnight couldn't come fast enough. He prayed he wouldn't get called out tonight. He had to keep that meeting with her. Perhaps what she would tell him, along with what he suspected, would be enough for the investigators to swoop in and make an arrest.

The horse car clanged to a stop, and Michael climbed aboard. His mouth fell open when he found Willie and Charley seated near the back. His tongue dried out. Yet here was his opportunity to talk to them, to perhaps glean more information from them. Maybe to include or rule out one of them as a suspect.

They were in public, the car almost full on this Saturday afternoon. The crowd included men in dirty work pants and stained hats; a woman in a purple and white striped day dress, a mound of packages at her feet; and a priest dressed in black save for the white square of his collar. When another woman in a pale blue gown stepped aboard, he motioned for her to have the seat he was about to take.

Why did his heart pound like a hammer against a nail? He glued on a smile and staggered toward the back.

"Have room on this bench for an old friend?"

Charley's face lit up with a smile. Willie's expression didn't change. No smile, but no frown. He was the one who answered. "Sure. Move over." He elbowed his brother.

"Thank you. I appreciate it."

Michael sat down beside Charley, and Willie leaned over his brother to speak to Michael. "It's been a while since we've seen each other."

"That it has. I trust your family is well."

Charley nodded. "What a relief when each day passes and no one else falls ill. Though we walk about holding our breath. We went months between Lizzie and Tommy's illnesses. You never know."

"I'm praying you'll all stay healthy."

"Funny thing for a doctor to pray for." Willie cleared his throat.

"Yes, maybe it is, but I know that my services will always be needed. There will always be babies being born and old people dying."

He nodded. "I suppose you're right."

"Gracie says she misses you," Charley went on. "Mentioned last night at dinner something about you being at the house yesterday."

Michael swallowed hard. He glanced at Willie. Again, the man's face remained unreadable, though he clenched his fists in his lap. How much could he trust him? Did he dare?

"Don't worry about him." Charley gave his brother a pat on the shoulder. "He can keep a secret better than anyone I know. He won't say anything to Mama, who was out of the room when Gracie said something about you. Mama's the one you have to watch out for."

"Oh." That was an interesting statement. "Why is that?"

"You know what a battle-ax she can be." Charley kept his voice light and low. "She's protective of her children. Can you blame her? She's lost five already and most of the rest of her family. Whatever it takes, she's going to protect who's left. And I'd hate to see anything happen to anyone, especially Gracie. She's the youngest and most innocent of us all."

"We'd all hate for anything to happen to anyone." Willie's voice was flat.

Michael rubbed the goose bumps from his forearms. "Of course."

"So, were you at the house yesterday?" Charley slid forward on the seat.

"Yes. Harriet and Gracie were playing on the porch."

"They were outside?" Charley's blue eyes widened. "Good for her not listening to Dr. Beers."

"Your mother can't keep them holed up in that boiling hot apartment all summer. With this heat, it must be stifling. Not to mention that school will start again in a few weeks. What will happen to Gracie then?"

Willie shrugged. "Mama will figure out something. She always does."

"She has ingenuity and strength, that's for sure. My mother wouldn't have been able to endure the amount of loss your mother has." In fact, she hadn't. When Pop died, Mom curled into a little ball and never paid Michael much mind from then on. Pop had been her world. Soon afterward, she'd entered the institution.

He had never measured up to Pop in her eyes. Even when he'd told her he was going to be a doctor. She had patted him on the head during that visit too, but never said a word. Never even smiled.

"She's had her share of struggles, that's for sure. Imagine leaving home when you're but fourteen and traveling across the ocean alone with your younger sister, leaving behind everything you know. They scraped for every penny they could get, just to keep from starving. Mama is a survivor, that's for sure." Charley beamed.

A survivor, yes. Something more? Still to be determined.

"We don't like Dr. Beers." At Willie's unsolicited words,

Michael sat up straight.

"Why not?"

"Don't be so critical, Willie. Just because he's not Papa doesn't mean we shouldn't like him."

"That's not it. I don't care for him. He's the puppeteer, and Mama's the puppet."

Another strange thing to say. Between this and the doctors at the hotel, Michael had a raging headache. This conversation got him no closer to any answers. The family stood up for each other, that's for sure.

The horse car slowed to a stop. Charley and Willie rose. "This is where we get off."

Michael came to his feet so they could pass. He gave each of the brothers a hearty handshake. "It was good to see you again. Give your mother my regards." He almost added Harriet to that statement but clamped his lips shut in the nick of time.

He rode the rest of the way home by himself on the bench, staring out the side as Somerville went by in a blur.

No. No matter what those other doctors thought, no matter how devoted Charley and Willie were to their family, someone was poisoning those people. No one would be able to convince him otherwise. All he needed was proof. Not a gut feeling about Willie or Mrs. Robinson or Dr. Beers, but solid details that pointed the finger straight at them.

Perhaps tonight, Harriet would bring him useful information. Anything that would get them closer to who was committing these crimes before they acted again.

With his thoughts consuming him, he almost missed his stop. He hopped off just as the driver clucked to the horses to get them moving along. Though the car had been close because of the number of passengers, it was no match for the hot late-afternoon sun which blazed on his black bowler hat. He removed it and wiped the sweat from his brow.

When he arrived home, he left the sign in the window declaring the doctor was unavailable. He retreated to his office, filled his ink-well, and gathered a sheaf of papers. He set to work, documenting every detail he knew about the case, the similarities to little Samuel's death, and the suspicions he had about each member of the household. Much as he hated to do it, he even included Harriet on the list.

The next time he glanced up, darkness had invaded the small room. He lit the lamp. Before he returned to his seat, a knock came at the door. Oh, no. Not a patient. He couldn't miss this meeting with Harriet. He had to hear what she had to say.

Then again, he couldn't turn away someone in need. He went to the door and didn't find a patient but Chief Parkhurst. "Come in, come in. You're about the only person I care to see right now."

The chief removed his tall blue hat with the black brim and stroked his bushy beard. "We've been working the case but haven't come up with much. I was wondering if you have any new details you could share with me."

Michael led him into his office. "Have a seat." He shoved the sheaf of paper containing his scribbles into the chief's hands. "Here's everything I know." He filled Parkhurst in on Samuel's death. "I'm meeting Harriet tonight, in just a few hours. She knows something, and she's going to share it with me."

The chief sat back, almost tipping over the chair. He gazed at the ceiling and stroked his beard once more. "Are you sure you want to do this?"

Michael nodded. "Of course."

"I would proceed with caution, if I were you. There is new information we've just discovered."

Chapter Nineteen

Harriet slid from beneath the sheets, careful to move slowly enough not to rock the bed and wake Gracie. As she stood beside the mattress, she held her breath. Good. The little girl slept. She crept across the room, then turned the door handle little by little.

Outside the window, an owl hooted. Harriet's heart might just beat so hard it would pound through her ribs and out of her chest. She stood still a moment to allow her breathing to return to normal.

She tiptoed down the hall. Just as she reached the parlor, a floorboard creaked. Another long moment passed as she stood statue still. No one moved about. She exhaled. Just as she was to the stairwell, someone reached out and grabbed her.

Stifling a scream, she whirled around. Willie stood there, dressed in nothing more than a pair of pants. Harriet stared beyond him so she didn't see his bare chest. He held a lamp, the dim, flickering light casting eerie shadows over his face, accentuating his long, beaked nose, much like his mother's. On the wall behind him, a long-legged, long-armed shadow writhed in a macabre dance.

Harriet's chest heaved as if she'd run a mile.

"Where are you going?"

"What are you doing in the hall? And why did you grab me?"

"I'm on my way to the privy. I thought you might be an intruder."

"An intruder? Me?" Harriet's voice squeaked.

"You haven't answered my question."

"You frightened me half to death."

"What are you doing up and dressed?"

"I, uh, I haven't been to bed yet. I've been working on a hat."

That was the truth.

"Then why not bring your lamp with you?"

Why did he keep throwing these questions at her? "Um. . ."

"How could you see to work on your hat?"

"I left the lamp in the room." Again, the truth.

"You're nothing more than a foolish woman. How you manage to care for Gracie, I have no idea. I can't imagine why Lizzie charged you with looking after the children. Here, take the lamp, and please hurry in the necessary. The air is heavy. A storm may be rolling in."

"I have no need of it. You go ahead. I, uh, am fine.

"Oh."

At least this way, she could sneak out while Willie was in the privy.

"Suit yourself." Willie shrugged and started toward the stairs, the shadow on the wall fading until the light cast over a bronze figurine. The one that had created the shadow on the wall.

Once he had exited the house, she counted to twenty, then dashed down the stairs, keeping her steps as light as possible. As if the specter chased her, she was out the door and down the street in no time.

She didn't stop until she rounded the corner. Then she leaned forward to catch her breath. From several blocks away, the church bell chimed midnight. She didn't have time to rest. If she didn't get there soon, Michael might not wait for her.

The clocked chimed again. It was time for her to tell what she knew.

As she made her way through the quiet streets of Somerville, lightning flashing in the distance, she kept to the shadows, away from the puddles of light pooling under the gas lamps. What she suspected was going on in the Robinson household was best kept to the dark corners.

Light couldn't tolerate the evil in the home.

She scurried down the streets, much like the rats which infested the night. Though the humid air sent shivery beads of sweat racing down the sides of her face, she pulled her shawl tighter around herself, covering her head. At last, much later than she had anticipated, she arrived at the old stone church. A stroke of lightning illuminated the tall center tower looming above the rest of the building.

She raced up the stone steps and pulled open the massive arched doors that came to a point at the top. Either Michael had found a way to open them or the pastor kept them unlocked day and night. Whatever the case, she slipped into the dim interior, candlelight flickering in the front of the church, illuminating the colored figures painted on the wall behind the altar.

There, a few pews in front of her, sat Michael, his head bowed. Though she could only see the back of him, there was no mistaking his dark wavy hair.

Keeping her shawl over her head, she slipped into the pew beside him. He squeezed her hand, his warm and sure, while hers trembled. "Willie almost caught me leaving the house."

"He must have spooked you." Michael slid closer to her, heat radiating from his body.

"Yes, a good deal."

"How did you get out?"

"When he went to the privy, I slipped away." She couldn't keep her legs from quivering. Was this the right thing to do? How could she betray the very people she'd come to love? They hadn't thrown her out. She had lost her first family. The Robinsons were all she had left.

Then Gracie's laughter filled her head. For her. For Tommy. For Lizzie. All the innocent ones. That's who she was doing this for. If someone else died because of her inaction, their blood would be on her hands.

"Tell me." Though gentle like water over smooth stones, his voice held a hint of insistence.

She drew in a deep breath and steeled herself. All she had to do was to force the words through her lips. Just start talking and it would be over. "I may know why someone is poisoning the Robinsons."

He squeezed her hand a little harder.

His silence gave her a chance to gather steam. And courage. "Everyone in the household carries a life insurance policy. When Mr. Freeman passed, little Tommy received that inheritance. That's why Tommy needed to die." She choked on the words.

She closed her eyes and allowed the peace of the place to wash over her. Before she began again, she pursed her lips. "Lizzie also had a life insurance policy. I heard Mrs. Robinson and Dr. Beers speaking with the agent from the Order of Pilgrim Fathers, an organization I believe Mr. Smith also belongs to."

"What about you?"

She wiped her sweaty palm on her navy-blue skirt. "Several months ago, Mrs. Robinson insisted that I also purchase a policy. She argued that if anything happened to me, they would need the money to pay my medical bills and bury me."

She bit her lip.

"What's wrong?"

"Signing those papers for the insurance policy was so unnerving. Just thinking about my death and what comes afterward turns me icy cold."

"I think if affects us all to a degree. You love the Lord, so you know you'll go to heaven."

"That's just it. Do I love Him enough for Him to accept me into His eternal home? Have I been good enough?"

"You aren't asking the right question."

She turned to stare at him. "What question should I ask?"

"Did He love you enough to send His Son for you?"

"What?" She tipped her head.

"He did, didn't He?"

"Yes."

"Then that's all you need to know. No more fear. Because, though I pray the Lord gives you many more years here, when it is your time to leave this earth, you can have assurance of where you will spend eternity. It's not what you did. It's what He did."

So easy to say. So much harder to grasp and believe. A long moment stretched between them.

He shifted his weight in the seat. "So you got a life insurance policy."

"I owe them a great deal. It was a sensible thing to do." Was she trying to convince him or herself?

"Oh Harriet, how I fear for you." His words quivered, and his body shook.

Like puzzle pieces falling into place, the entire scheme came together in Michael's mind. Someone in that house was cashing in on the life insurance policies. Profiting from their family members' deaths.

He clenched his free hand.

Despicable. How could a person's heart be so twisted and contorted that they justified and rationalized the deaths of those they supposedly loved? How could they sit across the dinner table from their next victim and look at them, knowing what was coming?

And Harriet. A tremor ran through him from head to toe. Because she too carried a policy, she was a potential victim. One of the residents of that house didn't see a beautiful, charming, caring young woman but a bag full of money. He hardly dared to voice the question. "Who?"

"I don't know."

"You must have some idea."

"It's too horrible to contemplate. I'm sorry I ever doubted you. You've been right all along." Her words were thick with tears.

"Hush, hush." He pulled his handkerchief from his pocket and handed it to her. "I know this is frightening."

"Who is going to be next?" She dabbed her eyes.

How Michael prayed in that moment there would be no more victims. "Maybe the reign of terror is over."

She wiped her nose. "I fear it's not."

A crack of thunder sounded, muffled by the church's thick stone walls. He shuddered, sharing the same fear. Whoever was feeding the poison to their family members had done it numerous times already. Had gotten away with murder for some time. Now, they were emboldened. Hardened. By this time, they had lost any conscience and any heart they may have had. "Who has the most to gain? When Lizzie and Tommy died, who received the money?"

"I'm not sure. Willie, Mrs. Robinson, and Dr. Beers were all in the room with the agent." Her words flowed now. No more hesitating. "They all spoke to Mr. Bugbee and urged him to complete the payout quickly. Mrs. Robinson and Willie said they were low on funds."

"Okay. That's good information." Charley was appearing less and less like a suspect. You could never tell, but he was a nice chap. "That gives the police a name to check with on the insurance policies. What do you know about the other deaths? Like Mr. Freeman's?"

"Not much. I was busy working at the department store at the time as an apprentice, many long hours. When I was home, it was only to sleep, so I didn't see much at that time. Afterward, Lizzie said it was horrible to watch him die, and so much like the manner in which her father and her aunt passed away."

"So she was Mr. Freeman's caregiver?"

"One of them. Mrs. Robinson was very devoted to him. Lizzie told me that, even though her mother worked all day, she spent her nights with him. But it can't be her. She wouldn't commit such a despicable act. She wouldn't take Tommy's father away from him." Though her words were strong, her voice warbled.

"I know. I know. But we have to look at all the possibilities. Everyone in the house is under suspicion, with the exception of Gracie. She's too young."

"Even me?" Now there was no denying the trembling of her voice.

Her fright cut Michael to the heart. He had to reassure her. "I believe you to be innocent. There is no way you could have perpetrated these crimes. You haven't been associated with the family that long. Have you?" The moment the question slipped from his mouth, he bit his tongue. If only he could drag them back again. He shouldn't make her believe he questioned her innocence.

"You say you think I'm not guilty, but in the same breath, you question me. So you aren't sure, are you?" She pulled from his grasp and slid away from him, huddling on the edge of the pew. An emptiness washed over him.

"Yes, I am. I'm sorry."

"I've been part of the family for a number of years. I remember Mr. Robinson dying about three years ago. Then Lizzie's younger sister Emma, then the others." She hugged herself, shivering despite the humidity that clung to them. "So yes, I've been with them long enough to be involved in all of the crimes."

"They all died the same way?"

She nodded, the small movement barely visible in the weak light. "All suffered terribly."

"How awful for you to watch."

"Not for me. For them."

His heart beat a wild rhythm. More in the family had been killed than he had realized at first. His fuzzy mind couldn't figure the number, but it was several. "Could it be that the three of them are working together?"

"I don't know."

He turned to face her and pulled her shawl from her head, her midnight-black hair spilling over her shoulders. The way the uneven candlelight played across her delicate features sent his heartbeat skidding across his chest. She was breathtaking.

He couldn't lose her. "You have to get out of that house."

She slid backward even more, halfway off the end of the pew. "What did you say?"

Why would those words cause such a reaction? "You have to get out of the house."

"Please, don't think I'm crazy. Don't send me to the insane asylum."

"I would never think you're crazy. You're the most rational person in that house." Though that wasn't saying much.

"Inside my head, I keep hearing these voices. I know they're not real. It's not even voices. Or maybe it is."

He reached over and touched her knee. She stiffened.

"What do you hear?"

"Someone telling me to get out of the house."

"Then you need to listen."

"Do you think it's God?"

"I don't believe God speaks to us that way anymore. I think it's your own instinct telling you something is not right there. That instinct is given to you by God. You must pay attention to it. You must act."

"I can't leave. Gracie would be lost without me. Who would watch her while the others are at work? She's too young to be left alone. Mrs. Robinson is so afraid of contamination, she'll never allow me to come and go. I even broached the subject with her, but she begged me to stay. Pleaded with me until I had no choice but to relent."

"You're a grown woman in a free country. You can come and go as you please."

"I don't want to upset her or Dr. Beers."

"Why?" The word hung in the quiet, reverent air.

"Because. . ."

"Why?"

"I just don't." As another round of thunder rumbled, Harriet jumped to her feet. "I have to go."

He grabbed her by the wrist. "Wait. Please, listen to me. Listen to yourself. You have to get out. Before it's too late for you."

She wrenched from his grasp and raced down the aisle and out the door.

Dear God, protect her.

Chapter Twenty

Michael sat in the stiff wooden chair in the overcrowded room, the stale odor of too many unwashed bodies gagging him. Combine that with half-eaten pastrami sandwiches sitting on desks in heat that would melt flesh, and it was enough to make a man lose his lunch.

Or his nerve.

He shifted on the chair as he waited for Chief Parkhurst. Between the information the police had uncovered and the information Harriet had given Michael last night, perhaps progress could finally be made on the case. Perhaps an arrest would be forthcoming. Perhaps this entire nightmare would end without the loss of more life.

Of course, he had come here before with the same hopes, only to have them dashed.

The chief strode through the room, his height and muscular frame commanding attention and respect. The noisy precinct fell a notch quieter.

Michael stood as he approached. "Thank you for meeting with me."

Chief Parkhurst shook Michael's hand and motioned for him to be seated. "You said you had some information that might be of interest to us." The man didn't beat around the bush.

Michael would respect that and not waste his time. "Last night I met with Miss Peters."

The chief took out a pad of paper and scribbled a few notes. "She's the woman living with the Robinsons, helping to care for the youngest girl, correct?"

"That's right. Mrs. Robinson and Dr. Beers have forbidden her from leaving the premises."

"That right there constitutes kidnapping."

"She wouldn't see it that way. Despite the increasing danger I believe her to be in, she wants to be there. Or rather, she's been persuaded to stay. She's fulfilling a promise to the late Miss Robinson, her friend, to take care of the younger children. Now that only consists of Gracie. Though I tried last night to convince her to leave that place, she refuses."

"Out of fear?"

Michael nodded. "That might be at least part of the reason. She did start to say something about being afraid, but then she up and ran from the church without finishing."

The chief stroked his beard and waved for Michael to go on. "She told me that all of the victims, as far as she knew, had life insurance policies through the Order of Pilgrim Fathers. When someone in the household dies, there is a payout of money to help with funeral expenses and to help the family replace the lost income."

"I've heard a little bit about such things. They're a newer product, so I don't know much. But it's interesting. Could it be that someone is killing the others in order to get the money?"

"That's what I believe. Miss Peters seems to agree with me." Michael leaned in and lowered his voice. "Everyone in the house has a policy. Including Miss Peters."

In an even rhythm, the chief tapped his pen against the only clear space on his desk. "Which makes her as much a target as anyone else."

"Exactly."

"How recently did she get the policy?"

"I don't know the exact date. It was some time after Miss Robinson's death."

"Did she say who encouraged her to purchase one?"

"Mrs. Robinson and Dr. Beers were both present. She didn't indicate which one of them was the person pushing for her to purchase the policy. It could be that both of them are in cahoots.

They're my most likely suspects."

"Thank you for your detective work, doctor, but I'll keep track of the suspects. There is another young man living in the house, isn't there? Charles, I believe."

Michael leaned back and crossed his arms over his chest, working not to take offense at Parkhurst's words. He was right. He was the detective, not Michael. "Yes, there is Charley. But I don't believe he's responsible for any of the deaths."

"Why is that?"

"He's too kind. A genuinely nice young man."

"He needs to remain on the list. I refuse to rule out anyone in the house. Including Miss Peters. They might have their own policies as a smokescreen to throw off the authorities. You can't truly know any man's or woman's heart, Dr. Wheaton."

"We'll have to disagree on that point, Chief Parkhurst. Neither Charley nor Harriet would be capable of this kind of heinous act."

"Who had the most to gain?"

"Anyone in the house. After Mr. Freeman's death, they moved to a larger apartment and bought new furniture. That benefits all of them."

"Miss Peters wasn't living with them at the time?"

"No, which is another argument against her being party to these crimes."

"I see your point, and I'll note it." Chief Parkhurst leaned forward over his desk, now tapping the pen against his chin. "Between the work we are doing and what you have just given us, we really have something to go on now."

"But you won't share the new information you have with me."

"Unfortunately not. While you've been a great help to us, there are things I cannot tell you. Please understand that we have to maintain the integrity of the case."

Michael's stomach tickled. "Are you going to make an arrest?"

Chief Parkhurst shook his head.

Michael came to his feet and gripped the edge of the desk, his words as tight as his grasp. "Why not? Do you want to see someone else die?"

"Of course not." The inspector's voice was gruff. He cleared his throat. "You have to know, Dr. Wheaton, how the wheels of justice turn. I have no hard evidence. I have four or five possible suspects, not just one. Has anyone seen any of them administer this poison?"

It was Michael's turn to shake his head.

"Then, though I will continue to investigate the case, I cannot make an arrest at this time. The best you can do for me is to keep your eyes and ears open. Encourage Miss Peters to do the same and report any unusual activity to you or to me. Would she be willing to come to the precinct for questioning?"

"That might be quite tricky."

"Perhaps I could meet with her another way. You managed to see her."

"We met at a church at midnight."

A small smile crept from Chief Parkhurst's mouth to his eyes. "Ah, a clandestine meeting. Perhaps I could go there when none of the others are home."

"Gracie will be there. She's little and may not be able to keep the meeting secret. I know, because I tried that too. The rest of the household found out, only causing Miss Peters more grief and, I believe, putting her in increased danger."

"Perhaps another midnight rendezvous, then. It would be most helpful to me if I could speak to her. She's a first-hand witness. She knows what goes on inside that home. Who has the most to gain? Who has the most to lose?"

"I agree." Though it would soothe his nerves if Chief Parkhurst would take someone into custody so Harriet wouldn't be in danger any longer. "I'll do what I can to arrange a time for you to question her. But I want her out of the house."

"I can understand. You have some interest in the lady, do you not?"

Interest? It had gone beyond interest for Michael. If anything happened to Harriet, he would never forgive himself. His world would never be the same. Though he didn't get to hear it often, her laughter was music he could listen to every day. Her smile was a light he could live in every day. Her touch was a river he could bathe in every day.

This weakness in his arms and legs, is this what love was like? Could those be the feelings he harbored for Harriet?

Most definitely.

"So, Dr. Wheaton." Chief Parkhurst rose, and Michael also came to his feet. "This is where we are. We are getting closer to solving this case, but we aren't there yet. I need more evidence. Some kind of proof that these victims were poisoned. We'll work it on this side. You and Miss Peters work on it from the other. Warn her to be careful, though. A murderer lurks in that home."

Harriet's neck ached from hours of staring at the hat she was attempting to create. The flowers refused to stay tacked on, the ribbon wouldn't lay the way she had designed it to, and the feathers drooped. Much like she did.

At her feet, Gracie lay sleeping on the blue and red Oriental rug. In this kind of weather, no one wanted to do much of anything. Then again, she shouldn't complain about being penned up in the apartment. Charley and Mrs. Robinson had to go out, riding the crowded horse car to their jobs, and poor Willie had the unenviable job of driving horses all day under the blazing sun.

In the end, she didn't have it so bad. At least, that's what she kept telling herself. Ah, she'd poked herself with the large tapestry needle. A drop of blood pooled at the tip of her left pointer finger. She sucked on it to stem the tide and avoid soiling any of the hat materials. Mrs. Clarke needed this bonnet tomorrow. Harriet had to finish the purple creation with great feathers sticking out of it. Not her style, but what the client asked for. With her hours at the shop cut back, she needed all the work she could get.

It's all for Gracie. It's all for Gracie. She repeated the mantra.

The downstairs door slammed and footsteps jogged up the stairs until Charley burst into the parlor. In his hands, he bore a basket overflowing with ribbons and flowers and fabrics.

"Oh good, you brought me more to work with. Thank you so much. Mrs. Clarke's chapeau is taking more material than I had anticipated. Of course, she keeps adding to it and adding to it. I'm afraid she'll never be satisfied with the outcome."

"Are the others home yet?" He glanced about the room.

"Not yet."

"Where is Gracie?"

She nodded to the child on the floor. "She fell asleep while we were singing songs. Perhaps we should have picked something more rousing." Even with their conversation, Gracie didn't stir.

"Good." He set the basket on the floor beside Harriet. "You might want to double-check to make sure I got everything on your list."

She frowned. "You always do a great job of getting me what I need."

"Just do it."

"Now?"

He nodded.

Could it be that Michael had sent her another note? Her stomach shouldn't flutter the way it did at the thought, but she was helpless to stop it. Every time she was with him, he left her trembling and quivering. The other night, it wasn't just fear that did it to her. Sure, there was that, but she lived with that emotion every moment of every day she spent in this house.

No, there was another cause. A feeling she couldn't quite yet define.

She took a deep breath and searched through the finery loaded in the basket. Down deep, her fingers brushed a piece of paper. Though she tried to hold it back, a smile broke out on her face.

Another note from Michael.

"Thank you, Charley. I appreciate you bringing me what I really needed."

He winked. "I thought you might be happy about that. Of course, I wish it could have been Willie. You'd be my sister, then. But I'm glad it's Michael. He's a good sort."

"Thank you, Charley. That means a great deal to me."

He half grimaced, half smiled. "Go into the kitchen and read it. If anyone else gets home, I'll head them off."

She kissed him on the cheek. "I miss my little brothers, but you're just as good as them. Maybe better, because you never pulled my braids or put spiders in my bed."

His expression widened into a true, full smile. "I would never do anything like that to you, Harriet."

"And that's what makes you such a dear." He was so different from his brother. The complete opposite, really.

Gracie stirred. The others would soon be home. "Thank you again. I'm off to read my letter." She infused her voice with enthusiasm. Quite easy to do when she recognized Michael's writing on the envelope.

She refrained from skipping to the kitchen, no simple task. As soon as the door shut behind her, she tore open the envelope. Like someone stranded in the desert with no water, she drank in the words.

My dearest Harriet,

How I have missed you these days we have not been able to see each other. I cherish each moment we spend together, no matter how long or short the time we have. Just a glimpse of your beautiful face, your radiant smile, your kind heart is enough to sustain me. But only barely. I admit to being greedy, wanting to spend more and more time with you. Perhaps soon, the Lord will allow that to happen.

While many young ladies like to keep letters from their gentlemen friends, I urge you to destroy this one as soon as you have read it. Do not allow it to fall into anyone's hands. Not even Charley's. Will you promise me that?

Thank you for meeting me last night. It couldn't have been easy for you to get away, and it must have been difficult for you to share with me what you did. Loyalty to the Robinson family on your part is understandable. They have become your family, and you don't want to betray them in any way.

I have spoken to the police chief. He begs an audience with you so he might inquire if you know more about what is going on in the house and who could be responsible for those deaths. Again, it will not be easy for you. We both understand that. But it is crucial that you share what you know, if not with me, then with the authorities before more people fall ill, before another one dies. You and I both know it is only a matter of time until that happens.

Charley doesn't know the contents of this letter, nor do I wish him to know. I will come by the house tomorrow at 2 p.m. so I may speak with you on this topic. I look forward to seeing you once more.

My very best regards to you, my dearest Harriet,
Michael

He signed his name with a confident flourish. After another quick reading, she stuffed the paper into the stove and watched as the flames consumed it. Even after it was nothing more than ash, she stared at the fire, the way it ate everything in its path. It twisted and contorted and devoured. As it chewed through everything in its path, it was like the murderer. No thought for the next victim it attacked. No remorse for the ruins it left behind. No conscience to stop its vengeance.

She slammed the stove door shut and closed her eyes, but the image of the flames remained seared onto the back of her eyelids.

Dear Lord, grant me wisdom. Give me strength. Show me who is committing such heinous acts. And stop any more from happening. Help me. Help me. Help me.

More people clomped up the stairs. She opened her eyes and smoothed back her hair. The words she would pen in return to Michael wrote themselves on her heart.

Chapter Twenty-One

Except for the chirping of the crickets and the hooting of a distant owl, all fell silent around Harriet as she again snuck from the Robinson house to make her way to the nearby church. If this kept up, the police would be forced to make her an honorary detective.

Her stomach cramped, and she clenched her middle, hugging herself to ease the pain. Talking to the police, and the chief no less, was not high on her list of favorite activities. If anyone found out what she was doing, there would be dire consequences. A few weeks ago, she would have thought them to be along the lines of not being allowed to care for Gracie or Tommy anymore.

Now she knew better. The consequences of her actions tonight could well cost her life.

She kept her footsteps swift. The wind rattled the leaves in the trees overhead.

Snap.

What was that?

Snap.

Was someone following her?

Snap.

There had to be someone behind her. She'd been found out. Her heart beat in a strange, uneven rhythm. Though she pressed on her chest, it didn't still the quaking inside. What should she do?

The logical thing would be to return home. Pretend she couldn't sleep and had gone for a stroll. At midnight. Oh, they would never believe her. She'd been caught sneaking out once already.

Did she dare go to the church? No, she couldn't, because then she would give away the police chief. Then again, he would protect her from whoever now nipped at her heels.

She picked up the pace. The hairs on the back of her neck stood at attention. She stopped and held her breath. For a moment, a hush cloaked the evening. A far-off coyote's cry broke the stillness. But nothing else.

Maybe whoever was following her had also stopped. Little by little, she released her breath. In one fluid motion, she spun around.

No one stood in the street. The shadows were long and deep, cast by an almost-full moon. Her pulse pounded in her wrists. She had to keep going. There was no other alternative.

To keep from tripping, she picked up her skirts and made a mad dash for the church a couple of blocks away. What a relief when the large double front door came into view. She flew up the stone stairs, flung the door open, and sprinted into the sanctuary, the heavy door creaking shut behind her.

For a moment, she leaned against the back pew to catch her breath. She tucked an errant strand of hair behind her ear. When she could take a normal breath again, she moved forward. No one bowed in any of the pews. No one prayed at the front of the altar.

Had she gotten the time wrong? Had whoever been following her reached here first and done away with the chief? She covered her mouth to block the sound of her gasp.

"Psst."

The whisper came from behind a pulpit carved with the twelve apostles. There. A door cracked the tiniest of bits. She caught a glimpse of a few dark curls and unforgettable hazel eyes.

"Harriet."

The deep voice left no doubt. Why, that was Michael. She let her shoulders sag and her muscles relax. When he had stopped at the house this afternoon, he hadn't mentioned coming tonight. At least she wouldn't have to face the police chief by herself. Michael had come to be by her side. At least, that's what she allowed herself to believe in the moment. What she needed to believe.

She moved forward and slipped through the door. As soon as she entered, Michael locked it and stuffed a blanket between the bottom of the door and the floor to snuff out any of the dim candlelight that managed to escape the room.

He took her by the hand, first squeezing it, then leading her to a huge polished table surrounded by chairs. A tall, muscular man with a large beard sat on one seat.

"Thank you for meeting me, Miss Peters." His voice was rich and deep, soothing in a way. "I'm Chief Parkhurst. I know you've come here at great risk to yourself."

"I think I might have been followed." She informed them of what happened on the street.

"I'll check to see if anyone is lurking." The chief pulled a revolver from its holster and slipped from the room.

Michael embraced her, and she reveled in being ensconced in his arms. A safe place. A place for her heart and soul to quiet.

"I tried to be careful, but I heard noises behind me, so I ran a good part of the way to the church. I'm sorry if I've done anything to put either you or the chief in danger."

"I'm just glad you made it here in one piece, especially if someone was behind you. If there is anyone out there, Chief Parkhurst will find him. He's very good at what he does." The pale light from the candle danced in his eyes. "Even under the circumstances, I'm so happy you came tonight. Though you told me you would, I prayed you'd be able to make it out."

The moth wings that tickled her stomach had nothing to do with nerves and everything to do with the man who held her close enough for his breath to whisper across the top of her head. "I didn't expect to see you. What a nice surprise to find you here."

"I'm glad it was a nice surprise."

"Of course. Seeing you could be nothing else."

"I'm glad we've put away the earlier misunderstanding."

"I was horribly wrong."

They stood together in silence, Harriet drinking in Michael's nearness, his presence, the faint odor of leather and pipe smoke clinging to his wool jacket. Just being like this with him was enough. She glanced up only to discover him peering at her, his eyes wide in the soft light. No, now being held by him wasn't enough. She wouldn't turn him away if he tried to kiss her.

He pursed his lips, as if that same thought crossed his mind. He bent his head.

The door flung open.

As the chief strode in, Michael released Harriet, and she stepped backward.

"Nothing but a couple of feral cats roaming about."

"I could have been dreaming the snapping of the twigs. My mother always told me I had an overactive imagination."

"Could have been your nerves." Michael shrugged. "Just to be on the safe side, I'll walk you home." He held a chair out for her. To sink into it was just short of heaven.

The chief arranged a stack of papers in front of him. "Are you willing to speak to me about what you know about Sarah Jane Robinson, Charles Beers, Charles Robinson, and William Robinson?"

"I'll tell you what I can. I can't promise it will be helpful." She rubbed her throat in an attempt to ease the choking sensation.

"You never know what piece of information might be the one to bring the entire case together. That's what we're searching for, Miss Peters. Even if you think a detail isn't important, it might be, so I need you to tell me everything."

Again, she nodded. She glanced at Michael beside her, the flickering light playing off the angles of his face. In this setting, he was more handsome than even in the daylight. Strong, sure, and steady. Underneath the table, he held to her hand. Warmth and encouragement flowed from him to her.

Chief Parkhurst began the interrogation by asking her name, birth date, birthplace, occupation, and how she had become acquainted with the Robinson family.

"Now, what can you tell me about the deaths?"

"I met the Robinson family soon before Mr. Robinson became ill. They saved me from starving on the streets. Took me in. Mrs. Robinson got me a job at the department store where she worked. Anyway, Mr. Robinson had been a strong man, working as a carpenter. One terribly hot summer day, Lizzie said he came home from work very thirsty. According to her, he drank a great deal of cold water and ended up with awful stomach cramps, vomiting something terrible. I helped her when I could spare a few moments from my job. I've seen people die before, Chief Parkhurst, but never like this. Never such an agonizing death. They were all this same way. Emmie, Mrs. Freeman, Mr. Freeman, Lizzie, Tommy..."

Her tears flowed down her cheeks, and she could do nothing to stop them. "How could someone snuff out Lizzie's life? She was a beautiful person, both inside and out. She loved people. She helped them. How could they do that to her? And Tommy? He was nothing more than a little boy. Emmie so young too. How could anyone do this to any of them? It's unthinkable. Unspeakable."

Michael gathered her to himself, his wool coat rough underneath her cheek. She nestled against him, for the first time in a long time not alone in the world.

He rubbed her back until she managed to stem the tide of tears. She drew a handkerchief from her reticule and wiped her nose and eyes. "My apologies."

"Take all the time you need, Miss Peters."

The questioning continued for what must have been hours. Chief Parkhurst filled sheet after sheet of paper with notes, writing almost as fast as she spoke. From time to time, he stopped her and asked for clarification on this point or that. At last he laid down his pen. "That's all I have for you right now. I may need to follow up. Are you willing to make yourself available should that be necessary?"

"I am."

Chief Parkhurst gathered his things together, packed them in a briefcase, and exited the room. They had decided they should leave one at a time, especially since someone might have followed Harriet.

"Thank you for what you did tonight." Michael had yet to release his hold on her.

"I did it for Lizzie and Tommy and to protect Gracie. I did it for all the others who have been victims. This madness needs to stop, and it needs to stop before someone else dies." She prayed she had done her part tonight to put an end to these murders. Oh how she prayed the risk had been worth it.

"You need to be careful. You are worth as much to the killer as anyone else in the home."

"I know." Though she imbued her voice with confidence, she went cold inside. Gracie might not be the next one chosen. It might be her. How could she protect Gracie if she was next?

Despite the chief advising against it, Michael and Harriet left the quiet solitude of the church together. He refused to allow her to walk the few blocks home on her own. At one point before they turned the corner, she glanced over her shoulder. The church rose dark against the even blacker night.

Hand in hand, they traversed the streets, taking a winding, circuitous route toward Holland Street. At least this time, Harriet didn't have the pin-prick feeling of someone watching her.

"Do you miss your family?" Michael spoke the words low and soft. It would not do to awaken anyone or to draw attention to themselves from anyone up to use the privy or quiet a crying baby.

Harriet kicked at a stone in the middle of the street. "I think of them often, especially the children. My mother was busy. My father was cruel. When I got old enough to be married off, he promised me to an even crueler neighbor, a man I detested. So I ran away. . . That's a long way to say that yes, I do miss some of them. Still, I didn't stay to protect the younger ones. Maybe I should have."

"Is that why you won't leave Gracie?"

"You might be right." She hadn't thought about it that way, but it was the truth.

"Is that why you were attracted to the Robinsons?"

"Because they're a family?"

"Yes, I suppose that's what I'm asking."

"Lizzie was a friend to me. One of the few I ever had. I came into her life at a time when she needed me, not to cook or clean or do laundry for her but to be a friend to her. Mrs. Robinson took me in and treated me as one of her own. So yes, that's why I grew so close to the family. Which makes this all the harder." She sighed. "What about you?"

His steps stuttered. "My father died when I was a boy. My mother went crazy with grief." His grimace was apparent even in the pale moonlight. "I was taunted and bullied. So I became a doctor to show them all that Michael Wheaton was not worthless."

"And you're not. Not to me, not to your patients."

"Now I'm shunned by the medical community, because they think I'm as insane as my mother."

She sucked in a breath. When he had said his mother went crazy with grief, she assumed he had been using a figure of speech. "You mean that she really did go crazy? You aren't exaggerating?"

He stopped and held her at arm's length. "After what I'm about to tell you, I don't know if you'll want to have anything to do with me. I hope that's not the case. I hope you can understand that this is my mother, not me."

She pressed her lips together and nodded for him to continue.

He shifted his weight from one foot to the other, not gazing at her but at the ground. "My mother is a patient at the McLean Asylum for the Insane. Has been for years. In all likelihood, she will die there."

Another heartbreaking story.

"Will you shun me too?" His plea was that of a little boy longing for acceptance.

How could she withhold it from him? "Of course not. What an awful childhood you must have had. And the way the other children picked on you must have made life almost unbearable."

"If not for Grandpop, it would have been."

"I don't know how anyone could push you away because of that. You are not the same person as your mother. You aren't insane. Definitely not. She isn't an evil person. What happened to her isn't her fault."

"What if I go crazy later in life?"

"I don't think you will." She touched his sleeve. "In the time we've known each other, I've come to see what a caring, generous, and strong person you are. You have an unwavering faith, one that I know will see you through whatever trials lay ahead of you in life. None of us know what life is going to bring from day to day. We just live and walk in God's grace through it all."

"How beautifully put." He drew her close once more. She inhaled the fresh scent of rain-washed air. "If only the rest of the world saw me through your eyes. My own colleagues turn away from me."

"Why?"

"They don't believe anyone would be evil enough to murder their family members for money."

"You discussed the case with them?"

"Yes. I did so out of the hope that they would give me the answers I've been seeking. Instead, when I put forward my hypothesis, they ridiculed me."

"That's ridiculous." No one had the right to treat him that way.

"Not really. It's hard to believe such darkness resides in the world."

"But not unheard of."

"Absolutely not."

"I'm sorry you have to endure that. For what it's worth, I believe you. And I believe in you."

"Thank you."

They resumed their walk and soon approached the gray house, the fluted columns standing sentry in front of it. She stepped near to him. Would this be the time he kissed her? He bent toward her.

Her breath caught in her throat, every nerve ending alive.

"Miss Peters. What on earth are you doing?"

Chapter Twenty-Two

At the deep-throated question from the porch, Michael jumped away from Harriet, the blood pounding in his ears. He could do nothing more than stare at the stout older man in the doorway.

"I'll say it again, what is going on out here? Miss Peters? Dr. Wheaton? Do you have an answer for me?" Dr. Beers stood on the porch with his legs spread apart and his arms akimbo, his eyes narrow.

Harriet's mouth hung open. Though Michael no longer touched her, she trembled beside him.

Michael thought quickly. "Imagine my surprise when I couldn't sleep and was out for a walk, and I ran into Miss Peters having a similar problem. I believe the fresh air has now prepared us for a good night's sleep. When you came out, I was bidding her a pleasant rest."

"You certainly were, weren't you?"

Mrs. Robinson stepped from the doorway, wrapping her shawl around her shoulders. If anything, it wasn't chilly but rather much too warm tonight. "What is this ruckus? Gracie and the others are trying to sleep upstairs." Her gaze swept across the scene. Michael opened his mouth to speak, but she beat him to it. "Miss Peters, I'm surprised at you. Here you pass yourself off as a fine Christian young woman, and yet you go gadding about town in the middle of the night."

Michael bit the inside of his cheek. What was Dr. Beers doing leaving the Robinson residence at such a late hour? Mrs. Robinson had admitted everyone else in the house was asleep. If ever there was a case of the pot calling the kettle black, this was it.

Mrs. Robinson pinched her eyebrows together. "I have half a mind not to allow you inside the house again. Who knows what you picked up while you were out. Not to mention the tarnished reputation you now carry with you. Have you forgotten everything I've done for you? Now you've sullied this home."

Michael tugged on Harriet's arm and whispered in her ear. "Let's go. This is your time to get out. The perfect opportunity."

She struggled against him for a moment and wriggled from his grasp. "I can't." Tears laced her words. "I told you why I have to stay."

"Not like this. Please, don't."

"But I'm going to be gracious and give you one more chance." Mrs. Robinson didn't miss a beat, pretending like Michael and Harriet weren't having a conversation. "I'll allow you in my home this one time. Just this one time. I trust that this time you will not abuse my goodness to you and you will not bring shame on this house."

Michael could hold his tongue no longer. "If you think that little of Miss Peters, I wonder why you even allowed her in your house in the first place. I would think you would be eager to be rid of her."

"Michael, please." Harriet hissed the words at him. "I have a vow to keep. Gracie's life may be at stake."

"Lizzie wouldn't want you to do it at the risk of your own life." He kept his words low, so only she could hear.

"She would want me to do it to save Gracie's. She's nothing more than an innocent child who can't protect herself. She can't leave, and so neither can I."

Dr. Beers marched down the steps toward the street where Michael and Harriet stood. "You should be grateful Mrs. Robinson is so good to you. In kind, you should abide by her rules. And mine. For the welfare of everyone who lives here. That includes yourself."

Yet Dr. Beers came and went at will. Just when Michael had been sure Mrs. Robinson was behind the murders, Dr. Beers acted in such a way that threw the suspicion on him. The older doctor had been around the entire time, always hanging about the house, making odd comments, setting strange rules.

"Can't a body get any sleep around here?" Willie joined his mother on the porch. He glared at Michael and Harriet, shaking his head. "I should have known you would go behind my mother's back."

"I wasn't going behind anyone's back. If I need a walk to help me sleep, then I will take one."

Willie stepped forward. "If anyone saw you with this man, you would be a sullied woman. They may believe that already."

Michael leaned closer to Harriet. "Please, come away. If you're afraid to be on your own, my pastor and his wife would be more than happy to have you stay with them."

"I told you, I can't leave." She pleaded, almost begged him. To what? Understand the position she was in? He did. But he couldn't allow the woman he was falling in love with to stay in such a dangerous situation. "Come away. Please. This might be your last chance."

"I have to trust the Lord enough to do what is right. I can't turn my back on those who are innocent."

Dr. Beers approached and guided Harriet toward the house in a much too possessive manner.

As she climbed the porch steps she gazed over her shoulder at him. The moonlight played across her features. She knitted her brows together, her mouth pinched shut, her eyes wide.

She was frightened.

How could she not be?

"I hope never to see you around here again." Dr. Beers returned to the street, took Michael by the shoulder, and propelled him down the road. "If I do, I promise to ruin you. You will never practice medicine in the Boston area again. With such a besmirched name, I doubt you'll be able to practice anywhere, except perhaps Alaska. Maybe they haven't heard of you there."

"You wouldn't dare."

The older, more rotund man set his old-fashioned top hat on his head. "I would. You see, I know certain things."

Michael drew in a breath. No, he couldn't know. No one could know.

"You think I don't, but I have my ways of finding out certain matters. I'm a doctor, for goodness' sake. Do you think I've never stepped foot in that insane asylum?"

Michael fought to release his breath. "Asylum? I don't know what you're talking about."

"But you do, Dr. Wheaton. In fact, you're a regular visitor there, aren't you?"

"You followed me. You're nothing more than a snake in the grass."

"Better that than being loony. I wonder if it runs in the family. I think it must. If the physicians in this city already believe you to be off your rocker, wait until they hear about your mother. The one who can't keep her wits about her." Dr. Beers tipped his hat and strode away.

He wouldn't. He wouldn't go that far to ruin another doctor's reputation.

Would he?

August 11, 1886

Gracie stirred in the bed beside Harriet, who opened one eye. The sunlight streaming through the window sent shooting pains into her brain.

The little girl rolled over and hugged Harriet. "Good morning. I thought you were going to sleep forever."

"What time is it?"

"I don't know. But Mama and the boys left for work a long time ago. I heard them. Since you weren't awake, I laid here real quiet so I didn't bother you. I like the breakfast you cook for me better than the one Mama makes anyway." She giggled. "Don't tell her I said that. She'd get real mad."

"She wouldn't get mad at you. She loves you." Was that the

truth? With shadows casting a pall over almost everyone in the family, Harriet found herself glancing over her shoulder and peeking in dark corners all the time. This was no way to live. *Dear Lord, please help the police to catch whoever is doing this. We can't go on this way much longer.*

"Miss Harriet, wake up. You're closing your eyes again."

"I was praying, sweetie. Now, shall we get up and get ourselves some breakfast? Otherwise, they'll come home from work tonight and call us lazy bones."

Gracie laughed again, the beautiful melody of childhood. If only she could capture it and bottle it and store it up for when she was older and life got hard. The child bounded from the bed and skipped down the hall, through the parlor, and into the kitchen. Harriet followed, although at a more sedate rate.

She would enjoy today and the time she spent with Gracie. Neither Mrs. Robinson nor Willie had said anything about her late-night escapade after they returned inside. Since she had missed them this morning, her reprimand was sure to arrive with them this evening. That's when she would worry about it. No sense in ruining the day. Besides, she had a hat to finish constructing. If it would cooperate with her.

Harriet scrambled a couple of eggs and fried a few strips of bacon. Because of her late night last night, she brewed the coffee to be extra strong. Even at this early hour, the August heat seared the kitchen. Though she didn't wish to risk further wrath from either Mrs. Robinson or Dr. Beers, she and Gracie might just spend the afternoon on the porch. This heat wasn't good for anyone.

She fanned her face with a napkin though it did little to no good in stopping the perspiration from forming on her·forehead.

"What are we going to do now, Miss Harriet?" Gracie hopped from one foot to the other.

"I need to wash the dishes."

"Can I help dry? Please? I'm getting to be a big girl. Mama says so. She says I have to start working around the house like the rest of you."

Harriet handed her a ragged blue dish towel. "For this morning, I'll allow you to dry the silverware. We'll see how that goes first before we add dishes and cups."

A small pout burst on Gracie's lips, but she set to work and diligently wiped every tine on each fork.

Harriet had just hung the dishcloth from a rack to dry when the door downstairs opened and shut. Who was home at this hour? Every muscle in her body tightened.

Maybe it wasn't one of the family. Perhaps it was an intruder. Or maybe it was one of them come to get her and Gracie out of the way.

Harriet grabbed a butcher knife and motioned for Gracie to stay behind her.

She cracked the kitchen door.

"Harriet. Harriet." The weak male voice called from the stairwell. *God, no!*

She dropped the knife on the table and hurried to meet Willie as he staggered to the top of the stairs. "You're home from work early."

He gazed at her with glassy eyes. This young man, healthy enough last night to stand on the porch and scold her, now teetered before her, weak as winter's sunshine. "It's happening again."

"What is?" she asked, even though the answer was clear.

"The stomach pains. I lost my breakfast on the way home." He clutched his midsection. "Help me."

"Of course." She grabbed him under his arms and steadied him on his feet.

"What's wrong with Willie?" Gracie stood in the kitchen door, her ocean-blue eyes wide in her thin face.

"Stay in there, Gracie. You can play with the bowls and spoons." Harriet struggled under Willie's weight. He had at least six inches on her and many more pounds. "You have to help me. I'm not strong enough to carry you to bed."

Willie puffed out a breath. "I'm trying. The pain is unbearable. And I might be sick again."

They limped down the hall and to the bedroom the men shared. She set Willie down with as much gentleness as possible, trying not to jar him too much.

"Fetch the pail."

She ran to the kitchen and got back just in time for Willie to be sick again. Using the handkerchief in her apron pocket, she wiped his mouth. "Let me pull your boots off, and then you can lie down."

As she bent to unlace his shoes, he touched the top of her head. "Thank you, Harriet."

She pushed down the lump forming in her throat. "You're welcome. Now, lie back and rest. That's the best thing for you. I'll brew some tea." She pulled the thin summer blanket over his broad shoulders.

How could the poison work so fast in such a large, robust man?

Somehow, she had to get word to Michael and Chief Parkhurst. But how? Gracie was too little to go on her own. Wasn't she? But she might be Harriet's only hope. She didn't have to go all the way to Michael's office and the police station. All she had to do was get a message to Mrs. Joss across the street. The neighbor could send one of her older girls with a note for Michael.

Harriet cleaned up and sat at the parlor table to dash a note off to Michael. "Gracie, come here, please."

With her head bowed, the girl made her way from the kitchen to stand in front of Harriet.

"What is it? What's wrong, sweetheart?"

"Is Willie gonna die?"

"Not if I have anything to say about it." Not that she did. Willie's life was in God's hands. "You need to listen to me, though, and do everything I tell you. Go across the street and take this note to Mrs. Joss. Tell her Willie is sick, and I need her to get this letter to Dr. Wheaton right away. As fast as possible. She'll know what to do. You come straight home from there."

"Mama and Dr. Beers won't be happy."

"Do you want Willie to get better?"

She nodded, her mouth still turned down.

Harriet stroked her smooth, warm cheek. "If Willie has a chance to get better, then you have to do this. Can you? Please?" She proffered the note, and Gracie slid it into her apron pocket.

"I'll do it, Miss Harriet. Even though I might get in trouble, I want Willie to get better. If he dies, it'll just be me and Charley left."

"Go, then, as fast as you can."

Harriet prayed Michael would come in time.

Chapter Twenty-Three

Harriet held Willie by the shoulders as he emptied his stomach once again. She'd lost track of the number of times he'd been sick since he'd come home. At this rate, he wouldn't last more than a few hours. She settled him against the pillows and smoothed the blanket over him. "I'll make you some tea."

"No." His voice rasped.

"You have to drink. It's the only way you're going to get stronger."

"It'll just come back up."

"So be it, then. Maybe some will stay in you. You have to try. You can't give up. Think of your mother. Of Gracie."

"I'm trying."

"Good. Then you'll drink some of the tea I make you." Where was Michael? It had been almost thirty minutes since Gracie had arrived home after delivering the note.

The kettle had just reached a boil when a knock sounded at the door downstairs. Finally, Michael had arrived. "Gracie, would you answer that, please?"

A moment later, light little footsteps sounded on the stairs. Then several pairs of shoes clomped up. Harriet set the tea to steep and went to the parlor to meet Michael.

He wasn't alone.

He gave her a wan smile. "Miss Peters, this is Dr. White. I worked with him when Tommy was ill."

"Of course, I remember you, Doctor. Thank you for coming. Let me show you to Willie's room." As she brushed by Michael, heat coursing through her as their shoulders met, he pulled her back.

"How are you?"

"Fine. I can't believe, though, that we are reliving this nightmare. It never ends. The third time this year. When will it stop? The police have to do something to try to save Willie's life. We can't allow another member of this family to die. Now the list of possible suspects has shortened by one."

"I've let Chief Parkhurst know what's going on, but we need concrete proof of poisoning. Of deliberate poisoning. That's where Dr. White comes in. He's going to help us determine, first of all, if this is indeed poisoning, and what type."

"That's all going to take time. Time I'm not sure Willie has. Listen, we know it has to be either Dr. Beers or Mrs. Robinson. I refuse to believe it's Charley. Why not arrest them both? Even if they can't hold them, maybe it will be long enough for the proof to come. If nothing else, long enough for Willie to live."

"We're going to do everything we can to make sure he does. Trust me on this."

Before Harriet could inhale, Michael took off down the hall. Trust him? Yes. *Lord, please heal Willie.* She snagged the tea from the kitchen and followed.

When she entered the room, both Michael and Dr. White were hunched over the bed, examining Willie. She set the cup on the table beside the bed. The two continued without giving her a second glance, both intent on their work. That was as it should be.

"Miss Harriet." Gracie pulled on her skirts with one hand, twirling her hair with the other. This was the first time in a long time Harriet had caught her doing that.

"What, pumpkin?"

"I'm scared. What if Willie dies? What if I get sick too?"

How did Harriet answer those questions when the same ones ran through her own mind? She had to believe in Jesus' love for her, like Michael said. Knowing it and believing it, though, were two different things.

Gracie tugged on Harriet's dark skirt again.

She hugged the little girl. "The doctors are here now to take care of him. They are going to do everything they can to make him better." He had to get well. Surely, between the doctors and the police, they would be able to save Willie.

"But nobody else got better."

How well they all knew that. It had to be foremost in the doctors' minds. Harriet couldn't shake the thought. The two physicians completed their exam and stepped to the far corner of the room to confer.

Harriet knelt in front of Gracie. "The best thing you can do to help your brother is to go play quietly in your room. Say a prayer for him."

"I will, Miss Harriet." Gracie perked up. "I'll pray so hard God will have to make Willie better."

"We will pray that it be God's will that Willie lives." *Yes, Lord, please.*

The meeting in the corner concluded, and the doctors straightened beside Willie's bed. Michael nodded to Dr. White, who rocked back and forth.

"The amount of vomiting that you've done, Willie, is actually a good thing. It is flushing the poison, if that's what this is, from your body. What I'm going to do is take some samples and send them to Harvard. From your vomit, they should be able to determine if poison is present. Drink plenty of that tea Miss Peters is bringing you. If you ingest no more poison, you have a chance at recovery."

Willie moaned and curled into a ball like a baby. "What about this pain, this awful burning sensation? When will it go away?"

"It will ease as the poison leaves your system. Hold on for a few more hours. Let's see what happens. If you don't improve, we'll give you either bismuth phosphate to help the stomach pains or nux vomica to induce more nausea. I won't lie to you. It won't be pleasant. As of right now, I'm cautiously optimistic about your prognosis."

Harriet sagged and sat on the bed. Maybe Willie would live.

Perhaps Michael and Dr. White would be able to thwart the murderer's latest attempt.

The older physician took his sample, then snapped shut his black bag. "I'll leave you in Dr. Wheaton's capable hands. I'll be back later this evening to check on you, Willie. Dr. Wheaton, don't hesitate to send for me if you need anything. Anything at all." The older man cocked a graying eyebrow.

"Understood." Michael shook Dr. White's hand. Willie had fallen into a restless sleep, so both Michael and Harriet showed the doctor to the door. Michael, however, didn't leave. That alone lifted some of the weight from her chest.

After Dr. White departed, Harriet fixed lunch for herself, Gracie, and Michael. She seated herself across from him at the table, one ear attentive for any cry from Willie. "I guess we can cross Willie off the list."

Gracie hummed as she bit into her sandwich.

"Looks that way."

"Will we catch the culprit this time?" Harriet attempted to talk over Gracie's head.

"I hope so. I sure hope so. There aren't many left."

"True." She pushed her cold chicken around her plate. "Soon they'll run out of victims." She couldn't help but gaze at the sweet child across the table from her.

"Let's pray it doesn't come to that."

"I have been. I'll continue."

Michael consumed his sandwich in record time and wiped the crumbs from his long, thin face. "You finish your meal and rest for a while. I'll check on Willie."

"You don't have to stay. I can nurse him."

He cast her a sideways glance. "I'm not going to leave you alone in this house when Mrs. Robinson comes home. You're not going to get rid of me."

"You'll only bring her wrath on your head if you're here. I implore you, please go. I tell you what. I'll send you across the street to the Joss's house with a note asking them to extend hospitality to you. That way, if I need you, you're within a stone's throw. Gracie can always come get you."

"Are you sure?" He shook his head.

The last thing any of them wanted or needed was for Mrs. Robinson to get upset. Who knew what she would do then? "I am positive."

"Do me one favor. Do not let anyone—not you, Gracie, Willie, or Charley—eat or drink anything you don't prepare with your own hands. Can you promise me that?"

"Of course. That's only sensible."

"Good. I'll return this evening with Dr. White. Between the two of us, we can withstand whatever that woman has to dish out." He towered over her and brushed her hair back. Would he try to kiss her right here in front of Gracie? Her fingers and toes tingled.

"Harriet." The call came from Willie's room. "Harriet, I need you. Hurry."

As the afternoon progressed, so did the patient. Once Harriet had a simple potato and cheese supper started on the stove, Willie even felt well enough to challenge her to a game of checkers. In fact, in all the time she had lived there, he had never played any game with her. Perhaps his brush with death had improved his sullen disposition. Then again, she shouldn't judge. He had been through so much in his life.

Because of this unusual turn of events, she pulled in the parlor table and a chair without hesitation and fluffed his pillows under his head so he could reach the game pieces. He was weak from being so sick, so she set up the black and red pieces on the patterned board.

"See." He moved one of his playing pieces forward, pinning hers on the side. "This was nothing like what the others had. Just a little stomach upset. No reason for you to call for that doctor friend of yours. Gracie will chatter away and tattle to Mama, and it will cause an unneeded uproar."

"I'd rather deal with your mother then with your corpse." She pursed her lips and acted as if she was studying the pieces on the board and how to get out of her pickle. In fact, she was working not to remember what happened with Mr. Freeman. Trying not to remind Willie of how his case progressed. Lizzie told her that after he came home from work and was sick for a while, he was much better until the evening. Until everyone returned from work and Dr. Beers arrived.

When, or rather if, the police chief ever arrived, she would have to share that detail with him. It was something she had forgotten about when he questioned her.

Willie moved his black piece diagonally across the board. "There's something I have to say to you, Harriet."

She peered at him. "You do?"

"Um, this isn't easy for me. I, uh, don't talk much. Don't like to show my emotions much."

When the pause dragged on, Harriet slid her red checker into position.

"I know at times I've been horrid to you. Especially when you didn't want me to court you."

She gazed into his blue eyes, a sincerity there she'd never seen before. "You were hurt. It's understandable."

"But inexcusable. For that, I must apologize. I should have been nicer to you. Should have treated you better. Earlier today, I thought I might die, that's how bad the pain was. I wanted to die, in fact. But how could I stand before God with that on my conscience?"

"I've forgiven you. Let's move beyond this. Maybe now we can become good friends. Brother and sister, even."

"I'd like that." Willie returned his attention to the game, jumping one of her pieces and reaching her side of the board. "King me," he crowed.

Harriet giggled. "See, you're already acting like a brother."

As the shadows lengthened across the floor and the sweet aroma of bubbling potatoes and cheese reached them, Harriet squirmed in the seat. More than once, she jumped at a sound outside the apartment—the neighbor moving around downstairs, another neighbor's dog barking, a door slamming across the street.

Perhaps noises from Mrs. Joss's house, where Michael sat and waited for word from her. Before Mrs. Robinson and Charley returned, she should send him a note via Gracie to let him know how things were going, how much better Willie was doing. She should also let him know what she remembered. If the chief didn't come here, Michael could pass the word to him.

Just as she was blowing the ink dry on the paper, the door downstairs creaked open. She shoved the letter into her apron pocket and capped the inkwell.

Mrs. Robinson entered the apartment and dropped her almost-new reticule on the blue settee. "What a day. All I want to do is to put my feet up and take it easy. I smell supper going. That's good. Where is Gracie?"

"In her room. Whom you should be concerned about is Willie."

"What about him?" Mrs. Robinson narrowed her eyes.

"He came home this morning complaining of similar symptoms as Lizzie and Tommy had and the others."

Mrs. Robinson jumped to her feet, her lips parted. "My poor boy. Not again. This can't be happening again." She rushed to his room.

Harriet followed.

"My boy, how awful you've had to go through this."

"It's nothing to worry about, Mama, really." Willie's color had almost returned to normal. "Though I had a scare, it wasn't what everyone else had. Nothing but an off stomach. We're so jumpy now, no one can get sick without all of us rushing to conclusions, ready to call the undertaker at the first sign of illness."

"What an awful thing to say." Mrs. Robinson stood straighter, her head up.

Harriet leaned against the doorway. Was it possible that Willie had administered the poison to himself to throw the mantle of suspicion from him? No. It couldn't be. Could it?

Knowing what happened to Mr. Freeman, she wouldn't pass judgment until she saw for her own eyes that Willie had made a full recovery.

Harriet went to the kitchen and, with Gracie's help in setting the table, got dinner ready to be served. Mrs. Robinson came in just as she was about to pour the tea into the cups for herself, Mrs. Robinson, and Willie. "Dear, why don't you bring some bread and maybe even some of this dinner in to Willie. You've been busy caring for him all day. I'll get the cups while you pour the tea. You look like you could use some yourself."

"That would be delightful." Caring for Willie had tired her.

She brought him his dinner. "Here you go. . ." Steam rose from the china cup.

"You didn't have to do that, Harriet. I almost feel well enough to come to the table."

"Nonsense. We don't want you to relapse. You're going to take it easy for a few days, at least."

"Are those Dr. Wheaton's orders?"

"No, they are mine, and I'm a much stricter taskmaster than he is."

Willie smiled broadly at her. "I will follow your commands, then."

A great deal of time had gone by since she had last seen Willie in such good spirits. Was it because he believed he was no longer under suspicion, or because he realized he had cheated death?

Harriet heaved a sigh and returned to the kitchen to eat her supper. They were halfway through the meal when Dr. Beers arrived. He didn't even bother to greet Harriet or the others. He pulled Mrs. Robinson into the parlor. Because the door was shut and Gracie was chattering to Charley about her day, Harriet couldn't hear what they were saying.

Their conference didn't last long. Mrs. Robinson bustled around, fixing a plate for Dr. Beers. She peered into Harriet's teacup. "My dear, you haven't touched it. Come, drink it. You'll feel better once you have."

Harriet glanced at Mrs. Robinson. She might have slipped something into the cup while she was out of the room. Then again, the cup had been on the table the whole time Charley and Gracie had been in the room.

She sipped at the almost-cold drink. It tasted fine. No one had had the opportunity to taint it.

Michael and Dr. White would return soon. And the chief had yet to show up. It could be a long night of confrontation.

Harriet sipped some more.

Mrs. Robinson sank into a chair. "We can only pray Willie is truly on the mend. We all have to keep our strength up in case he has a relapse. If that happens, he'll need a great deal of nursing care, as you well know."

Just like this morning, Michael arrived as Harriet finished drying the dishes. Unfortunately, she wasn't the first one to the door. Charley was. He welcomed Michael and Dr. White inside.

"What brings you here?" Charley's voice floated into the parlor as the trio made their way up the stairs.

"We were here earlier when Willie fell ill." As he reached the top of the stairs and Harriet caught her first sight of him, Michael finger-combed his already mussed hair. Mrs. Robinson entered from the hall, the almost-completed green dress from the form in her hands.

Charley leaned forward. "How did you know about that?"

"I called for him." Harriet braced for Mrs. Robinson's wrath.

Good thing she did. Mrs. Robinson tightened her jaw. "Did you take Gracie out to get the doctor? Or leave her alone? Can't you follow orders? Besides that, we don't need these men. Dr. Beers is here if Willie should be sick again."

"Mama, Mama, hurry." Willie's cry came from the bedroom.

Almost as if his mother's words were prophecy.

Chapter Twenty-Four

Get that man out of my house," Mrs. Robinson screeched as she sat on the edge of Willie's bed.

Willie hugged his middle, crying in pain. Harriet restrained herself from covering her ears to shut out the woman. "Mrs. Robinson, get control of yourself."

She turned her burning gaze in Harriet's direction. "Don't you see what he did to my son? Look at him, just look at how much he's suffering. And I blame you." She pointed at Harriet, her finger long and spear-like. "You brought him into this house. You brought this curse on us."

"Willie was already sick before Dr. Wheaton came." Mrs. Robinson wasn't making sense. She couldn't see reason anymore.

"We have Dr. Beers. We don't need anyone else." She directed her steely gaze at Michael. "You are useless and worthless. If my son dies, the blame will lie squarely with you and your crazy, cockamamie ideas."

Michael paled. After what he'd told Harriet, it was understandable. Those words must have been like arrows to his heart. He moved toward the door.

"No, wait." Harriet reached out for him. "I live here, and you are my guest. I want you to be with me." With her back to the others, she mouthed, "Please," and prayed her face conveyed how she begged him not to go.

Michael peered over Harriet's shoulder. "Willie, what do you want?"

Harriet turned as Willie attempted to lift his head from his pillow, but only managed to raise it an inch or two. "Stay." His voice was again raspy.

"I will not stand for that." Mrs. Robinson straightened, royal and regal.

Willie clasped her by the hand. "I want him."

Several times, she glanced between her son and the doctor she hated so, chewing on the inside of her cheek. "Fine. For my son, I would do anything. You may remain, but Dr. Beers will be the lead doctor on this case. You aren't to touch anything, administer anything, say anything about my son's case. Is that clear?"

Then what was the point of him being here?

Harriet blew out a breath she didn't realize she'd been holding. If Willie had any chance of living, Michael had to remain. Even if Mrs. Robinson and Dr. Beers wouldn't allow him to act as a physician, he could have his eyes open for anything out of the ordinary happening. Dr. White had to hurry that test. With her chin up, Harriet marched into the hall, where she could keep her eye on Mrs. Robinson and Dr. Beers.

Michael exited after her.

"She shouldn't be treating you in such a manner."

"I'm used to it."

Harriet picked at a nonexistent piece of lint on her dark skirt. "I try to think that she's worried about Willie, that's all. She's never been the warmest person in private, but this is a new low, even for her. Who can blame her? She's in danger of losing yet another child."

"Is that the way a person who is concerned about their son's welfare would act, yelling and screaming at people who are trying to help? Shutting out a doctor who might assist one who hasn't been able to save any of her family members?"

"Different people deal with grief in different ways."

"But this is a person you're afraid of."

Harriet couldn't deny it. Though she longed to defend Mrs. Robinson, in truth, her behavior was bizarre. "Just promise me you won't leave. Please. Where is Chief Parkhurst?"

"Waiting for the results of the tests."

"How long will that be?"

"A few days."

Harriet steadied herself against the wall. "Willie might not live that long."

"I understand. In the meantime, we have to do whatever we can to keep Mrs. Robinson or Dr. Beers from administering anything to Willie. I know. It won't be easy, but we have to do it."

"Fine." Harriet glanced into the sickroom. "I'll try to convince Mrs. Robinson and Dr. Beers to rest for a while. That should at least buy us some time to get Willie feeling better."

"I'll stay out of the way as much as possible. If you need anything, I'll be in the kitchen, doing my best to behave." He flashed her a crooked, almost boyish grin.

Even in the grimmest of situations, he managed to bring a smile to her face. What would it be like to have that kind of love and support for the rest of her life? She'd never experienced anything like it before. Her heart fluttered at the thought. She clutched her chest in a vain attempt to still it. "I'll keep you apprised of Willie's condition."

Michael traveled to the kitchen and left her alone in the hall.

She shouldn't be thinking thoughts like that about Michael at a time like this. Before entering Willie's room, she stopped and inhaled several deep breaths. There. Much better. She could handle anything Mrs. Robinson and Dr. Beers could dish out. If only she could stop her hands from shaking.

She plastered a smile onto her face and entered the bedchamber. Mrs. Robinson sat with green satin material, the needle flying in and out of the fabric. "Mrs. Robinson, you must be exhausted after working all day and coming home to find your son so ill. Why don't you lie down for a little bit? Just an hour or two to refresh yourself."

"I'm fine, my dear. I'm sorry I got upset earlier. It's just with Willie now like the others. . ." She sniffled.

"With everything you've been through, I'm sure it's hard on you. I insist that you rest. You'll feel much better once you've had some sleep. It's nearly midnight."

Mrs. Robinson rubbed her eyes. "Perhaps you're right. It has been an exhausting day. I only have a bit left to sew on this vest I'm making for Willie. When he heals, he'll be so handsome in it."

"As for me, I'm not going anywhere." Dr. Beers crossed his arms over his ample middle.

"I insist. I'm more than capable of caring for Willie. After all, I did nurse Lizzie. Charley has put Gracie to bed and is sleeping on the davenport in the parlor, so I'm at liberty to care for Willie."

"You, a chit of a girl, won't be able to chase me from this room. Willie needs a doctor. I'm it."

"I can call for you if the need arises. Hopefully, Willie will get some much-needed sleep tonight."

The doctor shook his head. "You won't win this argument. I'm as stubborn as an old mule."

He was an old mule. Harriet quickly repented of that thought. "At your age, you need your rest." Oh no, how had those words come from her lips?

Dr. Beers puffed up his chest. "You are rude and uncaring. I told you I'm staying, and that is final. In fact, I would appreciate it if you would leave."

"Like you, I'm as stubborn as an old mule. You have yourself an assistant for the night." She turned to Mrs. Robinson, who hung about in the doorway. "Don't worry. Dr. Beers and I will take good care of your son. Dr. Wheaton has agreed to stay away." For now. "So you can rest easy."

"That does put my mind at ease. Thank you, Harriet. I don't know what we would do without you." Mrs. Robinson rose from Willie's bed and swept toward the door. As she exited, she cast a narrow-eyed glance at Dr. Beers.

One very pointed and full of meaning.

If only Harriet could decipher it.

Dr. Beers rose from his chair, came to her, and clenched her shoulder. "Willie should have some fluids. I'll get the tea."

"No, that's fine. I can do it."

"It would be my pleasure." His smile was as sweet as sugar, but the meaning behind it was as sour as a lemon. "I'll bring you a cup also."

How could she stop him from making the tea without letting on that she thought he might be slipping poison to Willie? That's right, Michael was in the kitchen. He would watch Dr. Beers and would make sure he didn't mix anything in the drink. "Thank you."

Michael sat at the kitchen table, working a crossword puzzle from yesterday's newspaper. He was about to fill in an answer when the kitchen door opened and Dr. Beers entered.

Michael didn't move his head but peered sideways at the doctor.

"Just came to get Willie and Harriet some tea. Harriet managed to get Mrs. Robinson to lie down for a while."

Chalk one up for Harriet. "That's good. We wouldn't want anyone else to get sick."

The doctor leaned over the table across from Michael, his face mere inches away, his onion breath strong. "No, we wouldn't, would we? Because enough people have died here. And I believe that you and Harriet are the ones who brought the contamination in this time."

"Not where Willie worked?"

"He doesn't work in a factory like his uncle. He's a teamster."

"You don't know where he makes his deliveries." Perhaps, at this late hour, the doctor would let some incriminating information slip.

"What's important now is making sure Willie gets better. Wouldn't you agree?"

"Of course." Michael sat back in his chair. "I'll leave you to it. Let me know if you need anything."

"What we don't need is you hanging around here. You're free to go anytime you like."

"I believe I'll stay. You never know when another pair of hands might be needed. If the time comes that you would like to rest as well, I'll be available to help."

"If you don't leave this house this minute, I will let the entire town of Somerville, the entire city of Boston and its environs, know about your mother. I'm not bluffing. With my connections throughout the area, your reputation will be broken beyond repair within hours. Is that what you want?"

Michael stiffened. Yes, Dr. Beers had hit a nerve. All these years, he'd worked so hard to keep the world from discovering his mother's lack of mental stability. The doctor could do it and would do it, no doubt about it.

What about Willie? Wasn't his life more important than Michael's reputation? Even more important than the career he'd longed for and labored hard to achieve?

It didn't take him long to answer that question. Of course Willie mattered more. "Threaten all you like, Dr. Beers. Go and tell the entire world my mother resides in an insane asylum. Has for years." Michael came to his feet. "I don't care. Sully me, ruin me, do whatever you want to me. But you won't get me to budge."

The old man huffed. "Well, well, well, perhaps it's time I got the police involved. You are trespassing on private property."

"Go right ahead. I've been invited into this home."

"And asked to leave numerous times. Yet you remain."

"Call for them. See what they have to say about my presence in this house." He'd been at the station often enough that most of the officers should recognize him. If there was a problem, he would invoke Chief Parkhurst's name.

Dr. Beers shook his head. "Suit yourself. I'm going to love seeing you dragged out of here by your hair." He poured the hot water, steeped the tea, and picked up the cups. They rattled in their saucers.

"Let me get the door for you." Michael hurried to help.

"I'm not an invalid. I'm quite capable." The man stomped off.

Michael wasn't about to let him out of his sight. He watched from the kitchen door until Dr. Beers disappeared into Willie's room. Then he followed down the hall and peeked inside. The doctor had set the cups on the table beside the bed and was helping Willie sit up to drink.

Nothing out of the ordinary. At least not this time.

One thing was clear, though. They had to get Willie out of the house. Now.

Because if they didn't, he would die.

Dr. Beers returned to the room with the two promised cups of tea. He set them on the table and helped Willie to a sitting position. "The more you drink, the better for you."

"I can't." Willie's voice was weak and weary.

"In order to keep your strength up, you must."

Willie opened his cracked lips when the doctor brought the cup to him. He took a few sips before pushing the cup away. "I'm not sure it's going to stay down."

"Just lie back and try to keep it in your stomach." The doctor adjusted the pillows behind Willie. When he had his patient settled, he handed Harriet her cup of tea. "You've been with him all day. You need to drink as well. Might help to keep you awake."

Did she dare taste it? She studied the cup in her hand. Surely Michael would have watched the doctor. Perhaps was still watching. When Dr. Beers turned around, she glanced over her shoulder. Sure enough, she caught sight of Michael's red cravat as he peeked into the room. If there was any poison in either of the cups, he wouldn't allow Willie or her to drink.

She blew on it, and when it had cooled enough, she gulped it down.

A few minutes later, Willie was sick again.

All through the long night, they repeated the process. Willie didn't improve. Toward dawn, the vomiting ceased, but the stomach pains worsened. He writhed on the bed in agony.

Pictures of Lizzie and Tommy suffering in such a way

overwhelmed her. This was the third time she'd had to watch someone she knew, someone she cared about, suffering such agony. How could she take much more?

As thin slivers of light snaked their way underneath the dark drawn curtains, the house stirred. Had Michael gotten any sleep during the night? Her own eyes burned, and she rubbed them in an effort to stay awake.

A short time later, Mrs. Robinson scurried into the room to her son's bedside. "How is he? Why didn't anyone wake me earlier? How could you have let me sleep so long? I should have been with my son. A boy needs his mother at a time like this."

Dr. Beers yawned and stretched. "About the same."

"His pain is worse." Why didn't the doctor mention that?

"It's all too reminiscent of what happened to the others. Why is my house so cursed?" With tears in her eyes, she fled the room.

After several minutes, pots and pans and dishes clanked in the kitchen, and then Mrs. Robinson returned. "I have some oatmeal for breakfast. Why don't you both come and eat some and then go to bed? Now that I've had a good night's rest, I'll watch Willie. Though I do need to go to work. I can't miss more time, or I'll lose my job, and this family would be destitute."

"Dr. Wheaton can stay with the patient while Dr. Beers and I sleep." That would be best. With the doctor sleeping and Mrs. Robinson gone, maybe they could even move Willie from the house to a safer location. Perhaps they would have those test results from Harvard today.

"I don't like that solution. Not one bit. I don't trust that man as far as I can throw him. No, we'll think of another way. Perhaps I'll stop on my way to work and have one of the church women come to sit. Or maybe Mrs. Joss could come, though something about that woman has always rubbed me the wrong way."

Harriet raised an eyebrow. Mrs. Joss was the sweetest, most pleasant woman Harriet had ever met. What could Mrs. Robinson have found wrong with her?

Harriet followed Dr. Beers and Mrs. Robinson to the kitchen. A steaming bowl of oatmeal sat at each place. Michael was still here, a bit bleary eyed, but spooning heapfuls of his breakfast into his mouth. Harriet relaxed her tense shoulders. If he could eat it, so could she. "Thank you, Mrs. Robinson."

She took her usual position at the table and tucked into the breakfast. In no time, she had it finished. Charley left for work, and Mrs. Robinson declared she would get Mrs. Smith from church to come and be with Willie while everyone else rested. With that, she swept out of the room, Dr. Beers following in her wake, leaving Michael and Harriet alone in the kitchen, the door downstairs slamming a moment later.

Good. Both of them were gone.

Harriet rose to place the dishes in the sink.

Michael came behind her and caught her in an embrace. She leaned against him, her body trembling, perhaps from his nearness, perhaps from extreme fatigue. He whispered in her messy hair. "This is our chance. We can get him out of the house."

"I was thinking the same thing."

"Good."

"If either one of them was poisoning Willie, wouldn't they want to stay with him? Why would they both leave, especially with someone from the church in charge?"

"Who knows."

"Have we been wrong all along?"

"Right now, it doesn't matter. We should have those test results back soon. Now that they have left, we'll convince Willie to allow us to move him."

"You're right. The rest is for Chief Parkhurst to figure out."

"Exactly."

He rubbed her shoulders. "Why don't you lie down for a bit? I'll keep Gracie busy with a puzzle. You look awful."

"What a way to charm a woman." Harriet couldn't help but laugh.

"My mother always told me I had a way with the ladies." His words were teasing.

"I think I'll take that nap now."

"I'll wake you when Willie is ready to go. We can take him to my office."

She turned and pecked him on the cheek. "Thank you. If not for you, I don't know what would happen to Willie. Or to the rest of us in the house."

In a matter of minutes, she was in bed, with just enough energy to kick off her shoes. She curled up on the mattress and allowed sleep to overtake her.

Get out of the house.

Get out now.

She awoke with a start. The world tilted and whirled around her. Where had that voice come from? It was so real. More than a dream.

Then a vise-like pain gripped her middle. Never in her life had she experienced such agony. Though she twisted and contorted into every imaginable position, the pain didn't cease. Her stomach churned, and bile rose in her throat. "Michael! Michael!"

She managed to yell for him just before she was sick.

Chapter Twenty-Five

Stuffy, clingy humidity wrapped itself around Michael. Willie's south-facing upstairs bedroom was stifling. Sweat poured down Michael's face and his back. He sponged Willie with cool water. The young man thrashed on the bed, groaning and screaming in pain.

The vomiting had stopped, but Willie wasn't improving. That wasn't a good sign. The poison had worked its way into his body now. They had no antidote. No bismuth phosphate or nux vomica would help. Willie had little time.

Another scream startled him. Not Willie's deep one but Harriet's feminine, high-pitched one. His pulse pounded in his ears so hard he heard nothing else. What could be going on in her room? He dropped the washcloth into the basin of water and rushed from the bedchamber.

She screamed again. Was someone trying to hurt her?

Though the dash across the hall was short, it might as well have been a million miles. He got to her side to find her hanging over the edge of the bed, having just been sick. Gracie came running and joined Michael beside Harriet.

He knelt at the foot of the bed and smoothed back Harriet's dark hair. "What's wrong?"

She gazed at him with shimmering eyes. "Help me." She clutched her stomach.

Gracie shouldn't see this. Then again, the child had seen too much of this. "Tell me where your mother keeps her rags. Then run across the street to Mrs. Joss's house and tell her to fetch Dr. White. Hurry. Go as fast as you can."

Once the child had torn from the room, he returned his attention to Harriet. Her face was devoid of all color. "Don't worry, my love, don't worry. I'll take care of you. I won't let anything happen to you. I'm going to get you out of here. I'll get some nux vomica for you. It won't be pleasant, but it will flush the poison from your system." At least he prayed it would.

Harriet reached out to him, and he held her by the hand. "Don't leave me. Please, don't leave me. They're trying to kill me."

"I know, sweetheart, I know. but I'm not going to let that happen. I promise you'll be fine. Let me go. I have to get the nux vomica. By the time it's done its work, we'll have you out of here. You'll be safe."

"Willie too?"

"Of course."

She curled into a tight ball. "The pain. Oh, I've never felt this kind of pain. Make it stop."

"I will." He wrenched himself from her noose-tight grasp and scurried down the hall to the kitchen. He located a loaf of bread and a knife. Once he had sliced a piece, he procured the bottle from his doctor's bag and squeezed a few drops onto the bread. Then he hurried to Harriet's room.

Gracie had brought the rags. Downstairs, the door banged shut. Good, she was on her way across the street.

He adjusted the pillows so Harriet could sit and handed her the medicine-laced bread. "I know you don't feel like eating, but it will get the job done."

"I don't know if I can."

He cupped her face and forced her to gaze at him. Her intense blue eyes were wild. "Calm down. Take a deep breath. If you want to live, you have to do this. For me. For us. I love you, and there can't be an us if you don't eat this. Decide now what you want."

With a trembling hand, she lifted the bread to her lips. She sputtered and gagged as she swallowed. As she did so, he cleaned up the mess and found another bucket in the kitchen. He peered into Willie's room. For now, the young man slept. What a blessing.

In short order, the nux vomica did its work. Though it was hard to watch Harriet suffer and wretch, the poison was leaving her system. That was a very good thing.

Gracie returned, red-faced. "Mrs. Joss is going to fetch Dr. White right now. I told her to hurry. Please, Dr. Wheaton, don't let Miss Harriet die. I couldn't stand it without her. She's like my big sister. I don't have a big sister anymore."

He took a second to kneel in front of the child, a smattering of freckles across her face. "I know. I'm going to do everything I can to make sure Miss Harriet gets better. Right now, the best thing you can do is pray for her."

They would also have to contemplate getting Gracie out of the house. Her life was as much in danger as Willie's or Harriet's.

He didn't have time to think or even to worry about either of his patients, especially the pretty one with the raven hair that flowed over her shoulders. Willie awoke in even more agony than before. The bismuth phosphate he administered did little good in combating Willie's pain.

Michael raced between the two rooms caring for his patients. After quite a while, he had them both settled and was on his way to the kitchen to make a pot of tea. Then again, maybe not. It could be that the tea leaves themselves were laced with poison, though he'd had some and was fine.

For now.

To be safe, just water for them.

As he made his way through the parlor, a ray of sunshine slanted across the room and landed on an amber bottle perched on the mantel. Was this the poison? Who would leave it sitting out? He picked it up and examined it. No label. No marking. He uncorked it. No odor. Perhaps Dr. White could send this to Harvard as well. Right now, whatever it was would have to wait. Michael slipped it into his coat pocket and returned to tending his patients.

A few moments later Dr. White knocked on the door, and Gracie let him in. The little girl was proving her worth today. Michael met him at the top of the stairs. "We have a situation."

"I heard from Mrs. Joss who heard from Gracie. So it's true?"

"Yes. I found this." He pulled the bottle from his pocket. "It was just sitting on the mantel."

"Interesting. I've seen arsenic bottled like this."

"You think that's what it is?"

"I have a very strong suspicion."

"Any word on Willie's tests?"

"Not yet. But soon. Patience, my friend."

"Patience isn't a commodity I have much of. I'm afraid it's just a matter of time for Willie. We have to get Harriet out of here. Immediately. While she still has a chance to live."

"Is she well enough to be moved?"

Michael rubbed his temples. "As well as she's going to be for a while. We don't have to go far. I believe we can trust Mrs. Joss."

"We can. I've known her family for a number of years. She's a good woman."

"Be careful. Looks can be deceiving." At this point, Michael didn't know if anyone was who they appeared to be. "But we don't have much choice. Can you stay here with Willie and Gracie?" The woman from church had never shown up. Perhaps Mrs. Robinson hadn't been able to persuade her to come.

"Of course."

"I'll take Harriet over there and be back for Gracie and Willie as soon as possible. I'd take the child now, but I don't want her under my feet as I carry Harriet."

The older man nodded his gray head. "You love her, don't you?"

"Who, Gracie?"

Dr. White tipped his head. "You know very well who I mean."

There was no denying the truth, one his heart had known for a long while. "Yes, I love her very much. And I refuse to lose her." He entered Harriet's bedroom. She remained in the fetal position with her eyes closed. With a light shake of her shoulder, he woke her.

"How would you like to go out for a while?"

"I can't."

"Are you feeling any better?"

"My stomach still hurts, but not quite so much."

"That's good. I'm going to get you out of here to somewhere safe before whoever is doing this gets more poison into you."

"Gracie?"

"I'll be back for her."

"Willie?"

"Him too." Jostling her as little as possible, he scooped her up in his arms. She was so light, so tiny and delicate, it took his breath away. With a light kiss on her forehead, he carried her from the room.

Gracie trailed him. "Where are you taking Miss Harriet?"

"I'm going to take her to a place where she can get better. Don't worry. Everything is going to be fine."

"Can I come?"

He shook his head. The last thing he needed was any kind of delay. Who knew when Dr. Beers might return. He had to get out of here. "No, you're going to have to stay here for now with Dr. White. But I'll be back for you in a little while, and you can see Miss Harriet very soon. How does that sound?"

"Okay."

"You just be good while I'm gone."

"Is Willie gonna die?"

How could he lie to her? "Maybe."

Her lower lip trembled. "I don't want him to. I don't want my brother to go to heaven. There's enough people there. Daddy and Emmie and Tommy and Auntie and Uncle and Lizzie. Don't you think God's got enough people up there He can leave some of us down here?"

"Everyone who loves Jesus is going to go to heaven someday. The Bible says God is building mansions there for each of us. Some people's mansions get done sooner than others." That answer would have to placate the child for the time being. "I have to go now."

"Hurry up."

"I will." Would he ever. Watching every step, he made his way downstairs. Harriet grew heavier by the minute. Then he faced the door. He hadn't thought about how he would get it open.

He shifted Harriet in his arms, just enough to free his right hand to turn the knob. There, the door gave way.

When he gazed up to see where he was going, his breath hitched. Striding to the door was Dr. Beers. "What is going on here?"

"Harriet is sick. I'm taking her away. And I'm coming back for Willie and Gracie."

The rotund man spread his legs and crossed his arms. "You aren't going anywhere."

"Yes, I am. There's nothing you can do to stop me."

"Oh, but there is."

Chapter Twenty-Six

Michael shifted Harriet's weight in his arms as he confronted Dr. Beers. "You have nothing that can stop me from leaving this place."

"The McLean Asylum for the Insane."

The one where his mother was a ward. He swallowed hard.

"Soon every doctor in the Boston area will know about it."

"What difference does that make?"

"Perhaps you are just as crazy as your mother. Not only would I spread the word your mother is there, I would make sure you end up in a cell next to her."

Michael shut out the taunts of his schoolmates from so many years ago. He gazed at the contorted, tortured face of the woman he longed to spend the rest of his life with. No longer did those play yard jests haunt him. No longer did he care what the good doctors of Boston thought about him. No longer was he going to cower to those bullies. Even those who wanted to institutionalize him.

At this moment, Harriet was all that mattered. "We'll be leaving now." Despite what anyone thought of him, despite what happened, he would do what was right.

Though well-advanced in years, Dr. Beers stood his ground. "You aren't taking her anywhere."

"You will allow me to pass."

Just then, Charley strode up the street and to the door. "What's going on? What's wrong with Harriet?"

"She has taken ill like the others. I'm getting her out of this house before your mother or Dr. Beers or whoever is poisoning your family members has the chance to kill her too."

Dr. Beers peered at Charley, his face full of thunder. "Whatever you do, don't let them out of this house." His words were a low growl.

Instead, Charley took Dr. Beers by the shoulder. "Let them pass."

"Do you believe the incredulous charges of an insane man?"

"I don't know what to believe anymore. I don't know which way is up and which is down, but we have no right to hold them prisoner. If it means saving Harriet's life, all the better. Now get out of the way. I don't want to have to accost an elderly man, but I will if I have to."

Dr. Beers whirled around, reached up, and slapped Charley across the cheek. Charley stumbled backward, but held firm to Dr. Beers, who tumbled with him.

This was Michael's opportunity. Leaving the men scuffling on the small patch of grass, he raced across the street to Mrs. Joss's house. He kicked at the door. "Let us in. Please. Hurry."

The woman with neat, graying hair and a clean apron opened up and ushered them inside. She stared at Harriet. "Oh dear. Gracie told me Miss Peters was under the weather, but I didn't expect her condition to be so grave. Why have you moved her?"

"There is no time to explain. I'm going to try to get back in and get Gracie and Willie out too. First, though, we have to get Harriet, Miss Peters, settled."

Mrs. Joss ushered them upstairs to a sunny, well-aired room. She flung back the patchwork quilt that adorned the bed and drew the shades. "What do you want me to do for her? First is that she appears to be in need of a clean chemise."

"Yes, get her changed. I'll mix up some bismuth phosphate for her to drink. Then I must get back to bring the others over."

"I'll be ready for them. But won't Mrs. Robinson be wondering where her children are?"

"My concern right now isn't Mrs. Robinson. It's the lives of everyone inside that house."

"What about Mrs. Robinson's health? Aren't you worried about her?"

"I believe she's the one poisoning her family."

Mrs. Joss covered her mouth but couldn't stifle her gasp. "No, I refuse to believe it. Such a sweet lady would never do such a dastardly thing."

"Outward appearances don't always reflect a person's character."

"You have me there. Go, do what you need to, and rest assured that Miss Peters is in good hands."

He held back from kissing the woman on the cheek. Instead, he flashed her a broad smile and hurried downstairs to prepare Harriet's medicine, all the while praying that it would be enough to save her life.

Then again, who was he? Was her life even in his control? No, God determined the number of a man's days. It wasn't the doctor's hands that cured, nor the medicine, but God.

Harriet's life lies with You, Lord. You will take care of her and bring her through this illness, either by receiving her into Your arms or by healing her and restoring her to those who love her. Restoring her to me. I submit to Your will. But if it be Your will, Lord, allow her to live.

With that prayer still echoing in his mind, he brought the drink to Mrs. Joss and gave her instructions for its administration. "I'll be back soon with Willie and Gracie. She's fine, but he's in a bad way. I don't believe there is much we can do to save him, but we have to try. If nothing else, we can make his last moments here on earth as happy as possible."

She smoothed the sheet over Harriet. "You are a good man, Dr. Wheaton. God go with you."

"I'll need Him. I can't do this in my own strength."

"I'll be praying."

"Thank you." With that, he was off, bounding down the stairs, out the door, and across the street. As he stood in front of the Robinsons' door, he inhaled a steadying breath. If he trembled in front of Dr. Beers, if he let the man see his fear, he would never get Willie or Gracie out of the house. Then again, it appeared he had Charley as an ally. That was good. He could help. Together, they would be no match for the old man.

Without knocking, he entered and crept up the stairs, careful not to make a sound. The element of surprise might be the difference between him getting Willie and Gracie out or signing their death certificates.

Gracie played on the parlor floor with her dolls. The moment she spied Michael, she ran toward him. "You came just like you said." She hugged his legs so he couldn't move.

"I promised I would."

"It's good to keep your promises."

"Yes, it is. How would you like to go to Mrs. Joss's house and play there for a while? She is taking care of Harriet, but if you are very quiet, I'm sure she won't mind you being there."

"Yes, I want to go."

"Then stay there until I come for you. Don't leave, even if your mother comes there."

"But I'm always supposed to listen to Mama."

Michael didn't have the time to stand here and argue with a small child. "Please, you have to listen to me. Just stay there until Charley or I come. Do you understand?"

She gave a solemn nod then streaked down the stairs, the door banging shut after her.

Dr. Beers peered out the bedroom door and down the hall. "What in tarnation are you doing back here?" His round face shaded from pink to rose to red to firecracker. The man had better watch his heart.

"I'm here to fetch Willie."

Charley exited his brother's bedroom and strode to the parlor. He raised himself to his full height and towered behind Dr. Beers. "And I'm going to help him."

Downstairs, yet another person arrived. By the voices, more than one person. Mrs. Robinson and Mr. Smith. In a moment, they both appeared at the top of the stairs.

The man with Mrs. Robinson beat out Charley by at least six inches and was lean. The size of his mustache rivaled that of any Michael had ever seen. Dr. Beers grinned a wide smile and, puffing himself up, went to shake the man's hand. "Mr. Smith, so good of you to come."

"When Mrs. Robinson called for me, I couldn't refuse. Even though there is no hope for Willie in man's eyes, prayer can work wonders. I'd like to lay my hands on him."

Mrs. Robinson eyed Michael up and down. "And just what are you doing here? Where is Miss Peters?"

"Miss Peters took ill. I've taken her away so she can get proper care."

She stepped toward him, her eyes burning. "I give proper care to all I nurse."

"Everyone you nurse has died."

Her chest rose and fell at a rapid pace, and a muscle in her jaw twitched. "How dare you stand here and say such things about me? To my face, no less. You are no gentleman, that is for sure."

"And you are no lady."

Mr. Smith pushed his way between Michael and Mrs. Robinson. "I have known this woman for many years. I'm the Sunday school superintendent at the church she faithfully attends. After she has suffered so much loss and is on the verge of yet another blow, I would thank you to treat her with Christian charity, if you possess any."

Michael bit his tongue so hard, the metallic taste of blood filled his mouth.

"And where is my Gracie?" Mrs. Robinson glanced about the room. "Gracie, Mama's home."

"She is at a place of safekeeping." Michael struggled to keep his words steady and even.

Mrs. Robinson's nostrils flared. She marched toward him, so close he was forced to step back. This continued until she had him pinned against the far wall, in danger of knocking down the dress form now sporting a completed green gown. "How dare you?" She stood against him, then choked him.

Harder and harder she pressed on his throat.

He fought against her. Tried to break her hold. Kicked at her. All to no avail.

She was a woman possessed. Strong. Stronger than he bargained.

Shouting in the background. Screeching in his ear.

He worked to pull in a breath.

Couldn't.

Dizzy.

Darkness coming.

Harriet's stomach burned as if it were on fire. Maybe it was. Everything was so hot. Blazing. Scorching.

Thirsty. Her tongue as dry as a cat's. Like that of a man in a desert without water for days on end.

Her head banged, like nails were being driven into it.

She fought the lightweight sheet. Batted it away. "Please, please."

A soft hand, a motherly one, one she hadn't felt since she'd left home, and even then many years before that, caressed her forehead. "It's all right, my dear. You're going to be fine."

The voice soothed, like cool water on a summer day.

"Dr. Wheaton says you'll recover."

Michael. She reached out for him but grasped only air. "Michael."

"He'll be here very soon. Gracie has just come, so I know he can't be far away."

Who spoke to her?

"Hot. Hot."

"I know. Here, I have some chipped ice from the icebox. It will cool you." The woman slipped a sliver of it between Harriet's lips.

Oh, so good. So wet. So cold. "More."

The woman fed Harriet more ice. Though it refreshed her parched throat, it did nothing for the inferno raging in her midsection. How to make her understand the intense pain.

Harriet forced one eye open and worked to focus. The fuzzy image came into view. A woman with a topknot. Dark blue dress. Hair threaded with gray. Mrs. Joss. That's right. Michael said he would bring her here. "Gracie."

"She's playing with my granddaughter now. We don't want to frighten her and let her see you like this. When you're feeling better, which will be very soon, she can come and sit with you. I know you'd like that."

"Stomach burns."

"I know it does, my dear, I know."

But she couldn't. There was no way to understand unless you were going through this yourself. Everyone else had died. She would join them soon.

Now that it stared her in the face, the fear dissipated. Jesus had paid the price, His burning pain far greater than her own. What He must have endured, all for her. He did it not because of who she was or what she had done, but simply because He loved her.

Amazing.

What a relief it would be, to be released from this agony in her stomach and her head. To float away into Jesus' arms.

Safe.

He would never leave her.

He would never hurt her.

"Have some more ice." Mrs. Joss forced the cold chunk between Harriet's teeth. She had no choice but to swallow the melting liquid. "You're a strong young woman and healthy. I know you'll be fine. Don't give up. You're in pain, but it will ease."

How could Mrs. Joss be so confident? If Harriet could but close her eyes and drift away. Far, far away.

"Surely you have something or someone to live for. Dr. Wheaton is quite handsome and cares about you a great deal. He's much more than a doctor to you."

Yes, Michael. The warmth inside at that thought had nothing

to do with her illness. Michael, with his long face and jutting jaw. The way a stray dark curl always fell over his hazel eyes. His jaunty bowler hat that he twirled more than he wore.

The man she couldn't live her life without.

Yes, Lizzie had been such a friend to her, true to the very end. How deeply they had loved each other.

These feelings for Michael, though, were not the same. Stronger, even deeper. True love.

If she couldn't live without him, maybe he couldn't live without her. The things he said pointed in that direction.

So for him, she had to fight. Fight with everything inside of her to get better. To get back to him. To have the life with him she'd always dreamed of.

The fight would not be an easy one, though.

She may never live to see that dream fulfilled.

Chapter Twenty-Seven

Though Michael battled the darkness, its pull on him was stronger than he was. No matter how he struggled against its power, it wrapped itself ever tighter around him. A noose tightening around him.

This was one battle he wouldn't win.

Oh Harriet. How he had failed her. Like he failed everyone.

"Stop!" The screech pierced through the enveloping blackness, though still far away, like it came from the bottom of a deep pit.

A pit he was falling into. Helpless. The pull so strong he couldn't fight it.

And then, all of the sudden, the pressure on his throat let up. In a rush, air filled his lungs, inflating them. His hungry body sucked it in. He slid down the wall until he crouched on the ground. Colors swam in front of his eyes like a kaleidoscope, and the world around him buzzed.

Someone had saved him. Stopped Mrs. Robinson's lunacy.

Charley appeared in front of his clearing eyes. "Are you okay?" He smoothed back his blond hair.

"Now I am." Michael cleared his throat. It must have been Charley who screamed for his mother to stop choking him. Michael owed the young man his life. "Thanks." How inadequate the word.

Charley pursed his lips and sucked in his cheeks. "I can't believe ... I mean, how could she?" His voice was little more than a whisper. Behind him, his mother still glowered at Michael.

Mr. Smith steered Mrs. Robinson by the shoulders toward the hall. "Your son needs you right now. Let's go pray for him."

Michael peered at Charley. "Don't let her in there."

Charley knelt in front of him. "Is there any chance my brother will survive?"

"As long as he has breath in his body, there is always a chance. God could choose to heal him."

"I was just sitting with him. He has to labor for every breath. He isn't conscious, and he's stopped writhing."

"Then he isn't in pain anymore."

"Even if. . . Even if she's the one doing this, what more can she do to him now? I want him to go, and I want him to go in peace." The young man's summer-blue eyes shimmered with unshed tears. He must have cried far too many in his life.

Michael clapped him on the shoulder. "I understand. His final minutes or hours should be strife-free. Go, be with your family."

"Will you be okay?"

"I'll be fine. You've done what you could for me. Now you need to do what you have to do for your brother. And yourself."

"Thank you. This is the last time it will be like this."

While Charley's meaning was muddy, Michael nodded. Whether he referred to his brother's coming death or the arrest of the culprit, he was right.

Charley followed his mother, Mr. Smith, and Dr. Beers into Willie's room. After they left, Michael grabbed several deep breaths and scooted up the wall until he was on his feet. For a moment, the room spun, but he soon got his bearings and made his way down the hall. He didn't enter the bedroom but remained outside, peering in.

The group surrounded the bed, Charley and Mr. Smith with their backs to Michael, Mrs. Robinson and Dr. Beers facing him. The young man's mother wiped away tears, her hands shaking. She fell to her knees at his side. "My boy, my boy. You did nothing to deserve this. Your father is calling for you. I hear his voice. He's reaching his hand out to you. Go to him. Go. Go."

Willie sat up straight in bed. "The old lady dosed me." Then he fell against the pillows.

Mrs. Robinson covered her head. "He's delirious. He's delirious." But there was no doubt about what Willie had said.

Though the room where Harriet lay with its heavy brocade curtains and the mirrored dressing table loaded with little bottles was unfamiliar, the voices floating toward her, niggling her to wakefulness, were ones she recognized.

"My brother is going to die." That was Gracie, her voice flat. Rather matter-of-fact. She had seen so much and been through so much in her seven years, it was like calluses had grown around her heart to protect her from all the loss.

"Oh sweetie, I hope not." That mature voice Harriet recognized as Mrs. Joss. The dear, kind lady who was doing more in this moment to save lives than she might realize.

"Dr. Beers brings Mama medicine to give to them, but they always die."

Medicine. Medicine. What was it about medicine?

Yes, she had seen Dr. Beers carrying the medicine in a little amber bottle. Was that it? Was that the key to everything? Could he be the one supplying the poison? Perhaps Mrs. Robinson wasn't a part of it. Yet Dr. Beers hadn't been there this morning when she had eaten and then gotten sick.

How had that even happened? Michael had been in the kitchen the entire time, watching Mrs. Robinson prepare the breakfast. If it was Mrs. Robinson committing the murders, she was sneaky. Very wily.

Harriet's head spun. The headache still pounded in her temples, muddying her thoughts. How could she figure this out if she couldn't even think straight?

If Dr. Beers wasn't there this morning, then it must have been Mrs. Robinson who poisoned her. It was only herself, as far as she knew, who had gotten sick, besides Willie, of course. Gracie was downstairs and healthy. Charley had gone to work, and he hadn't come home.

That medicine was the key. Of that, she was sure. Leave it up to little Gracie to provide a very important clue.

She had to get back to the house across the street. She had to tell Michael what she knew before it was too late. Before anyone else suffered the same fate as too many other members of that family.

Her stomach didn't burn as much as it had before. Thank the Lord the pain had eased. She wouldn't have been able to stand it a minute more. Even if she had to crawl, she had to get herself across the street and tell Michael what she knew. The information may not help her, and it may not help Willie, but it may help Charley and Gracie.

Little by little, she sat. So far, so good. The world didn't whirl too much. She scooted to the edge of the bed. The cool floor sent a shiver through the soles of her feet and across her body, despite the heat in the upstairs bedroom. Shuffling, holding onto pieces of furniture as she went, she made her way out of the bedroom and to the stairs. By the time she arrived, she was huffing and puffing.

With all of her might, she grabbed the handrail and steadied herself. She couldn't do this. She wouldn't make it.

"I wish Miss Harriet was better. She's the nicest person I know. Well, my sister Lizzie was nice, but she died. And my brothers are nice too. But they're big and have to work all the time. Miss Harriet plays with me and lets me help her cook and reads to me."

For Gracie. For Gracie. That's who she had to do this for. For Gracie.

She mustered her strength and rallied her flagging spirits. One step at a time, she made her way down the stairs. She glanced at her attire. A clean nightgown, one that didn't belong to her. Though the neck was high and the sleeves were long, it wasn't anything she should be wearing out of the house. This, however, was not an ordinary time. A life was more important than even her reputation.

By the time she reached the first floor, she might as well have walked across the country. The room tilted. Or was it her tilting?

"Miss Harriet? Miss Harriet!"

And then the floor rose up to meet her.

Was Mrs. Robinson truly as broken up about the condition of her son as she seemed, or was she frightened for herself after her son pointed his finger right at her heart?

In the midst of the commotion, a quiet knock came from downstairs. No one in the room moved. Perhaps with Mrs. Robinson's cries, they didn't hear it. Michael slunk down the hall to answer the door.

As he made his way, from the corner of his eye, he caught sight of a bottle glinting in the darkness of the room. Clouds had rolled in and hidden the sun. The bottle that always showed up when a member of this family fell ill. The one brought by Dr. Beers. Though Michael had already pocketed one, another one had appeared. Curious. The powder inside resembled talcum or flour, but that didn't mean it wasn't lethal. He slipped this new bottle into his pocket too.

He opened the door to discover Chief Parkhurst, who doffed his hat and combed back the few wisps of hair remaining on the top of his head. "Dr. Wheaton. How is the patient?"

"I'm afraid it's a matter of time. Thankfully, Harriet is safe across the street."

"Miss Peters?"

Heat rose in Michael's neck. "Yes, Miss Peters. She fell ill this morning with the same symptoms as the other victims. I haven't even had a chance to notify you. Thank the Lord, I believe she'll pull through."

"That is an item of praise." Chief Parkhurst replaced his hat and stroked his bushy beard.

Michael stepped outside and closed the door. "Willie woke up for a moment and pointed the finger at his mother. Said she was the one who had dosed him."

The chief nodded. "You witnessed this?"

"Yes."

"That could be important if you're called on to testify in the case."

"I also found these." He withdrew both amber bottles from his pocket. "Dr. Beers brings them every time someone gets sick." He handed the vials to the chief.

"What's in them?"

"I'm not sure at this point. Perhaps Dr. Wood from Harvard would be able to analyze the contents of these as well."

"We will need to have him do that. In the meantime, I have a pretty good idea what they contain." He rubbed his deep-set eyes.

"Really? That has piqued my interest."

"I thought that might."

"You have the test results back from Willie's stomach contents, don't you?"

"I most certainly do. I think you'll be quite interested in what they are."

Michael couldn't help but take a step forward. "And?" He held his breath. This would be the moment his suspicions would either be validated or condemned. If this didn't turn out to be poisoning, he would be labeled as insane as his mother.

Of course, if this wasn't poisoning, there was no evil in this house. That would be a very good thing, especially for the remaining family members. Innocent little Gracie.

His heart, though, told him what the results would be.

A gut-wrenching cry came from upstairs. "My boy, my boy! What am I going to do without him? Moses, why do you keep taking them?"

Michael spun, raced inside, and flew up the stairs. Chief Parkhurst thumped behind him.

Charley met them in the parlor, tears streaking his cheeks. "He's gone." His voice cracked on the last word.

Michael clapped him in a hug. "I'm sorry for your loss."

Charley stepped back and motioned in the chief's direction. "Who is this?"

Parkhurst stepped forward. "Chief Parkhurst from the Somerville Police Department."

"I know why you're here."

"Is your mother in the room with your brother?"

Charley nodded and led the way down the hall.

Chief Parkhurst strode into the room and stationed himself at the foot of the bed. As soon as Mrs. Robinson gazed up, her tears dried. She came to her feet and straightened.

"Mrs. Sarah Jane Robinson? And Dr. Charles Beers?"

They both nodded in response to Chief Parkhurst's questions.

"Dr. White took a sample of Willie's stomach contents."

"Wait." A weak but familiar and too-lovely voice came from the hall.

Michael whipped around. There, supported by Mrs. Joss and her daughter, was Harriet. "You shouldn't be here."

"I'm fine. I want to hear what the chief has to say."

Chapter Twenty-Eight

Though her arms and legs trembled, Harriet leaned on Mrs. Joss and her daughter and nodded at the man in the blue uniform, two rows of brass buttons down the front of it, a badge on the left breast. Chief Parkhurst had a presence about him that commanded attention and demanded obedience. Both necessary qualities in a police officer.

Michael furrowed his brow, though a small smile crossed his lips. Just him standing there, gazing at her the way he did, made her stomach flip in a way that had nothing to do with the poison she had been administered earlier that day.

She nodded again. "Please, go on. I'm sorry to have interrupted."

Mrs. Robinson's face was as white and stiff as a starched sheet. No flicker of any emotion crossed her features, the earlier tears vanishing in a split second. She was as cold and calculating a human being as Harriet had ever met.

Chief Parkhurst cleared his throat. "As I was saying, Dr. White sent a sample of William's stomach contents to Dr. Wood at Harvard University. He has examined them and determined that the young man's stomach was saturated with arsenic."

Harriet couldn't help but gasp. All along, Michael had been right. Mrs. Robinson had poisoned her family. Her husband. Her sister. Her own children.

Even Lizzie. Harriet's eyes watered. How could she have done that to such a sweet, loving soul as Lizzie? Even Willie, though he didn't show it often, had a good heart. He didn't deserve the kind of death he got. His suffering must have been many times greater than her own. So, so terrible and awful.

And Tommy. Nothing but a child. Several tears slipped down her face. That poor tyke. Though she had witnessed his incredible suffering, she now understood so much better what he had endured. It was enough to break the strongest man. How much worse for a defenseless child.

She allowed her tears to flow freely. All of them had deserved better.

"Mrs. Robinson, I'm placing you under arrest for the murder of William Robinson along with the attempted murder of Miss Harriet Peters. Dr. Beers, you are also under arrest for the same murder and attempted murder."

Mrs. Robinson, as stiff as a board, fell to the floor, thunking as her body hit the ground. Charley rushed to her, but Chief Parkhurst pulled him out of the way.

Charley fought back. "Let me take care of my mother. Whatever else she has done, she is the woman who gave me birth. I owe her this much."

The chief backed off and allowed Charley to attend to Mrs. Robinson.

Dr. Beers, just the opposite of Mrs. Robinson, paled and swung his attention from the young man now dead in his bed to the policeman to Harriet, and back again. His mouth hung open. "Why me?"

"You have been present at each of the deaths."

"Yes, what you say is correct, but I have been here as a healer, to save precious lives. That is all, I swear to you. God knows the truth."

The officer with the bushy beard harrumphed. "God certainly does know the truth. And it is one we will know ourselves very soon. If you are innocent, you have nothing to fret about. If you aren't, you had better make peace with your Creator. This will likely be a case of capital murder."

Dr. Beers fell on the bed, across Willie's body, sobbing and moaning.

Harriet's own tears continued to flow. No matter which way you looked at it, it was a tragedy. The Robinson family was forever shattered. There would be no piecing it together again.

Never.

None of it had to happen. Lizzie could be happy and married to Fred Fisher and living in Cambridgeport by now. Tommy could have grown into a fine young man. Perhaps he would have been a lawyer or a doctor or any number of things. Willie could have helped to provide for his family and maybe have found love of his own. All of it was so senseless.

Several more officers arrived, stomping up the stairs. Such a good thing Gracie wasn't here to see what was happening to her mother.

Charley exited the room as the officers entered. Mrs. Robinson must have recovered from her fainting spell or whatever it was. Harriet reached out and touched his arm. "How are you doing?"

Red rimmed his eyes. "Awful. How do you survive something like this? Why did she do it? How. . . How could she do it?" He gasped for air.

"Only God knows the answer to that question."

"My own mother. My own mother." He hunched over as if the pain was too much for him to bear.

It probably was.

"Either you or Gracie would have been next. She was running out of victims. When you've been poor all of your life, having money becomes very attractive. She wasn't living the life she thought she'd have in America just by working, so she had to try to get as much cash as possible. Never in her life has she had it easy. You can see it in her care-worn features."

"Money?"

"All that life insurance."

A light dawned on his face. "Yes, that. She insured my life at the same time as Willie's."

"Then thank God you are alive. She could have just as easily poisoned you."

"What kind of life will I have without my family?" He glanced over his shoulder to the room where Michael remained, then turned to her.

"You will have the best life you possibly can. You're a good man, Charley. God has spared you for a reason. Don't throw away this chance at life. Not to mention that you have a very important job now."

He raised his fair eyebrows. "What is that?"

"You have to take care of Gracie. Because you are the only two left, you must be there for each other. She's going to need you. She's going to depend on you."

"Oh Gracie." Now tears coursed down his cheeks. "My poor dear. I can't do it alone. I can't raise her by myself."

Harriet rubbed his arm. "You won't. I'll be there for her. I can help you take care of her. You're going to be fine. Both of you will be. Time will help you cope with these wounds. Now, more than ever, is the time to lean on the Lord. He will take care of both of you."

"She's going to be devastated to lose Willie."

"That little one has been through so much in her life, but she's stronger than you may think her to be. You can comfort each other."

"I have to go to her. I have to explain. Then I have to take care of my brother."

"Then go."

He wiped the tears from his face and straightened his shoulders. "Thank you, Harriet, for everything. Without you. . ."

"Just give Gracie a hug and kiss from me."

Charley leaned over and pecked her on the cheek, then disappeared down the stairs.

Michael left the room, followed by Mrs. Robinson and Dr. Beers, held by the collars by the police, their hands cuffed behind their backs. When Mrs. Robinson passed in front of Harriet, she stopped. "That green dress on the form?"

Harriet glanced at it, the material shimmering in the waning summer light. "You finished it."

"Yes, I did. It was to be your burial shroud."

Michael stood in stunned silence as the police carted away Mrs. Robinson and Dr. Beers. Mr. Smith blubbered after them, proclaiming that Mrs. Robinson was innocent.

While Mrs. Robinson's footsteps still echoed on the stairs, Harriet held herself straight and tall. How could she do that when Michael's heart slammed into his ribcage? Especially after that vicious woman spat those hateful words at her.

He held his breath until the door downstairs slammed shut and the voices on the street faded. Once they had, he released his breath in a whoosh.

Harriet sagged against him in a quivering heap. He caught her just in time to keep her from falling to the floor. The heat had plastered her black curls against her forehead and the nape of her neck. Praise the Lord she had survived.

She peered at him, her lashes so long they almost swept her neat eyebrows. "All along, she intended to kill me. She's been working on that dress since Lizzie died."

He kissed the top of her head. "Yes, it looks like she did."

"I'm the only one to survive the poison."

"For that, I'll be eternally grateful. Now, you need your rest." Before she could protest, he swept her into his arms and carried her to the settee in the parlor. Mrs. Joss's daughter left soon after the police, and the older woman faded into the background, a chaperone for them but not a distraction.

A soft roll of thunder sounded in the distance, moving away. A sudden cool breeze blew through the window, fluffing the white curtains. Harriet lay back and closed her eyes. "Is it really over?"

"It is. I'm only sorry it took so many deaths to put a stop to her rampage. If only the earlier doctors who treated Mr. Robinson and the others years ago were suspicious and had run tests or alerted the police."

She opened her eyes, the color of the Boston bay, then reached up and cupped his cheek. "Do you know why that was? Because they were all afraid to speak up. They didn't want to appear foolish or crazy in front of their colleagues. But not you. No, even though you had been picked on in school, even though Dr. Beers threatened to expose the secret you held about your mother, you stood your ground. You fought for Lizzie and Tommy and Willie and me. No one blames you."

He kissed her hand. "Thank you for that."

"I know it wasn't easy, but you did the right thing. In the end, you did save lives."

"No. I failed three people."

"You did what you could. No one could expect more than that. Think of the lives you saved."

"The ones I saved?"

"If you hadn't intervened, I would have died. No doubt about that. And what about Charley and Gracie?"

"Charley had taken out an insurance policy."

"He would have been next." She held his gaze, hers intense and raw. As she opened her soul to him, so he opened his to her. "And then Gracie. Don't think Mrs. Robinson would have spared her. You saved their lives as surely as you saved mine."

"I suppose I did." Perhaps he had done something good. Something right.

"None of those doctors who ridiculed you, who shunned you, none of them did anything to stop this crazy woman. Only you."

"You, Miss Peters, are a remarkable woman." One he would be a fool to let go. There was no way he could allow her to walk out of his life. "I can't imagine spending another day without you."

The color in her still-pale cheeks deepened. "Oh Michael."

"I know this isn't the place or time, but when the time is right..." He swallowed hard. "I love you, Harriet Peters. More than I have ever loved anyone in my life."

"And I love you with all of my heart."

"Even with a mother in an insane asylum?"

"Because of that, because I see how much you care for her and love her. If you give such tender attention to her, I can depend on you to give me that same love. No matter what comes. I will do the same for you. No matter what."

"Then soon, very soon, the time will be right. Until then, you need to regain your strength. It's a wonder you can even carry on a conversation right now."

"I'm never too tired for you." Though her words were strong, her smile waned. She'd need time for the rest of the poison to leave her body.

"Why don't I make you some tea?"

She bolted upright. "No!" She fumbled with the lace at her neck. "I never want another cup of tea again. Nor a bowl of oatmeal."

He chuckled. "Very understandable. Perhaps it's best not to eat or drink anything in the house."

Mrs. Joss spoke up from the chair in the corner. "A wise decision. Will you two be coming along soon?"

"Very shortly, Mrs. Joss. Harriet needs some food in her stomach and a good night's rest."

"I agree. I'll go home and warm the stew I had on the stove."

"Sounds heavenly. I can almost smell it."

Harriet laughed, music to his ears. "So like a man."

Mrs. Joss straightened the pillows on the chair she'd just vacated. "From the sound of things, you'd better get used to it. Only a few minutes more, understand? I will not have a young lady's reputation ruined on my watch." She cut the strict words with a small wink.

"I promise not to tarnish Harriet's good name."

Mrs. Joss left, and Michael turned his attention toward Harriet, her eyes fluttering shut. "We'd better get you across the street."

"That sounds even better than stew."

Once more he scooped her up, and she leaned against him, tucked into him just right. Made to fit there. "Then let's be on our way. Say goodbye to this house. I'll send Mrs. Joss's daughter here to gather your belongings."

"I can't say that I'm sad to go."

They crossed the room and passed the dress form with the green gown adorning it.

"One more thing, Michael."

"Anything for you."

"Burn that dress."

Epilogue

S irs, if it would please you, I'd like to help my wife to the stand."
Michael stood tall and broad, so very handsome in his new
dark gray suit.

Harriet smoothed her pale blue dress over her much-expanded
midsection, the place where the child God was granting to her and
Michael lay. The one who would be named Elizabeth if she was a
girl and Thomas if he was a boy. She adjusted her white hat adorned
with light blue feathers.

The judge, perched on his bench, stared down at them, the white
wig on his head a little askew. "That's fine, Dr. Wheaton, but then
you must take your seat with the rest of the gallery and not disrupt
the proceedings."

She leaned over to whisper in Michael's ear. "Really, you don't
have to make such a fuss over me. I'm fine."

"No arguing."

Well, it was nice to be pampered. Getting around was getting to
be a chore. Even sitting on the stool in her shop was uncomfortable.
In a little while, the apprentice she'd hired would have to take over
while Harriet enjoyed her confinement. Leaning just a little of her
weight on Michael, she waddled to the stand, passing Mrs. Robinson on the way.

The woman had lost none of her regal bearing. In fact, with
plenty of food to eat in prison, she'd filled out some. Her face
remained expressionless. She stood at the bar without so much as
blinking. At the sight of her, the child in Harriet stirred, as if shuddering along with Harriet. A wave of nausea passed over her, and
she moved on.

Michael delivered her to her seat and returned to his chair. His absence sent a shiver through her. She took a single deep breath to calm herself. All night, she'd been up, pacing, blaming her inability to sleep on the coming child. That, however, wasn't what weighed on her mind.

Her testimony was critical to a guilty verdict for Mrs. Robinson. Already, one trial had ended in a hung jury. That couldn't happen again. As it was, Dr. Beers was exonerated without any consequences. She settled in the straight-back chair and steeled her spine.

The district attorney, Mr. Stevens, approached her, his dark hair wild, his eyes deep-set. It was a good thing she had met him before. With the perpetual scowl he wore, he might have intimidated her. That must be what made him good at his job. "How long have you known Mrs. Robinson, Mrs. Wheaton?"

"About four years."

"Upon what occasion did you meet her?"

"I met her at her church. I was hungry and alone. She took me into her home and helped me get a job."

"And what year was that?"

"It would have been 1883."

"Then you have known her five years."

Harriet's hands trembled, though she clutched them together in her lap. "I suppose that's right. Almost five years."

Mr. Stevens turned up the corners of his mouth a bit. "And when did you go to live with the Robinson family for the second time?"

"I moved to my shop in the summer of 1885 and returned to the Robinson household after Lizzie's death in February 1886. I went to help with the care of the children, Thomas Freeman and Grace Robinson."

The questioning continued in much the same way for several more minutes before Mr. Stevens got to the point. "When did you become ill?"

"I fell sick the day after Willie did, on August 12, 1886."

"Describe your symptoms." Mr. Stevens stood back, his right hand stuck between the buttons on his vest.

She did as requested, reliving the horrible burning pain. Pain she never wanted to go through again. Even childbirth, no doubt, would be easy compared to that.

"What did the tests that Dr. Wood from Harvard College order on your stomach contents reveal?"

"That I had been poisoned with arsenic."

"Who made your breakfast that morning?"

"Mrs. Robinson made oatmeal, and I ate it."

Mr. Stevens sat down, and Harriet blew out a breath. That was, until Mr. Goodrich, the defense attorney stood. He didn't come to face her but remained at the table where he was seated with his associate. His old-fashioned mutton chops were graying. "Did the rest of the family eat the oatmeal on the morning of August 12, 1886?"

"Yes." The tremors returned, not only to her hands, but to the rest of her body.

"Did anyone else fall ill?"

"No."

"Did you ever see Mrs. Robinson put poison into anything?"

"No."

"Thank you. That is all."

One of the two judges nodded to dismiss her. By the time she came to her feet, Michael was again at her side. She didn't chide him now. Her shaking knees wouldn't hold her.

Michael led her from the courtroom, their footsteps echoing on the marble floors, and situated her on a bench in the hall. "You were magnificent."

"I don't know. I didn't see anything I could testify to."

"You did your job, just as Mr. Stevens prepared you to do. You even knew what the defense would ask."

"But I got so nervous."

He pulled her close. "You have nothing to worry about. It doesn't all rest on your shoulders."

"Thank you for being there for me."

"I wouldn't be anywhere else."

February 11, 1888

Harriet tensed as the jury entered the courtroom. A hush fell over all gathered. Justice Knowles received the paper from the foreman and instructed Mrs. Robinson to stand.

Harriet grabbed Michael by the hand and held fast. His palm sweated a little. Or maybe that was hers. Or both of theirs.

"As to the count of murder in the first degree of Prince Arthur Freeman, we the jury find you, Mrs. Sarah Jane Tennent Robinson, guilty."

All the air rushed from Harriet's lungs, and she collapsed against Michael's shoulder.

The proceedings continued, but Harriet heard little of them. "It's over," she whispered to Michael. "It's over."

"Yes, dear heart, it is. She won't ever hurt anyone again. She'll be hung and will have to face the ultimate Judge."

"We must pray for her soul."

"Have I told you how much I love you?"

He had, many times over. This coming child was a sign of that. Still, she never tired of hearing it. "We'll live the rest of our lives in peace and treasure every day the Lord gives us together."

The bailiff led Mrs. Robinson away. As she went by, Harriet swallowed the lump in her throat and spoke. "May God have mercy upon your soul."

List of Sarah Jane Robinson's Victims

- Oliver Sleeper, 72, Sarah Jane's landlord, died August 10, 1881
- Moses Robinson Jr., 45, Sarah Jane's husband, died July 23, 1883
- Emma M. Robinson, 10, Sarah Jane's daughter, died September 6, 1884
- Mrs. Annie Freeman, about 45, Sarah Jane's sister, wife of Prince Freeman, died February 28, 1885
- Prince A. Freeman, 33, Sarah Jane's brother-in-law, Annie's husband, died June 27, 1885
- Elizabeth A. Robinson, 24, Sarah Jane's daughter, died February 22, 1886
- Thomas A. Freeman, 7, Sarah Jane's nephew, Prince and Annie Freeman's son, died July 23, 1886
- William J. Robinson, 22, Sarah Jane's son, died August 12, 1886

Author Notes

After the results of the tests that Dr. Wood from Harvard performed on Willie's stomach contents showed they contained arsenic, the bodies of Sarah Jane Robinson's husband Moses, sister Annie, brother-in-law Prince, daughter Emma, and nephew Tommy, were all exhumed. Each of the bodies was found to contain arsenic. For the readers' ease, I didn't include Sarah Jane's year-old niece, Elizabeth, in the cast of characters. It was growing to be unwieldy. Elizabeth died soon after she, her brother Tommy, and her father Prince, arrived in the Robinson household upon the death of her mother. Her body was not exhumed. There is debate whether the child died of natural causes or if she was also poisoned.

Moses and Sarah Jane Robinson had a total of eight children. In addition to Lizzie, Willie, Emma, Charley, and Gracie, there were twin daughters, Robina and Margaret, who were born on February 25, 1867. They lived to be eight months old and died within a week of each other. There was apparently another child who died at birth.

It is believed that Sarah Jane's first victim was her landlord, Oliver Sleeper. She killed him and extracted $50 from his family for the nursing care she supposedly gave him. $3000 was also missing from his personal effects and never found.

Sarah Jane Robinson's first trial on multiple charges ended in a hung jury. For the second trial, instead of attempting to convict her on charges stemming from multiple deaths, the prosecution only tried her for the death of her brother-in-law, Prince Arthur Freeman. (Prince was his first name, not his title. He was, in fact, extremely poor.) She was convicted on the date I list in the book and sentenced to death by hanging. By November of that year, however, public sentiment swung in her favor, and her sentence was commuted to life in prison. She died there in 1906.

Dr. Charles C. Beers or Bearse—the spelling in the transcription of Sarah Jane's second trial spells his name Beers, although multiple census records have the spelling as Bearse—died on February 24, 1889, a little more than a year after Sarah Jane Robinson was found guilty of Prince Freeman's death. He was 76 years old. He was never convicted in any of the deaths, his case being dropped before Sarah Jane's first trial. He did spend some time in prison in New York in the 1870s for robbery.

I took some fictional license and shortened the duration of Lizzie's illness to just a couple of days. She actually lingered for about three weeks. I also took license with the character of Dr. Emory White. He was a Boston-area physician who consulted on William Robinson's illness. Instead of being older and retired, however, he was just thirty-seven at the time. It worked better for the story to have him be Michael's mentor. The real-life Dr. White died suddenly on April 29, 1915, at the age of 66.

The relationship between Sarah Jane and Dr. Beers is played up somewhat. He did call at the house on a regular basis. He was not necessarily the doctor who attended each of the victims. He did bring a vial of something to the house and set it on the mantel. Apparently, he and Sarah Jane met on the horse car soon after Sarah killed her husband, though it seems they had known each other years before that, before Dr. Beers moved to New York and was imprisoned.

Dr. Beers was, in fact, a married man. There is some doubt as to when Sarah Jane discovered this. Some of the witnesses at the second trial testified that she had known all along. According to Sarah Jane's testimony, she didn't discover this information until much later in this relationship, after he had proposed to her several times.

Mr. Thomas Smith was also a historical figure. He was present at each of the deaths, having come to lay hands on and pray for each of the victims. He was the Sunday school superintendent at

Cottage Street Methodist Church, the church the Robinson family attended. In fact, it was he who was arrested with Sarah Jane upon Willie's death. Dr. Beers wasn't apprehended until a few days later. As with Dr. Beers, Mr. Smith never faced any formal charges.

R.H. White was a real Boston department store and the one at which Sarah Jane worked for a number of years. The store operated from 1853 to 1980.

Willie worked at several jobs, including the railroad, but was a teamster at the time of his death. One source (though I question its reliability) said that just before Willie was poisoned, he injured his leg on the job when a box fell on him. The source also said he was taken to the hospital as he was having terrible convulsions and stomach pains, and he died there on August 12, 1886. Willie's death certificate, however, lists his place of death as Holland Street, the location of his family home, so I tend not to believe that he died in the hospital or that he was ever taken there. The family wouldn't have had the money for it. The certificate doesn't list a cause of death or a duration of the illness. He was known to be quiet and sullen.

The police became suspicious of the family after Tommy's death and were quietly investigating the case. Authorities watched Willie when they learned of his illness, but by that point, it was too late for them to save his life. In the book, I have Michael and Harriet keeping watch over Willie, still giving Sarah Jane the opportunity to slip Willie the poison.

Charley worked at a bookstore and at other shops. He was known to be more gregarious and outgoing than his brother. He did have a very close relationship with his uncle, Prince, and walked to work with him the morning that Prince fell ill. The two of them also were together the night before Prince's illness at a church function. In the trial transcript, Charley refers to his aunt as Auntie, and his uncle as Uncle, so that is how I refer to them in the book. It is said that Charley was Sarah Jane's favorite son. Sarah Jane was kind to her brother-in-law in public, but in private, she loathed him.

Elizabeth (Lizzie) was being courted by Fred Fisher and was speaking of marrying him and moving to Cambridgeport. Though Lizzie was a valuable member of the household, Sarah Jane was once again being pressed by her creditors, and so she killed the daughter who was about to leave her.

Of course, killing her family wasn't Sarah Jane's only option for handling her financial woes. She didn't stand to gain anything by her sister Annie's death, since the money from her life insurance policy went to Annie's husband, Prince. After Annie's death, Prince was speaking of taking his two children and moving in with his sister. That would have freed Sarah Jane from having to care for the three of them.

Though none of the Robinsons made a great deal of money, their combined incomes should have been enough to keep a roof over their heads and food in their stomachs. In the end, we're left to conclude that Sarah Jane killed her family members out of pure greed.

Acknowledgments

Thank you, first of all, to Becky Germany at Barbour Publishing. The idea for this story was yours from the beginning. What a great premise. All I did was run with it. I appreciate all you have done for me over the years. As always, it is a joy to work with you.

To my readers, a huge thanks. You are the reason I do what I do and why I love to do it so much. Your encouraging words mean more to me than you will ever know. I appreciate and cherish each and every one of you.

Thank you to my outstanding critique partners, Diana, Jen, and Jenny. Yes, Diana and I get confused all the time! You all are the best any author could hope for. I owe the three of you such a debt. My career would be nothing without your help.

Thank you to my fabulous agent, Tamela Hancock Murray. What a ride it has been these past years. The best part about being your client? The chocolate you send every Christmas. And I'm only half kidding about that.

A shout out to Ellen Tarver, my terrific editor. Your keen eye and gentle spirit are so much appreciated. I'm always happy to find out each time you get to be my editor. And a special thank you on this book, for your quick work so that I could get this finished and spend some time with my family over the holidays.

And my family – I just can't gush enough about each of you. Doug, my ever-supportive husband, you are the best. I thank God for you each day. Brian, Alyssa, and Jonalyn, my amazing children, I truly am blessed to be called your mother. Each of you is such a miracle to me. That God brought you to me from halfway across the world amazes me. Thank you all for being you and allowing me to love you.

And thank You, Lord, for granting me the deepest desire of my heart – this job of writing stories. Most of all, thank You for granting me forgiveness and the peace that passes all understanding. You have replaced my fear of death with the joy that I will one day go home to be with You forever.

Liz Tolsma is a popular speaker and an editor and the owner of the Write Direction Editing. An almost-native Wisconsinite, she resides in a quiet corner of the state with her husband and their two daughters. Her son proudly serves as a U.S. Marine. They adopted all of their children internationally, and one has special needs. When she gets a few spare minutes, she enjoys reading, relaxing on the front porch, walking, working in her large perennial garden, and camping with her family.

True Colors. True Crime.

The Black Midnight (August 2020)
by Kathleen Y'Barbo

Could a series of murders in London in 1889 be related to unsolved murders in Austin, Texas, 1884? Queen Victoria wants to know and asks her granddaughter—who left the queen's good graces by going off to America to become a Pinkerton agent—to quietly look for any connection. The catch is the queen doesn't want her to do it alone. Alice Anne must find her former Pinkerton agent partner—now an attorney in Austin—and enlist him in the hunt. As the pair get closer to finding their suspect, their lives become endangered, but they refuse to be intimidated. Can this case be solved?

Paperback / 978-1-64352-595-2 / $12.99

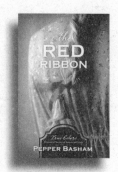

The Red Ribbon (October 2020)
by Pepper Basham

In Carroll County, a corn shucking is the social event of the season, until a mischievous kiss leads to one of the biggest tragedies in Virginia history. Ava Burcham isn't your typical Blue Ridge Mountain girl. She has a bad habit of courtin' trouble, and her curiosity has opened a rift in the middle of a feud between politicians and would-be outlaws, the Allen family. Ava's tenacious desire to find a story worth reporting may land her and her best friend, Jeremiah Sutphin, into more trouble than either of them planned. The end result? The Hillsville Courthouse Massacre of 1912.

Paperback / 978-1-64352-649-2 / $12.99